T0165596

OFF RAMP

A Frivolous Tale of Roguish
Senior Citizen RVers

Donald E. Chandler

iUniverse, Inc.
New York   Bloomington

OFF RAMP
A Frivolous Tale of Roguish Senior Citizen RVers

iUniverse books may be ordered through booksellers or by contacting:

iUniverse
1663 Liberty Drive
Bloomington, IN 47403
www.iuniverse.com
1-800-Authors (1-800-288-4677)

Because of the dynamic nature of the Internet, any Web addresses or links contained in this book may have changed since publication and may no longer be valid. The views expressed in this work are solely those of the author and do not necessarily reflect the views of the publisher, and the publisher hereby disclaims any responsibility for them.

ISBN: 978-1-4401-2649-9 (pbk)
ISBN: 978-1-4401-2650-5 (ebk)

Printed in the United States of America
iUniverse rev. date: 2/24/09

ⅠⅠⅠⅠⅠⅠⅠⅠⅠⅠⅠ PROLOGUE ⅠⅠⅠⅠⅠⅠⅠⅠⅠⅠⅠ

Louann, Marguerite, and Prudence

Prudence hobbled as fast as her arthritic legs would propel her through the front entrance of the Texas Hill Country Guadalupe Retirement Center. She stopped in the lobby to catch her breath. As she stood panting she heard her friend, Louann, call out to her. "What's all the rush about, Prudence? You raced in here like you were running from the devil!"

Prudence looked across the room and studied Louann for a moment as she caught her breath and dabbed her forehead with her lace handkerchief. *Louann is looking kind of frail today. It's Wednesday. I should think she'd rather be up in her room taking a nap or watching some drama on Montel's show, but there she sits analyzing and judging everyone who ventures through the front door; and she's wearing those stupid athletic shoes. Marguerite and I just can't seem to get her to buy and wear sensible SASs like us. Oh well,* she pondered. Then she straightened up as tall as she could and made her way across the lobby to Louann's chair. All the residents made an effort to claim specific lobby chairs for themselves. Louann decreed that the armchair farthest from the front door of the Retirement Center was to be *her* chair during the afternoons because she had been there longer than most and that location protected her from the rush of hot and humid outside air during the Texas Hill Country summers and the cold breezes during the winter 'northers' when the automatic doors opened to let the residents and their visitors in and out. *But it was just after the lunch hour*, Prudence considered. *Why was she sitting down here in her chair now?* Prudence stopped and nodded to herself. *She's sitting there to snoop on me,* she deduced.

"What are you doing down here in the lobby this soon after lunch, Louann?"

Louann raised her chin and assumed a righteous pose. She peered intently over the top of her bifocals. "I can be anywhere I want when I want. Now what on earth have you been up to?"

Prudence sniffed, then leaned over as close as her curved back would allow, and whispered: "I walked up the block to the taco place just now to have myself a proper taco. I just got fed up with the tasteless lunches they're serving us here lately." She shook her head. "They never should have gotten rid of that Mexican chef we had. I don't care if she was a wetback."

"They're called 'illegals' now-a-days," Louann answered abruptly. "Marguerite and I worried about you when you didn't come to the dining room. You ought to tell us when you're not going to join us."

"Whatever," Prudence said, "but this new cook fixes

our food so's it's bland, you know, like the northerners like it."

"You mean to tell me that you walked to the corner in all this heat just to eat a taco?

"Yes, I did, and it tasted real good."

"So, what about all that rushing about in the heat of the day you were doing just now?"

Prudence leaned closer to Louann's good ear. "I need to tell you and Marguerite, at the same time, what I just overheard in the Taco Shack. It's shocking!"

"Shocking, you say? Well *who* in heaven's name did you eavesdrop on now, Prudence? You know that folks around here in the home are beginning to call you the 'Gossip Queen'."

"It's *not* about anything or anybody in the home, Louann. It's about something real big, and I mean *big!*"

"Well, you know that this is Marguerite's nap time and that she gets pretty cranky if anyone disturbs her," Louann said.

Prudence straightened as tall as her spine would allow. "I guarantee you that Marguerite will be *more* than upset if I don't tell both of you, at the same time, what I overheard in the Taco Shack just now. You know how irritated she becomes if I tell *you* something first."

Louann grasped the arms of her chair and leaned forward. "Oh, alright. Here, help me out of my chair. We'll go up to her room together." When she found her balance she turned to Prudence. "This better be good," she said.

Louann had spent her married life as the wife of a United States navel officer. She was accustomed to receiving respect from junior officers' wives - and girlfriends - and offering respect to the senior officers' wives and girlfriends. Her associations had been carefully calculated to help further her husbands's career and assure her proper 'pecking order' in the ebb and flow of the unique society of officers' spouses. Expertise in the playing of the card game, bridge, had been a 'must', as well as asserting her proper station amongst the officers' mate hierarchy. In her retirement home association with Pauline and Marguerite, Pauline had decided that she was the 'alpha lady', but her military-wife experience had taught her that successful relations require flexability. So, she acquiesced occasionally, to the pecularities of her two retirement-home friends.

#

Louann knocked the trio's secret code on Marguerite's door and stepped back beside Prudence in the hallway. They waited silently for a few seconds, then, with a sniff of impatience, Prudence stepped forward and pounded on the door.

"Oh, my," Louann mouthed, then turned to Prudence and said: "Marguerite isn't going to like *that!*"

Prudence snorted, "Well, she doesn't hear well and she takes a shot or two of that gin she keeps in her side table before she goes down for her nap. It takes a lot to rouse her before her rest time is over."

A few moments passed. Then they heard Marguerite's thin voice through the door. "What is it?"

"It's me and Louann, Marguerite, open the door!"

The two waited as she unlocked the door's handle, lifted the chain latch off it's catch, removed the back of a side chair from under the door's knob, and tapped the wood wedge from under the door with her foot. "What on earth has gotten in to you two?" she said crossly as she pulled back the door and peered through squinty eyes; first at Prudence, then Louann.

Louann trudged past her into the apartment followed by Prudence. "Prudence here has heard something that she deems to be of shocking interest to us, Marguerite, and she's just panting to get it off her chest."

"Well, for heaven's sakes," Marguerite said, "couldn't it wait till I finished my nap," she waved her right hand, "you know I don't like to be disturbed during my afternoon rest."

"No, this can't wait, Marguerite," Prudence said with a glare, "it's too important."

Marguerite took a deep breath and shook her head. Her short hairstyle - which was cut so that it never varied more than a quarter of an inch - reflected a dark red hue complementing her vibrant demeanor. "Well, why don't I fix us a cup of tea. Then we can all sit down like civilized ladies and you can tell us your *big* news." She turned toward her kitchenette.

"We don't have time for that, dear," Prudence said quickly, "sit down you two and I'll tell you what I overheard two shady looking men talking about while I was eating my taco over at the Shack just now."

Marguerite stared with disbelief in her expression at Prudence. "You walked up to the Taco Shack in all this heat?"

"Yes. Now sit down and listen to me. I heard those two swarthy looking fellows whispering about where one of them, just this morning, hid a sleeping bag."

"For God's sake, Prudence, have you lost your mind?" Louann exclaimed.

Marguerite rolled her eyes and shook her head.

"Now just you two listen to the rest of what they said," Prudence continued.

"Prudence, what in the world were you thinking to listen in to other folk's private conversations?" Marguerite said.

"I couldn't help overhearing them," Prudence said. "You know how the center booths in the Taco Shack just hold two seats each and are lined up side by side with those fake flowers between them? Well I was seated on one side and those two were just next to me on the other side with the flowers hiding us from one another. I was just finishing my taco when I heard one of the men tell the other that he had hidden '*the*' sleeping bag temporarily in a safe place with '*all the cash*' in it."

Marguerite shook her head and looked at Louann. "Can you believe this? Prudence has gone and lost her mind." She shook her head and said quietly: "I've noticed that she's been acting a little senile lately."

"Now you two just listen to me," Prudence proclaimed, "I'm telling you that one of those two hoodlums hid a sleeping bag containing half a million dollars - I heard him say - of ill-gotten dope money and I learned where they hid it!"

Stunned silence.

After a few moments passed, Marguerite said: "So? What in tarnation does that have to do with us?"

Louann gave a disgusted glance at Marguerite and said, "Well, dear, it's obvious to me that we need to call the police and tell them what Prudence overheard those two men talking about."

Prudence shook her head vigorously. "No, no, no. Don't you *get* it? *I* know where all that money's *hidden*!"

"Marguerite said, "So?"

Prudence stared back at her, then looked at Louann. She took a deep breath and exhaled loudly. "You two are going to have to try harder to keep your minds sharp. I said: *"I know where all that money's hidden!"*

"*So?*" Marguerite repeated.

"Oh, I get it!" Louann exclaimed, "Prudence wants *us* to go find the money and hand it over to the police!"

Prudence turned her back to Marguerite and Louann and looked up at the ceiling. "I said: 'Half a million American dollars in cold…hard…*cash*'!"

"We heard you both times, Prudence," Louann said as she glared at Prudence's back, "we both have our hearing aids on."

Prudence spun around, placed her fists on her hips, and glowered at the two women. Louann shrugged back at her as she held the palms of her hands upward and said, "We don't understand what you're trying to tell us, Prudence, other than you overheard two hoodlums discussing where one of them secreted a sleeping bag, of some sort, full of illegal dope money."

"And Louann suggested that you wanted to steal it from the hoodlums and turn it in to the authorities," Marguerite added, her eyebrows arched.

Prudence slowly shook her head from side to side as she studied her two companions. Marguerite had her hair styled to a short, stylish cut. Prudence had never seen her with a different hairstyle. Her blouse was brightly colored in a flowered pattern, and her brown slacks complimented the green stems of the flowers. She was a good-looking woman, Prudence reflected, and dressed fashionably, but oftentimes she acted naïve. Then Prudence focused on Louann. She, too, was attractive and just as innocent as Marguerite. *I'm just going to have to spell it out in simple-to-understand language to them,* she reasoned to herself.

"What I'm attempting to get across to you two is that I now *know* where five-hundred thousand U.S. dollars is stashed and *we* can go fetch it for ourselves this very afternoon!"

Marguerite glanced at Louann. She said in a whisper: "And do *what* with it?"

"Spend it, you silly woman!"

"On what?" Louann whispered.

"On *us*!"

Prudence shook her vigorously and began pacing back and forth across the room. "Just look at the three of us," she said, her face contorted into an earnest expression, "holed-up in this old folk's fantasy of a ritzy retirement complex." She spread her arms and affected a clown-like smile, "We nibble our cereal and sip our black coffee alone each morning in our rooms as we watch Regis fumble things up and Kelly grin and giggle for us, then we primp ourselves, to look like painted dolls, to meet in the dining room for a bland lunch planned to not give us indigestion, then we rush back to our 'cells' to nap so's we can better concentrate for our afternoon bridge game with old folks with bad breath who don't know how to bid properly…"

Louann pursed her lips and struggled from her chair.

"Now you just listen to me, you rebellious old woman," she interrupted, "we three are doing just fine here in the Guadalupe Center!" She peered down at Marguerite and questioned: "Aren't we?"

Marguerite wrinkled her nose and looked away. "If you say so," she muttered.

"Well, *I* say we *are* and I don't understand what on God's earth has gotten into Prudence's craw, for heaven's sake!"

Prudence stopped pacing and stood with a determined stance, her fists on her hips, and said to her companions: "Well, ladies, I guess you two have given up 'the ship of living', so to speak, and are resigned to spending your so called 'golden years' sitting on your rear ends." She sniffed loudly, "So I'm saying: 'Adios, amigas' to the two of you. As for me, I'm escaping from this boring facility and heading for Las Vegas and parts West!" She added with a sniff: "Old age only happens when you lose your dreams."

Louann raised her brow. "Prudence, you know that we don't tolerate or appreciate language like that. You weren't raised to speak that way and neither were Marguerite and I."

"Didn't you digest one thing that I'm telling you two? We three can grab that money and get the hell out of here and *live large* for a change!" Prudence shouted.

Louann lowered her chin and said: "Didn't you hear what I just told *you*, Prudence? We weren't raised to speak…"

"Shut up, Louann," Marguerite exclaimed, "I want to hear more about what Prudence is trying to tell us about half a million dollars, living *large*, and Las Vegas."

"Why, Marguerite," Louann sniffed, "I'm shocked and ashamed of you and Prudence for even considering, for one moment, such thoughts."

Prudence looked deep into Louann's eyes and said: "I haven't gotten this stimulated since Clark Gable told Vivien Leigh in 'Gone with the Wind': 'Frankly, my dear, I don't give a damn', and jerked her up against his body and began to…"

"Me, too!" Marguerite interjected as she twirled about laughing.

"Well I'll be," Louann said as she frowned and shook her head at Marguerite and Prudence.

"Perhaps we should discuss this development further and sleep on it," Marguerite suggested to Prudence.

"Maybe we should simply call the police and tell them about what you overheard and be done with this nonsense," Louann said.

"We don't have the luxury of time to '*sleep* on it', dear. That hoodlum said that he was going to retrieve the sleeping bag early tomorrow. He told his companion that he was driving over to a recreational vehicle sales lot on Sidney Baker Street this afternoon to trade his pick up truck for an older model Winnebago motor home he spotted as he drove past the dealership. He was talking about how much easier it would be to secrete the sleeping bag with all that cash in it in an RV rather than inside his pick up when he crosses the border into Mexico down in the Rio Grande Valley at the Nuevo Progresso crossing."

"Well, just where *did* the man hide this sleeping bag with all that money?" Louann said.

Prudence smiled broadly and said, "Across the street

from us inside the old abandoned Ritz Theatre underneath the old popcorn popping machine!"

Louann snorted. "Now just how did he do that?"

"He's a criminal…they know how to do those things."

"Hooray for us!" Marguerite bellowed, "We're headed for Sin City where 'what happens there stays there'!" She jumped from her chair and grabbed Prudence by the arms and the two began dancing about the room.

Louann leaned back in her chair and watched the brief celebration for a moment. "Now just how do you plan to steal that ill-gotten money and get ourselves *to* Las Vegas, if I may be so bold to ask?"

Prudence stopped her dance and grinned widely, "In dear old Mr. Jones's luxurious motor home."

"Old man Jones? The old coot in room one-thirty-one, on the first floor, who was always sniffing around you?" Marguerite asked as she struggled to catch her breath.

"But he passed away last month," Louann said.

"Yes, but he didn't have any survivors," Prudence said, "so, because I was kind enough to always let him be my bridge partner when others wouldn't - and he remembered that my late husband and I had spent our last five years together full-timing around the country in our own motor home as he and his wife had done, and that I knew how to do all of the driving and hooking up and such - Mr. Jones willed *his* motor home to me."

"To you? You didn't tell Marguerite and me about *that*!"

"I didn't think that it was any of your business.

Anyway, he requested that I sell it and gift the money to the charity of *my* choice if I felt that I wouldn't drive it."

"Well, for goodness sakes, Prudence, aren't you going to fulfill his request?"

"Certainly. What kind of person do you think I am, anyway?"

"We can't run away in Mr. Jones's motor home if you intend to honor his dying wishes," Louann said.

"Oh, I'm going to honor his last wishes for sure," Prudence said with a twinkle in her eyes, "I'm donating the motor home to *my* favorite charity: *Us.*"

Marguerite and Louann, with their eyes as wide open as possible, stared in total silence at Prudence for a moment, then howled with laughter.

"But wait! What shall we tell the folks here at Guadalupe River Center?"

"We'll just inform them that the three of us are going on a long vacation outing and that we're not certain as to when we'll return."

"Won't everybody be curious as to what we're up to?"

"Who cares? We're adults. We can do as we wish. Besides, it'll give all the old coots here at the retirement home something to gossip about."

Now let's get to our rooms and pack up our medications, some clothes, and necesities, then inform the front desk that we're going to be away on an extended vacation!

#

Prudence, followed by Marguerite and Louann, struggled

their way out of the taxi. Prudence turned to the driver, paid him his fare, and instructed him to drive away from the RV storage lot which was located in the rear of the Rio Oak Mobile Home Park.

"How're you three ladies gonna get back to the retirement home?" the cabby asked.

"That is none of your concern," Prudence replied.

The driver shrugged and said, "Suit yourselves, then," and pulled away from them.

"Which one of these motor homes is it?" Marguerite asked.

Prudence stood and studied the giant busses for a moment. "Mr. Jones said that it was blue and white with a streak of red that looked like a lightening bolt along its sides."

"My word, Prudence, these vehicles are as big as the old Kerrville Bus Company tour busses!" Louann said as she stared at the array of motor homes and travel trailers lined side by side on the storage lot. "Have you ever driven one of these monsters?"

Prudence straightened her body as tall as she could, looked straight into Louann's eyes and said: "Yes, there's nothing to it. It's just like driving an enormous car… only longer. And don't forget: After my Elmer retired we drove our motor home all across the country for several years."

"I thought you and your late husband were ranchers."

"We sold the ranch and went camping when Elmer got fed up with smelling cow poo-poo all day every day."

Marguerite pointed and muttered: "There's a large red, white, and blue one. It sure does look fancy."

The trio turned and stared at the huge vehicle for a few moments, then Prudence rummaged through her purse and pulled out an enormous ring of keys. She studied the tags on the keys a minute, then proclaimed: "That's it. The license plate has the same numbers as this tag with the keys."

"There's one of those Volkswagen bugs affixed the the rear of it."

"Mr. Jones said that would be the 'tow car'," Prudence said.

"What's it for?"

"It's to ride around in when we get to Las Vegas or wherever."

"Are you sure about all this foolishness?" Louann said.

Prudence turned and confronted Louann and Marguerite. "We either get in that monster right now… or spend the rest of our days wishing we had…now what's it going to be?"

"Let's do it," Marguerite said.

Marguerite had always been an agreeable and optimistic person. She had come to the United States as a young bride who always afforded positive thoughts for everyone she encountered. Having been born with a happy outlook on life and a quick sense of humor, she was a favorite of all who knew her. Her good nature and natural beauty captivated her friends and acquaintances as well as strangers.

Louann shrugged and started walking toward the RV.

Prudence nodded firmly and fell in behind Louann. Marguerite giggled and followed the two elderly ladies across the lot.

When the three reached the motor home Prudence selected the door key and unlocked the door. For several minutes they stood and peered inside. "Well, let's get on with it," Louann said.

They climbed up the automatic door steps that lowered when the door was opened and perused the interior of the bus. "My heavens," Marguerite exclaimed, "it looks just like what a fancy hotel suite should look like!"

Prudence wriggled into the driver's seat and studied the dashboard while Marguerite and Louann investigated the interior. She figured out how to start the giant rear deisel engine after several minutes of confusion, closed the door and sat studying the gages.

After several minutes passed, Marguerite said: "Well? Aren't you going to drive it?"

Prudence answered: "Mr. Jones explained to me that seasoned RVers always allowed their diesel engines to idle for a prolonged period of time before moving them."

"Why?" Marguerite said.

"He didn't know why," Prudence answered, "He said no Rver knew why. He thought, maybe, it was because the eighteen wheeler truck drivers did it." After several more minutes elapsed, she slowly edged the behemoth from its parking space.

"Oh my God," Louann exclaimed as Prudence slowly guided the motor home around the storage lot. "Where are you going, Prudence?"

"I'm just circling the other RV's for a few minutes

until I get the feel of this thing. I've driven tractors on our ranch, and I drove a school bus for a few weeks after Elmer and I sold the ranch, but I've never driven one of these fancy motor homes."

"What now?" Marguerite asked.

"We drive to the old abandoned Ritz Theatre and steal that money."

"How are you proposing that we break in that building, Prudence?"

"I've already figured that out. We'll simply drive up to the back door, tie a rope from the theatre's door handle to the bumper on the back of the Volkswagen tow car, and pull the door till it breaks off."

"Are you crazy?" Louann exclaimed.

"Nope, just inspired," Prudence said with a cackle.

|||||||||||||||||||| 1 ||||||||||||||||||||

Rose and Aldo Chambers

Rose jerked her head to the left and whacked the back of her hand against Aldo's right shoulder. "Hey! Did you see that?" she shouted.

Aldo fought to keep their camper inside the right lane of Interstate I-10. "Dang it, Rose," Aldo shot back, "you nearly caused me to swerve off the highway." He blinked rapidly, "We're going almost fifty miles per hour, you know!"

"Well, didn't you just see what I just saw?"

"Obviously not," Aldo mumbled.

"See that humongous motor home up ahead that just now passed us?"

"Yeah. What about it?"

"There was a little old lady riding in the front seat of that little Volkswagen Bug it was towing!"

"So?"

"She was screaming, honking its horn, and waving her hands!"

Aldo squinted his eyes and peered intently at the rear of the tow vehicle gradually being pulled away from their camper. "Yeah, I see the back of her head now."

"Well don't you think we should do something about that?"

Aldo turned his head toward Rose and studied her expression. The two had been married for fifty-eight years and he still marveled over her enthusiasm for life. Her energy. And, especially, her awareness of everything. *Take this instance,* he ruminated, *I just know from hard earned experience that Rose is going get the both of us involved in something that just isn't part of our affair, but there isn't one cotton picking thing I can do to avoid it.*

"Tell you what, Rose, I think that you and I should just keep on chugging along toward Junction, stop at Benson's Bar-B-Que up ahead, and each have us a nice beef brisket sandwich, then simply erase from our minds what we saw just now."

"That's it?" Rose asked incredulously. "Your solution to rescuing that old lady in distress is to stop and have a brisket sandwich?"

"OK, Rose, just what is it that you suggest we do?" Aldo shook his head. "That motor home's going at least seventy miles an hour. I'm afraid to drive this old 1978 Chevy pick up with our big old camper sitting on it that fast." He licked his lips, "And as a matter of fact, I'm a bit nervous about driving it at fifty miles an hour with all the whitetail deer crisscrossing I-10 as it is!"

Rose studied her husband for a brief moment. He had to sit on a cushion in order to properly see across the top of the steering wheel as well as having to position the seat bench to its closest position to the dashboard. He was short. But she was shorter. Their old time friends, the Hill Country Heller Biker Club members - *the ones who were still kicking* she mused - said that she and Aldo reminded them of the movie stars, Rhea Perlman and Danny Da Vito. But that didn't bother Aldo or her. They admired Rhea and Danny, *mostly because their sense of humor was a bit askew. Plus they were rich and famous.*

Aldo had been a house painter most of his adult life. Rose couldn't remember a time when he didn't have paint somewhere on his clothes or skin. But she loved him, kookiness and all, in spite of his idiosyncrasies.

"What we're going to do, Aldo, is follow that motor home until it has to slow down for something, then drive up to the side of it and honk until we get the driver's attention. Then I'll motion them to stop on the side of the highway so we can rescue that frightened little old lady!" Rose looked ahead and sat forward. "Look, look, look. They're slowing. I see their brake lights."

Aldo leaned forward and squinted. "There's a big old extra wide rig up ahead of them. Looks like it's hauling oversized tanks of some sort…probably gas storage tanks for a new gas station."

"That's great!" Rose exclaimed, "we're catching up with them now."

"What should I do?"

"Pull along side of the motor home and start honking." Rose rolled down her truck window and commenced waving her arms and shouting: "Pull over! Pull over to the side of the highway!"

#

Prudence slowed the motor home. She couldn't decide whether she should pass the pick up truck in front of her with its sign, 'wide load', and its blinking lights, or just follow slowly behind it.

Suddenly Louann jerked forward and turned toward Prudence. "Prudence!" she shouted, "There's an ugly orange vehicle beside us and a woman's in it waving and shouting at us!"

"What in the world is the matter with that crazy woman?" Prudence said as she swiveled her head and stared with astonishment down at Rose's frantic antics. "I think that that silly woman wants us to pull off on that off ramp just ahead!" Louann exclaimed.

"My God," Prudence mumbled, "do you think they could be part of the dope smuggling gang from whom we stole the sleeping bag full of money out of the movie house?"

Louann wrapped her arms across her chest and cried out: "Oh, dear! I just knew we should have turned all of that illicit money over to the Kerrville Police!" She leaned toward Prudence and slapped the air next to her shoulder and angrily said: "See what you and Marguerite have gotten us into now!"

Prudence said, "Shut up, Louann, we're in a pickle here!"

Louann unsnapped her seat belt and struggled to get out of her huge upholstered seat. "I better go back to the bedroom and awaken Marguerite."

"Well what do you think we should do?" Prudence said.

Louann stood unsteadily in the moving motor home and glared down at Prudence. "We? We have to take that off ramp, stop and give them back the money we stole from them…and, maybe, just maybe, they won't kill us!"

Prudence said: "We're busted!"

Louann stopped struggling and glared back at Prudence and stated with vehemence, "Prudence! You know we *weren't raised* to use language such as that, and I'm just…"

"Oh shut up, Louann, and go fetch Marguerite!"

Prudence slowed the giant motor home and steered it carefully down the off ramp. She brought it to a stop on the shoulder of the ramp and turned off the engine. The brief moments of silence were shattered by a hideous croak from inside the rear of the RV. Prudence spun about in her seat and gaped back.

Louann rushed forward wringing her hands shouting: "Marguerite's not in the motor home! I've looked in the bathroom…everwhere! She's vanished!"

"I thought that she was back in the bedroom taking a nap," Prudence said. "You don't suppose we left her behind at the service station, do you?"

Louann stopped shouting and placed her hands, palms facing backward on her hips, and tilted her head. "Now that you mention it, I don't remember," she said with a thoughtful expression.

There was a knock on the side of the motor home. Louann spun about and goggled at the door.

"Well, open the door. We might as well deal with whatever is going to happen to us right this minute," Prudence sighed resignedly.

"What about Marguerite?" Louann said.

"Forget about Marguerite. Just open the door and let's get this over with," Prudence mumbled.

Louann leaned forward and released the latch. As the door swung open Marguerite shouted at them from the shoulder of the highway: "You two crazy old ladies drove off with me inside that stupid little Volkswagen back there!" She turned to Rose and Aldo who stood beside her. "If it wasn't for these two kind citizens I would have probably died of carbon monoxide poisoning or, worse yet, fright!"

Prudence took a deep breath, exhaled loudly, and hollered, "Hallelujah!"

"Well you *should* be happy to see me," Marguerite huffed.

"Prudence isn't happy to see *you*, Marguerite," Louann said with a laugh, "she's happy that we aren't going to be shot…or worse."

"What, for heaven's sake, are you babbling about, Louann? I've just been drug behind this monster bus in that stupid little car for near half an hour honking its silly sounding horn, screaming my head off, and waving my arms for help and you two twits didn't even know that I was missing and in dire distress!"

Prudence stalked to the doorway and asked, "Marguerite, what in the world were you doing back there in the Volkswagen, anyway? Louann and I thought you had gotten in the motor home and went back to the bedroom to nap."

"I went back to that awful little car to take that stupid sign you gave me to put in its rear window, Prudence!"

"What sign?" Louann said.

"The sign that says: 'Tow Car', dear. "I forgot about

telling Marguerite to do that during all the excitement, and all, about the four hundred and thirty-six dollar fuel charge."

"What's that about 'getting shot…or worse?'" Aldo stepped forward and asked.

Marguerite turned back to Rose and Aldo. "Oh dear," she said, "I've forgotten my manners. These kind folks who just saved my life are Aldo and Rose Chambers from Kerrville." She smiled, then faced back to the motor home's door and said, "And these two ladies are my dear friends: Prudence and Louann."

"Glad to meet you," Rose said, then frowned and parroted Aldo: "What's that you said about getting shot…or worse?"

|||||||||||||||||| 2 |||||||||||||||||||

Jesse and Humberto

Humberto braked to a sudden stop behind the old Ritz Theatre and gawked with disbelief and horror at the shattered rear door. He jerked his head to the passenger seat of the 1978 Winnebago motor home, for which he had just traded, and stared with an expression of abject fear at Jesse. "The door's busted open!"

Jesse stiffened into a rigid, seated, statue. Copious tears instantly flooded down his bearded face. He screamed: "If that sleeping bag with half a million large has been snatched from us we're dead meat!"

Humberto jumped from the Winnebago and ran to the back entrance and peered inside. "Maybe it's still in there!" he shouted, "I stuffed it underneath an old greasy popcorn machine...nobody, I mean, nobody would be poking around underneath that...would they?"

"How the hell would I know, you stupid idiot?" Jesse said.

"Come on," Humberto declared, "let's go see!"

Jesse struggled from the motor home and followed Humberto into the old theatre. The two stumbled through its dark, cluttered interior to the front lobby. Humberto raced to the popcorn popper, dropped to his knees, and began thrusting his hands frantically under the machine. "Caramba!" he exclaimed, "The money's all gone!"

Humberto turned and began stumbling back toward the rear of the old movie house.

"Hey, man…where're you going?" Jesse hollered.

"I don't know, but I'm getting the hell away from you and your compadres and finding someplace far away where you'll never find me."

"Wait, man!" Jesse yelled, "We gotta find out who snatched the money and steal it back!"

Humberto stopped and looked back at Jesse. "Are you crazy? How're we gonna do that?"

Jesse poked Humberto hard on his chest. "We have to, man. There ain't no place on earth we can hide from those guys we were supposed to take it to." He wiped the tears from his eyes and peered into Humberto's face. "Those dudes are real bad-asses, man…they'll hunt us for the rest of our lives, and if they don't find *us* they'll find our mommas and daddies, and brothers and sisters, and cousins and…"

Humberto slowly sank to the floor and covered his head with his arms. "This is all *your* fault, man," he interrupted, "you told me that all we had to do was deliver that sleeping bag across the border to Nuevo Progreso; that there was no problem; that it was a 'sure thing', and that your friend, Turk, would pay us lots of cash for doing it," he glared at Jesse.

"And I *told* you that it was a dumb thing to do

when you said that you busted in this old theatre to hide that money while we traded my pick- up for the Winnebago!"

Humberto squatted next to Jesse. "I know, I know, amigo, but how'd I know some low life thieves would break in here and steal from *us*? Huh? Just tell me how I would know that?" He shook his head. "Man, I don't know what this old earth is coming to with all the thieving that's going on nowadays."

Jesse dropped his arms from his head and stared wide-eyed at Humberto. "Shut up," he said, "we gotta figure something out right now. He reached down and took a grip on Humberto's right arm. "Get up. We'll go out and scout around the theatre. Maybe someone saw or heard something." He sniffed several times. Then he tugged Humberto's arm. "Whoever the crooks were who broke in here and robbed us had to have made a big commotion and a lot of noise busting open that back door like they did."

"So?" Humberto snorted.

"We find out if someone around here saw who they were?"

"Then what?"

"Then we'll figure out a way to find them."

"Then what?"

"Hell, I don't know, man…we steal the money back!"

Humberto peered intently into Jesse's eyes. "You think?"

"It's either that or we die real *baaad*, estupido." Jesse stood and intently studied Humberto. "You know what, man, you gotta shave off that dumb mustache. It's disgusting to watch you eat. And you gotta stop wearing that dirty old necktie around your head. You look like a Mexican bandit, or something, in an old western movie. Ain't you noticed that folks avoid walking close to you?"

Humberto glared back at Jesse. "Hey, you piece of white trash. Don't you start on *me*! Just look in a mirror, man."

"Yeah?"

"Yeah. That freaking ear thing you wear. It dangles down your tattood neck like a piece of dirty ice. As a matter of fact, it's filthy. Don't you ever take the stupid thing off and clean it?" Humberto said.

"Hey! Hey! We have to stop this fussing and do something about the sleeping bag!" Jesse exclaimed as he shook his head. "Let's get out of here and look around out back and see if there's anyone who seen or heard something. You know, like someone jerking that back door off with a truck or something."

#

Humberto and Jesse stood near the trash dumpster behind the Taco Shack and watched the kid who worked there empty the trash. The employee turned to them and said: "What?"

"We was just wondering if you or any of the other employees here seen anything unusual over there behind that old theatre building across the street last night or early this morning," Jesse said.

The kid picked at a pimple on his neck for a moment, then answered: "Not me. I don't work those shifts. But old Craig does. Maybe he seen something."

Jesse grinned. "Old Craig? You mean to tell me that there's an *old* guy who works in this fast food joint?"

"Yeah," the teenager said, "he the night janitor. They say that he used to make a lot of money, but he burned out."

"Where can we find this Craig?"

"Craig? Oh, he's inside the Taco Shack now having coffee before he goes on home."

Humberto and Jesse hustled around the the front entrance of the Taco Shack and peered through the glass door. "That must be him," Jesse said, "the skinny guy wearing that dirty Texas University bill cap."

They pushed through the door and hurried over to the booth where the man was sipping his coffee. "Hey, friend," Jesse said, "me and my buddy here was wondering if you seen or heard anything last night or early this morning over there behind that old theatre building."

Old Craig looked up at Humberto and Jesse. "Why?" he asked.

"*Why?*" Humberto exclaimed. You're asking *us why?*"

Jesse stepped between Humberto and old Craig and pulled Humberto away from Craig. He offered a wide smile. "We've been hired to fix the busted theatre door. It was pulled off the building sometime during the last couple of hours and we was just wondering how it happened."

"Well, now that you mention it, I saw a big ol' red, white, and blue motor home with a little ol' Bug hitched behind it, about an hour or so ago, back behind the theatre over there. That big deisel engine in the motor home was making quite a racket. I just figured that it was a couple of Winter Texans parking there to cop a freebie overnight stay."

"A big red, white, and blue motor home pulling a Volkswagen Bug," you say?" Humberto asked.

"You know what?" Old Craig said, "you jokers oughta learn to listen better."

"Thanks, buddy," Jesse said as he turned and pushed Humberto toward the entrance, "we have to go find that motor home."

They hurried from inside the Taco Shack and stood a moment in the parking area looking around. Jesse pointed across the intersection to a service station. "Let's run over there and see if anyone remembers seeing that motor home."

The two frantic miscreants ran across the road to the gas station and burst through the front entrance. "Mam," Jesse said to the woman behind the counter, "did a big red, white, and blue motor home pulling a little car drive in here and fill up during the last hour?"

The clerk stepped back a couple of feet and said: "Hey, dude…you think that I remember every dadgum vehicle that comes through here?"

Jesse caught his breath for a moment and said: "Please, mam, it's important. My elderly momma and her two friends are driving it and they forgot to take their medicines along," he affected a frantic expression. "Momma will die if she don't get her heart pills right away."

The woman stepped forward and placed her hand on Jesse's hand. "Oh, my goodness," she said, "let me check." She turned and called out to the other clerk: "Hey, De Lynn, you were working the register earlier.

You remember seeing a big red, white, and blue motor home?"

De Lynn approached the counter holding a large cup of steaming coffee. "Yeah. About an hour ago. I remember 'cause three hysterical looking little ol' ladies were driving it." She guffawed, "You should of seen the expressions on their faces when I handed them the four hundred and thirty-six dollar bill to top their diesel's fuel tank!"

"Do you know which way they went?" Jesse asked.

"Yeah, as a matter of fact, they asked me if they could get to I-10 west from the corner up there by the super market on Harper Road."

"They're heading out I-10 toward El Paso," Humberto said.

Humberto turned to Jesse and furrowed his brow. "Three little old *ladies*? You think that three little old broads stole our money?"

De Lynn turned back to Humberto and Jesse. "Money? Well, all I can tell you about money is that those little old gals had plenty of it. When I showed 'em their diesel bill they commenced to argue about who's credit card they were gonna use, then the one with the cane gave out a big ol' whoop and said: 'Hey, wait a minute girls,' we have a ton of cash in the motor home!'"

Jesse looked at Humberto and frowned. "They are the thieving rascals! I just know it!" Then he thanked the two clerks and hurried from the counter. "Come on, Humberto. Those old broads got a head start on us. We gotta hustle to catch up with 'em before they turn off I-10 to who knows where!"

||||||||||||||||| 3 |||||||||||||||||||

Prudence, Louann, Marguerite, Rose, Aldo

Aldo took a deep breath of the hot and humid Central Texas air, wiped the perspiration from his forehead with the back of his arm, and turned to peer back toward I-10 and the beginning of the off ramp where his and Rose's camper was parked on the shoulder behind the huge red, white, and blue motor home.

"You know what, ladies, I think that we should move these two RVs off this ramp before some wired up trucker comes barreling down it." He licked his lips, "We didn't leave much room for an eighteen wheeler to squeak past." He continued, "Whichever one of you ladies is driving that big monster just ease it on down the ramp here and park along the side of that access road. I'll just tag along behind. Oh, make sure that you leave enough room for me to park my camper behind you."

Louann, Prudence, and Marguerite turned to step up into the motor home. Prudence looked back toward Rose and said: "Come on in with us, Rose. You can help me decide where to park this thing."

Rose said, "Why, certainly, Prudence." She nodded at Aldo and climbed into the motor home behind Marguerite, Louann, and Prudence.

As Prudence carefully steered down the ramp and turned onto the service road, Rose asked a second time: "Now what about this business Louann just said? Something about: 'getting shot…or worse'?"

Marguerite stared at Louann. Louann stared back at her. Then both stared at Prudence. Prudence parked the RV, shut down the diesel engine, and glared back at her two conspirators. "We agreed to not tell anyone about the money," she said angrily to Louann.

"*What* money?" Rose said.

"The sleeping bag full of five hundred thousand dollars that we just stole from two narcotics smugglers!" Louann blurted forth followed by a loud sob.

Rose furrowed her brow and blinked rapidly. "You *what*?"

"It's true," Prudence said in a quiet voice. "Early this morning, not more than two hours ago, the three of us pulled the back door off an abandoned theatre with a rope tied to the rear of the VW on the back of this motor home and sneaked in and stole half a million dollars of dope money that was stuffed into an old dirty sleeping bag under the popcorn appliance."

Rose stood and slowly shook her head from side to side. "Surely you're pulling my leg. Why that's not even *funny*, ladies. I mean: if you three like to joke around some, and act silly, you shouldn't do it so that it's about a life-losing situation." She peered into each of their eyes for a moment. "By heavens, you're serious, aren't you?"

"Yes," Marguerite said as the trio nodded their heads.

Rose licked her lips and slowly sank back into her seat. Aldo and I have gotten into some serious doo-doo, during our fifty odd years together, but none of it has been as smelly as this stupid thing you ladies just did."

There was a knock on the door. All four women jumped. "Don't open the door!" Marguerite shouted.

"Hey in there," Aldo called from the outside, "what's going on?"

Prudence opened the motor home's door. Aldo peered in at the alarmed foursome. "What?" he said.

"These three ladies here are in some deep 'you know what'," Rose said.

Aldo grinned and said: "What'd they do? Outrun a highway patrolman?"

"I'm serious, here," Rose said, "they just ripped off half a million dollars cash from a couple of dope smugglers."

"Now *that's* a hoot!" Aldo chortled, "Half a mil! Why, if they did *that* they'd already be greeting ol' St. Peter at the Pearly Gates!"

"They're serious, Aldo."

Aldo studied Rose's expression. He had learned, the hard way fifty-eight years and eleven months ago, to not ignore that particular expression. He turned to the other three women and said hurriedly, "Me and Rose are pleased to have met and helped you three charming ladies…now we've got to skedaddle on up the highway to Quartzsite, Arizona so's we can get a good spot before the late summer boondockers swarm in."

"Wait!" Prudence said, "Do you *really* believe that we're in a deadly situation?"

"Does a cat have an ass?" Aldo said.

"Oh my, oh my, oh my…," Marguerite exclaimed, "…what are we to do?"

"Run like the wind," Rose said.

"Where to?" Louann said.

"We don't want to know," Aldo said, then turned to Rose, "let's go, momma, before we get caught up in their mess."

Rose stood. "Good luck, ladies."

"Oh my," Marguerite said again, "don't just leave us here out in the Hill Country next to the highway. Please stay and help us decide where to go and what to do."

"You should have figured *that* out before you swiped half a mil from those bad hombres," Aldo said.

"We didn't have *time* to think it through," Louann said, "Prudence and Marguerite were *hell bent* on grabbing that money." She stiffened, "They wanted to escape from the retirement home. Prudence said to me - rather nastily, I thought - that we were just 'sitting idle on our tired rear ends during our golden years.' I told them that we were doing just fine at the center, but no, they just had to go and get greedy." Louann huffed, "Las Vegas, my ass!"

Marguerite jumped up and gave Louann a startled look. "Louann! You know we don't speak in that manner!"

Louann glared back at her. "Hey…we're part of the nouveau rich now…I'll say whatever the devil I want to."

Aldo turned to Rose. "See what happens to otherwise

nice folks when they suddenly come into a lot of money that they didn't earn." He continued with a sigh, "Mohandas Gandhi once proclaimed that the number one of *his* version of the seven deadly sins was: '*Wealth without work*.'"

"Now just where did you read that?" Rose said.

"On a bumper sticker on the back of an old pick up truck. There was a tiny line beneath that read: '*And I'll kiss your ass - no matter how you got your money - if you'll inherit me and leave me some of it,*'" Aldo quoted between chuckles.

Rose stepped down from the motor home and shielded her eyes from the bright morning sun. She studied a large sign on the opposite side of I-10. It read: 'Segovia Truck Stop and RV Park'. "Why don't you three ladies move your motor home over across the highway to that RV park and try to chill out a bit. You can spend a day or two over there and try to plan how to get yourselves out of this mess you made for yourselves."

Louann struggled from the motor home and grasped Rose's hand. "Please, Rose, don't you and Aldo just drive off and leave us out here!" She turned and pointed toward Prudence and Marguerite. "Those two scheming old ladies got the three of us into this fix and they don't have one notion as to how in the world we're going to rectify our sins of greediness and thievery, much less save us from those hoodlums we stole that illicit money from."

Rose glance at Aldo. He shrugged his shoulders. Rose turned back and looked up into the motor home. Marguerite and Prudence stood in the door opening. Prudence was glaring at Louann. Marguerite was wringing her hands and quietly repeating, over and over, a mantra of sorts: "What are we to do? What are we to do? What are we to do?" Rose glanced back at Aldo and offered him 'the *look*'. He lowered his chin and slowly shook his head back and forth, then stooped and picked up a pebble and pitched it across the road. "OK, OK…everyone just relax a moment." He turned to Rose and said: "How about we invite these three ladies to follow us on out to Quartzsite, Arizona? We can park side-by-side out there amongst the thousands of other poor misguided RVers and try to figure out how to help these three ladies save themselves from the wrath of the drug dealers they stole that cash from." He nodded his head. "There isn't a human being on the face of this ol' planet who could find those three gals out amongst the thousands of silly boondockers parked out there in that miserable desert."

Prudence motioned for Louann and Marguerite to huddle with her on the steps of the motor home. After brief moments of verbal exchange she turned to Rose and Aldo and said: "We've agreed to offer you one fifth apiece of our stolen money if you'll help us out of this predicament."

Aldo furrowed his brow and cogitated one full minute, then   grinned broadly toward Rose and said: "I suppose that one hundred thousand tax free dollars for each of us of these lady's ill-gotten loot would be acceptable, considering the peril they'd be subjecting us to, don't you, Rose?"

Rose smiled brightly. "I suppose so."

"Shucks, pumpkin, let's throw logic to the winds and go for it."

Rose grinned. "What the hell - let's do it!"

More huddling.

"Then it's a firm understanding?" Prudence turned and said.

"Oh, it's a deal for sure, Prudence," Rose said.

"Alright, then," Prudence sniffed. "I suppose that we all suffer the consequences of our wants and desires," she mumbled. Then she turned to the motor home and said: "Now let's get these two RVs onto I-10 and head out to that Quartzsite, Arizona place you suggested. Those two ruffians may already be on our trail."

Aldo scratched his head and said in a soft voice: "Well I reckon that *I* would be looking for *you* if that was *my* half a million smackaroos."

"Well let's not just stand here!" Marguerite exclaimed wringing her hands.

Rose and Aldo hustled to their camper and headed it around the three ladie's motor home toward the next on ramp where they could drive back onto to the westbound I-10. The three ladies followed in the giant motor home. Just as they slowly guided their Rvs to the freeway on ramp, Humberto and Al sped overhead in their Winnebago oblivious to the fact that they had just passed their quarry who had stolen their half a million dollars in cold cash.

ⅠⅠⅠⅠⅠⅠⅠⅠⅠⅠⅠⅠⅠⅠⅠ 4 ⅠⅠⅠⅠⅠⅠⅠⅠⅠⅠⅠⅠⅠⅠⅠ

Humberto and Jesse

"Can't you make this old Winnebago junker go any faster?" Jesse mumbled to Humberto.

"I got my foot to the floorboard," Humberto blared back, "and we're going as fast as it'll go!"

Jesse swiveled his head from left to right. "Just shut the hell up and keep a look out for that red, white, and blue diesel motor home. They might of pulled off the highway for something." He stared at Humberto's face for a moment, then shook his head and returned to his perusal of I-10 and the Hill Country. He had often been this far west of San Antonio and he always marveled at the green thickness of the cedar and oak covering the Texas hills. During the thirty minutes they had driven onto the highway he had mentally tabulated twenty-two dead Whitetail Deer crumpled along the freeway's shoulders that the truckers and other travelers had struck. He spotted few animals on the ranch land. Mostly sheep and goats. The evening before, as he sat sipping coffee in the Taco Shack, a local had told him that the cedar trees had sucked up most of the ground water and starved the grass that had dominated the hills. He guessed that was the reason there weren't more cattle. That, and the rocky soil. The local had told him that a couple of hundred years earlier the hills had been covered mostly with tall grass and oak trees prior to the cedar invasion. It had been a 'Mecca' for the Comanche and several other American Indian tribes for there was plentiful water, grass, and wildlife for them until the German settlers, and others, shouldered them off the land. He noted that there was still an abundance of White Tail Deer, but not much water. And no Indians.

"Hey!" Humbero shouted, "That sign says that there's a state park south on Highway 83. Do you suppose that they're headed there?"

Jesse sneered back. "Are you nuts? They wouldn't be going camping in Garner State Park just after stealing half a million bucks. They'd be heading somewhere where they could spend some of it…like southern California or Arizona…places where they could live it up."

He snatched an old road atlas he spotted between the seats and paged to the United States map. Running his forefinger along I-10 he snagged a ragged finger nail on a loose staple as he perused each city along the route. "Ft. Stockton? Naw…El Paso? Maybe…Las Cruces? Nope… Lordsburg? Hell no…Tucson or Phoenix? Hmmm." He sat back and scanned the overall western part of the map, then he jerked forward in his seat and stabbed excitedly at the atlas. "I think I know where those old thieving broads are headed!"

"Where?"

"Vegas!" Jesse shouted, "Where 'what happens there stays there'! That's where I'd be headed!"

Humberto was silent for a moment, then he said: "I don't know, man. They're probably well behaved old gals. Those kinds of broads are generally boring. Vegas just don't seem to fit with of old broads."

"Who knows what goes on inside their heads? They filched our money, didn't they?"

"I just figure that maybe they are just pissed 'cause they wasted so much of their life being pious and politically correct and missed out on the *fun* things."

‖‖‖‖‖‖‖‖‖‖‖‖‖ 5 ‖‖‖‖‖‖‖‖‖‖‖‖‖

Rose, Aldo, Prudence, Louann, and Marguerite

Aldo repeatedly glanced into his rear vision mirror.

"Why're you looking back so often, Aldo?" Rose asked, "You think the bad guys are on our tail?"

"No. I'm watching those twitchy women back behind us. I'm scared that Prudence woman is going overtake us. She's got a heavy foot on her gas peddle. I'm hoping that she don't ram into the back of us."

Rose peered into her side mirror. "Pull off to the rest stop up ahead. I'll run back and tell her not to follow so closely."

Aldo flicked up his turn indicator and began slowing for the off ramp. Prudence followed him off I-10. There were several eighteen wheelers and a couple of motor homes parked in the rest area. Aldo carefully guided his camper between an older motor home and one of the giant trucks and turned off his engine, then studied his rear side mirror watching for the three women to pass behind to park their motor home. After a moment passed he said to Rose: "Where are they? I didn't see them park."

"They missed the turn for truck and camper parking. They're pulling in over there in the spaces reserved for automobiles. Boy, are those automobile travelers going to be mad. I bet that monster motor home of theirs is taking up ten of their parking spaces."

Aldo twisted an scanned the area. "I don't see them."

"You can't see them now. They're on the other side of the restroom building."

Aldo turned of his engine and took a deep breath. "Rose honey, do you think we're doing the right thing here? You know, like helping those three ladies get away with stealing all that dope money from those punks?"

Rose sighed as she reached over and took Aldo's hand in hers. "Aldo," she said softly, "we can hardly get by anymore, what with medical bills and all, so I say 'let's go for it' and let the chips fall where they may. We're going be eighty years old before we can blink our poor old sad eyes. We did our best to hang in there with the rest of the folks all our years. We just didn't have the smarts to make big money, the luck to inherit a bunch, or get in on some retirement plan. In my humble opinion, I'd rather share that half a million with those sweet naïve old ladies and raise a little *whoopee* with however few years we got left on this old planet, than turn over all that money to those dope dealers…or the pencil pushers in D.C."

"But don't you consider the *morality* evolved here?"

"Nope."

"I do," Aldo said.

"Aldo, we've been together close to sixty years. I know you like the back of my right hand." Rose grinned and squeezed his wrist, "You don't give a rat's ass regarding the *morality* of this situation. You're just voicing out one of those stupid *politically correct* statements."

Aldo affected an exaggerated expression of chagrin. "Ya think?"

Rose turned to open the camper's door and glanced at the motor home parked on her side of the camper. "Hey, Aldo, look at that old Winnebago motor home next to us. I bet that RV has over three hundred thousand miles on it."

Aldo leaned forward and perused the antiquated Winnebago. "Those two guys sitting in it look kinda 'iffy'. Don't have eye contact with them," he said.

Just after that moment one of the Winnebago occupants waved at them and hopped out to the tarmac. "Hey lady," he called out as he trotted to Rose's side of the camper, "did you old timers happen to notice a big red, white, and blue diesel pusher motor home with three little old broads pass you headed west or anywhere on or off I-10 the last three hours or so?"

Rose squinted back at the fellow. "Who, me?"

"Who in the devil else am I talking to, woman. Yes, you, or your runty little old man there in the driver's seat."

Aldo leaned forward and smiled. "No, sir," he said politely, "we haven't noticed any motor home like that on the road today."

Rose faced the fellow and let her eyes quickly scan the man's face. "I bet that you'd look halfway civilized if you'd shave off those stupid, scraggily face whiskers, lose that cheap glass earring, and take a bath."

Jesse grinned and looked across at Aldo. "Hey, man… you got yourself a feisty little old broad here."

Humberto called from the Winnebago: "Come on, Jesse, we don't have time to screw around with those two old fossils."

Jesse returned to the Winnebago, got in, and said to Humberto, "You know, man, the old people in this country are starting to get real smart-alecky lately."

"Yeah, I've noticed," Humberto said, "they steal money, talk back, and are just plain ornery."

"Go figure," Jesse said as Humberto steered the Winnebago from the rest stop back to I-10 west.

"Are you *crazy*?" Aldo asked Rose as the Winnebago pulled away.

Rose watched the Winnebago drive onto the freeway. "What?" she said sarcastically, "I wasn't going to let that jerk call you a 'runty little old man' and let it pass!"

"Didn't you *hear* what he asked us?" Aldo wiped the perpiration gathering rapidly on his forehead, "Those are the two creeps who are chasing our three little old ladies who swiped their drug money!"

"Holey moley," Rose mouthed. "It's a miracle that they didn't see the gals pull in to this rest area. The women are lucky that they parked in the wrong spaces over there behind the restroom building."

Aldo took a deep breath and mumbled: "Well, at least we now know what the bad guys look like and that they are ahead of us rather than following behind."

"What should we do now?" Rose asked.

"Let's walk over to where the three gals parked and

let them know what just happened. Then we'll have to figure out how to get on out to Quartzsite without running across those scalawags again."

Rose and Aldo hurried across the rest area to the three women in the motor home.

"Hey, ladies, Rose and I think that we just met the two dope smugglers you stole the money from," Aldo said as Prudence opened the motor home's door."

"Oh my! Oh my! What are we to do?" Marguerite gasped as she wrung her hands and turned in circles.

Louann said: "Shut up, dear, and let the Chambers finish telling us what they just saw!"

"My Lord!" Prudence exclaimed, "Where are they now?"

"Try to relax a moment," Rose interjected, "they're gone. They just now drove an old Winnebago motor home onto I-10 headed west."

"How do you know it was them?"

"Well, one of them walked up to our camper and asked if we'd seen a big red, white, and blue motor home with three little old ladies in it this morning…headed west on I-10."

"What did you tell them?" Marguerite sputtered.

Rose gave Marguerite a disgusted look and ignored her question.

"I told them 'no'," Aldo said.

"Oh, thank you, Aldo," Marguerite sniffed, "you just saved our lives."

"No," Rose said, "we just saved the five of us one-hundred thousand tax-free dollars each."

"We have to figure out some kind of plan to get the five of us to safety out in Quartzsite," Aldo said, "there's hundreds of miles of open freeway between here and Quartzite."

"I just thought of a plan, of sorts," Rose said. "Since those two bad guys are ahead of us on I-10 we'll just watch out for them and try to spot them before they spot us."

"How?" Prudence said.

"Well, I figure that Aldo and I will keep the lead position on the road and keep a sharp eye out for them and if we see their old Winnebago we'll stop and flag you gals down."

"Then what?" Marguerite said.

"We'll keep them in sight until they get on ahead of us a few miles and then keep on driving til we get to Quartzsite and vanish amongst the multitudes in the Arizona desert."

Louann straightened her shoulders, raised her chin, and announced: "Well, if you want *my* opinion, I think that we should take the bull by the horns and hunt them down and shoot them before they get the jump on us!"

"Louann!" Marguerite said, "What on earth has gotten into you?"

"Money," Aldo chuckled. He turned to Rose and said: 'Remember what I told you about 'see what happens to nice folks when they come into a lot of money that they didn't actually earn'?"

"Do you have a gun, Mr. Chambers?" Louann said.

"Just call me Aldo, Louann, and no, I don't have a gun."

Rose said: "We have to figure out a way to communicate with each other while we're driving."

"Do you have a cell phone?" Prudence asked Rose.

"Heavens no," Rose laughed, "Aldo and I could never figure out how to use one of those stupid things."

Prudence turned to Louann and Marguerite. "Did you bring your cell phones?"

"I brought mine," Louann said, "Marguerite could never learn how to use hers."

"Give it to Rose. We'll communicate back and forth with her phone and mine."

"I just told you that Aldo and I don't know how to use those dumb things."

Prudence glanced around the rest area. She spotted a senior citizen woman walking a fluffy looking little dog. A young boy, who she estimated to be about eight years old, was tagging along behind. Prudence called out to the woman. "Excuse us, lady, could we ask your grandson to teach this nice couple here how to use a cell phone?"

The woman smiled back and said to the boy: "Honey, would you please go over and help those folks?"

"Sure, Grandma," the boy said with a smile. He trotted to the quintet of elderly folks and said: "Hand me your cell."

||||||||||||||||||| 6 |||||||||||||||||||||||

Turk, Beto, Junior

Turk leaned back in his chair and studied the interior of Arturo's restaurant in the Mexican border town of Nuevo Progresso. He liked the ambiance. The tile flooring. The Mexican décor. Not the smells permeating the bar and dining room, though. *A tiny scent of a Mexican border town was expected,* he thought, *but this was way beyond his nostril's acceptance.* He was becoming increasingly apprehensive. He and his two associates, Junior and Beto, had been waiting in the cantina, from the moment its doors opened, for Jesse and his buddy, Humberto , to walk in the front door with a bag containing half a million American dollars. They were late, and he was becoming incrementally angry as each minute passed off his Rolex watch.

"Hey, Turk, don't get all riled up, man. Jesse and Humberto are going to walk in here any minute now with that moola and we'll be on our way to Bogota and the *good* life. They know what you'll do to them if they don't show," Junior said as he mimicked an action of slitting his throat.

Turk shrugged and continued his perusal of the popular restaurant. He watched a foursome sitting at an adjacent table. 'Windshield farmers' from the Rio Grande Valley just across the border, he surmised. Arturo had explained to him that they were called 'windshield farmers' because it was their modus operandi to drive about their farms in their leased vehicles early each morning motioning instructions through their windshields to the illegals who actually worked the land. After that they would meet at the cotton gin and play gin rummy until noon. For lunch they would meet at here at Arturo's and loaf the remainder of the day having a few drinks and gossiping until departing for dinner time in their lavish homes back in the Rio Grande Valley. Turk was envious of them, but he knew, in his heart, that their grand life would bore him to lunacy.

Turk's gaze returned to Junior. "If Jesse and his pal don't walk in that front door within the next minute or two, I want you to call his cell phone one last time. If he doesn't answer we're leaving here to hunt them down. I'm thinking that something's happened that'll make me want to get real nasty. He called me last night and said everything was going smooth. He said that he was in Kerrville in a taco joint across the street from an empty theatre building and had just traded his pick up to an RV sales lot for an old Winnebago motor home so's he could easily hide the bag of cash to sneak it across the border to us. And he assured me that he'd be here at Arturo's by midday. So call again…I'm starting to get bad vibes."

Junior picked up his cell phone and dialed. A tense moment passed. "Nope," he said, "he's not answering."

"OK, that's it. Let's go find 'em and get our money," Turk said as he pushed back his chair and pitched some bills on the table.

‖‖‖‖‖‖‖‖‖‖‖‖‖ 7 ‖‖‖‖‖‖‖‖‖‖‖‖‖‖

Jesse and Humberto

"I'm getting hungry, man."

Jesse glanced at Humberto. "Every time we have to pull over and stop, those old gals could just get farther and farther away. We gotta keep focused here and catch up with those old biddies or we'll never get Turk's money back." He furrowed his brow, "And you *know* what'll happen to *us* if that don't happen."

"We have to stop for gas, don't we? I'll run in the station and pick up some snacks while you fill the gas tank." Humberto furrowed his brow, "They gotta stop for gas, too, ya know."

Jesse glanced at the fuel gage. "OK, we'll stop up here at Ozona, but make it fast."

"Why would anybody name a town 'Ozona?" Jesse mumbled.

"Don't ask me, man. Why would anyone name a town 'Balmorhea'?" Humberto replied as he ran his forefinger along I-10 on the atlas in his lap.

Jesse steered the Winnebago onto the off ramp and began scanning the area for a convenient gas station. "Over there," he said as he pointed.

"Does it look like we can buy some snacks inside?"

"Yeah." Jesse squinted. "I gotta take a leak before I fill up."

"I'll get us coffee and some eats," Humberto said.

Jesse pulled the Winnebago next to a gas pump and turned off the engine. "Hurry it up, now," he said as he exited to go to the restroom.

#

"Look! Look!" Rose shouted into Aldo's ear.

"*What?*"

"Down there in that Exxon station!" Rose exclaimed. "It's that old Winnebago those two creeps are driving. The ones who asked us about the motor home with the three women!"

Aldo clicked on his right turn signal and braked hard as he fought to swerve the camper down the off ramp.

"What are you doing?" Rose questioned.

"Grab that cell phone and call the gals…tell them to stay on I-10 but slow it down some. We going to stop here and figure out some way to distract those two vultures."

"Have you lost your senses? How on earth are the two of us old has-beens going to deal with the likes of those two hoodlums?"

"I don't know right now, but we can surely figure out something or other. We learned a lot of 'tit for tat' things hanging out with the Hill Country Heller bikers all those years. We'll have to start thinking like *they* think."

Aldo turned toward the gas station and drove slowly past as Rose dialed the ladies who were trailing a couple of miles behind on I-10. He watched the two fellows get out of their Winnebago and hurry toward the store.

"Hey, Prudence," Rose said into the cell phone, "Aldo and I are stopping here in this little town for a moment. You just keep on driving on I-10, but slow it down some so we can catch up with you after a while. OK?"

"You two aren't abandoning us are you?" Prudence cried.

"Heck no we aren't. You gals have *our* share of the loot, remember? We just spotted the two dudes who're looking for you. Aldo's going to figure out some way to delay them or something."

"Oh my lord," Prudence said to Louann and Marguerite, "Rose and Aldo just saw the hoodlums. They're going to…"

Rose jerked her cell phone from her ear as Marguerite and Louann screamed in panic. "Hey! Calm down ladies. We'll take care of this problem one way or another, so just try to relax and keep on driving!" Rose yelled into the cell phone.

Aldo circled the block and parked next to the curb adjacent to the gas station. He and Rose studied the scenario for a moment, then Aldo turned to Rose. "Climb over here in the driver's seat and keep the engine running when I hop out. I'm going around back to the camper and get in my tool chest."

"Now what cockamamie thing are you fixing to do?"

"You just do what I say and be ready to skeedaddle soon as you see me come running."

"Oh boy," Rose sighed.

"Focus on you and me pocketing a hundred thousand dollars each, momma. That's what keeping *me* motivated."

Aldo slipped out of the camper as Rose slid over behind the steering wheel. He surveyed the scene for a moment, then leaving the passenger door open, hustled to the rear of the camper and located his tool chest. He grabbed his wire cutter and hurried across the tarmack to the back of the Winnebago and clipped off the valve stem of its spare tire, then quickly stepped to the side of the motor home and cut off the valve stem of the rear right tire. Then hurried back toward Rose and their camper. As he approached the halfway mark Rose began honking the horn and pointing to the filling station. Aldo glanced back to see Humberto and Jesse walking toward their Winnebago. Humberto was gesturing toward the rear tire. Aldo hustled as fast as his arthritic legs would move. He scurried toward the door of the camper just as Humberto spotted the cut off valve stem on the asphalt, saw Aldo running with a wire cutter in his hand, and heard and saw the rear tire deflating. Rose watched Jesse grab Humberto's arm and point toward her and Aldo and the camper. She jerked the gear into drive and prepared to stomp on the accelerator.

"Hey! Hey! Hey!" Humberto shouted as he and Jesse sprinted toward Aldo and Rose. Aldo scurried to the camper and grabbed its open door. "Go! Go! Go!" he shouted to Rose. She stepped hard on the gas pedal. Jesse and Humberto ran diagonally across the corner of the station's apron and almost reached Aldo's backside. Jesse flung his styrofoam cup of hot coffee at the departing vehicle with his right hand and threw a banana with his left.

"Hey! Hey! Hey!" Humberto continued yelling as he slipped on the banana Jesse had thrown at the camper. Hot coffee splashed on him from his cup as he threw it toward the rear of the camper. He sprawled on the pavement and watched Rose and Aldo pick up momentum toward the on ramp to I-10 west. "Those are the two old codgers we questioned back at the rest stop!" he bawled at Jesse, "Why'd they flatten our tire? We didn't do nothing to them 'cept ask about three old biddies in a motor home."

Jesse stood and watch Rose and Aldo's camper move quickly onto the freeway. "I betcha I know why," he murmured.

‖‖‖‖‖‖‖‖‖‖‖‖‖‖ 8 ‖‖‖‖‖‖‖‖‖‖‖‖‖‖‖

Turk, Beto, Junior

Junior stopped Turk's rented Hummer next to the Departing Gate at McAllen International Airport. "Drive on back to Nuevo Progresso, Junior, and get a room near Arturo's. Beto and I will keep in touch with you on our cell phones."

"How long you gonna be gone?"

"Hell, man, I don't know," Turk said with a disusted tone, "as long as it takes to locate Humberto and Jesse."

Beto grabbed two carry-ons from the rear of the Hummer. "Let's hustle, Turk, the plane leaves in thirty minutes and we got to call ahead to San Antonio to make sure we got a rental car ready and waiting for us."

As Beto followed Turk through the terminal he felt a shudder course through his skeleton. He had rarely seen Turk become as angry as he was at this moment. And he knew that this was just the beginning of his jefe's boiling point. He had a moment of empathy for Jesse and Humberto, but it quickly dissipated. Those two estupidos

56

knew what they were getting into when Turk contracted them to sneak the half-million dollars to him across the Rio Grande to Nuevo Progresso. Beto wondered if they truly comprehended the consequences of not showing up at Arturo's with the five-hundred thousand at their allotted time. *Oh, well,* he reflected, *those two probably screwed up as far back as middle school. I figure that each of their teachers back then already had them pegged as 'losers'.*

#

Turk sped off I-10 at the 508 off ramp leading to downtown Kerrville. Beto's right foot ached from pressing hard on the rental car's floorboard as Turk braked to the stop signal at the bottom of the ramp.

"How're we gonna find that taco place Jesse called from last night?" Beto said.

"We'll look for an old abandoned movie house," Turk murmured, "with a taco joint across from it."

As Turk accelerated under the freeway bridge Beto pointed ahead. "Look there, jefe, there's a Kerrville Visitor Center! Someone in there should know where that empty theatre is."

Turk pulled off to the Visitor Center's parking lot and braked to a bouncing stop. Beto hopped from the car and hustled inside. "Where's the old empty theatre building at in this town?" he barked at a startled lady behind a desk.

The clerk, taken back by his sudden appearance and manner, asked: "The old Ritz Theatre?"

Beto leaned across the desk and glared into the lady's eyes and said with a sarcastic tone to his voice: "How many old empty movie houses does this little Hill Country burg have, lady?"

"Two…there's one down in old town and one out by…"

"Which one is across the street from a taco joint?"

"Oh, that would be the old Ritz theatre."

"Well? Beto asked.

She smiled sweetly - Texas style - and pointed toward the south. "Just drive that-a-way until you reach the stop signal at the intersection of Sidney Baker - that's the street out front here - and Main. That's where the old hospital building is. There's a lovely spanking brand new hospital now just across the Guadalupe River. You should visit it. It's lovely. Main Street is also called Junction Highway, it will take you to the quaint little Hill Country town of Ingram where there are some *marvelous* murals painted on the lumber yard building. You should see those, too. But that's just two of the many pleasures offered about the Hill Country. And before you consider viewing the murals…"

"I'm in a rush, lady, just tell me about the theatre."

"Oh, yes. Then turn to your right and continue until you reach a signal at Plaza Drive," Another large smile. "Then turn left. The Taco Shack is on the corner and the old Ritz is just down the street. You simply can't miss it. The movie theatre closed down recently, because…"

Beto turned and rushed out the front door and hopped into the automobile. He turned to Turk and said: "We drive on this street til we see an old hospital, then turn right and drive until we spot the Taco Shack!"

"Got it."

Beto exhibited an expression across his face. "Hey, Jefe, what good's it gonna do to find the Taco Shack?"

"Well just think it through, man. Somebody in that taco joint - a worker or someone - is bound to remember seeing those two jerks. How often do folks in a little one-horse town like this one run across dudes who look and dress like Jesse and Humberto, for cryin' out loud? Man, those two would stand out in San Antonio's River Walk Mud Festival."

Turk sped down Sidney Baker, turned right on Main, and raced to Plaza Drive. He turned into the Taco Shack, stopped in the center of the parking lot, shot a third finger to an elderly couple - in a late model Cadillac sporting a disabled license plate - who honked at him, and trotted into the café.

"Hey!" he hollored, "Anyone in here seen a couple of guys last night or early this morning who looked out of place or kinda strange?"

All movement in the Taco Shack came to a silent halt. Everyone stared at Turk. A male senior citizen slowly raised his hand and said: "I saw a couple of chubby men who had on kacki shorts, black socks, and wing-tip dress shoes."

The counter waiter said: "Oh, those were just Winter Texans who hadn't left to go back to Iowa yet."

"I seen a couple of fellers who was wearing dark business suits," a teenager offered."

"Yeah, I seen 'em, too," his companion added.

The counter waiter said: "Them two was headed to a funeral. We get a bunch of 'em every day since Kerrville became a sort of retirement center."

"I mean a couple of younger dudes with earrings and tatoos and all," Turk replied.

An older bald-headed man turned to Turk and said, "Yeah, I talked to 'em…they went over there to the corner gas station in a rickety old Winnebago RV. They was looking for three old ladies in a big motor home."

Turk pondered his thought, nodded, and hurried out to Beto who was waiting in the car. "Scoot over. Drive across the intersection to that gas station."

Beto shifted over to the driver's seat as Turk sprinted across the street to the filling station. Turk shouldered a patron away from the paying counter. "You see two earringed and tattooed jerks getting gas for an old Winnebago motor home earlier?"

"Who the hell wants to know?" De Lynn asked, thrusting her chin forward.

"Me, you stupid old broad!"

"How 'bout a hot cup of java?" De Lynn replied as she poured her steaming coffee onto Turk's crotch.

He jumped backward brushing wildly at his groin and glared at her. "You just got yourself into a world of hurt, woman."

The customer Turk had just shoved aside pitched his Stetson hat on the counter and grabbed Turk by the seat of his pants and the back of his collar and duck-walked him out the front door and kicked him in his rear. Turk sprawled on the pavement. Just at that moment Beto drove up to the station and hollered to Turk: "Get up, Jefe, that janitor dude from the taco joint just now told me that he heard that those two strange dudes drove west on I-10 early this morning in the Winnebago!"

Turk struggled to the car holding his left hand on his

butt and his right hand cradling his zipper and carefully slid onto the seat. "They got a couple hours head start on us. Drive back to that visitor center and find out if there's an air field around these parts."

As Beto swung the car around the station Turk proffered a third finger to the man who had thrown him out the door. "If we weren't in a hurry I'd go back and kick the livin' crap out of that jerk."

"Sure, you would, Turk," Beto mumbled to himself.

Beto slid the car to a halt in front of the Visitor Center building. Turk hopped out of the car and rushed inside. "Is there an air field around these parts?" he called to the clerk.

"Oh, yes," she answered with a sanguine tone to her voice. "It's a lovely flying field. Not too many years back they lengthened the runways so's bigger airplanes could take off and land. Just next door to the airport lies the Mooney Aircraft fractory. I'm told that the Mooneys are the fastest…"

"I don't have time to listen to all your crap, woman, just tell me how to get there."

The clerk tucked her chin to her chest and said: "You know, buster, you're the second asshole who's busted my chops this morning. She stood. "Now if you don't apologize to me this minute I'm gonna walk around this counter and kick your…"

"For cryin' out loud, lady…*I'm sorry*! So where's the airport?"

She briefly explained how to find Kerrville Municipal Airport. He hustled back out to the car. As he settled in the passenger seat he said to Beto: "Man, these folks out here sure like to kick ass!"

Beto opened his eyes as wide as his lids would allow. "She kicked your ass too?"

"Just shut up and drive. I'll tell you where to turn."

#

Beto parked near the office next to a large hanger. "Longhorn Charter Flying Service," he said. "How 'bout checking here?"

Turk hurried inside. "You people got a fast plane with a good pilot ready for hire right now?"

"As a matter of fact, we do," a smiling man said. "I have a hot little Mooney sittin' right out there on the apron fueled-up and ready to leave and I'm the pilot-owner ready to please."

Turk shook his head as he perused the pilot. "Excuse me?"

The pilot stopped smiling. "Just a little humor," he said.

"I ain't in a humorous mood," Turk said.

"Sorry," the pilot said, "where would you like me to fly you?"

"Can you fly that airplane out there without conversing with me or my sidekick?"

The pilot studied Turk for a moment. "Just exactly where do you want me to fly you in silence?"

"Follow I-10 to El Paso low enough so's that we can identify motor homes driving west."

"Are you searching for a particular motor home?"

"See," Turk said, "there you go, again, conversing too much. What you should be asking me is: 'Can you afford to charter me and my airplane, and do you have to pee before we take off."

"Can you and do you?" the pilot asked.

"That's better. Yes and no."

"OK, then…let's go," the pilot said with a sigh.

"You sure you have a current pilot's license?"

The pilot nodded his head slowly up and down and answered: "You got cash?"

Turk reached into his pocket and pulled out a large wad of cash.

"I'll start my check out," the pilot said.

Turk said: "Yeah, that's good. And just nod from now on." Then walked briskly to the door and motioned for Beto to take their small bags to the Mooney.

IIIIIIIIIIIIIIIIIIII 9 IIIIIIIIIIIIIIIIIIII

Rose, Aldo, Louann, Marguerite, Prudence

Aldo pushed the gas pedal to the floorboard as Rose focused ahead on the open stretch of I-10 West.

"I hope those three old ladies slowed up their motor home when we told them to," Rose said.

"Likely as not they sped up in a panic," Aldo answered as he crunched his brows together in concentration.

Rose leaned back into her seat and shook her head from side to side. "Hell, I don't blame them for getting all jittery. Those two hoodlums chasing after them looked awful mean." She took a deep breath. "And now they're after you and me as well."

Aldo glanced at Rose. "Momma...how on God's green earth do we, somehow, manage to get ourselves mixed up in stupid chenanigans such as this?"

"Well," Rose answered, "*this* time the off-hand mention of you and me collecting one hundred thousand dollars each in tax-free cash gave us a nudge, I suppose."

"I believe you're right."

Aldo focused on the highway, but his thoughts began to trail off to the predicament in which the three elderly women were caught, and now, he and Rose. *We're bound together with the three old gals for our mutual survival. If we split up each of us will be forever questioning: will one or more of us be found by those hoodlums and be forced to rat-out on the others? No,* he concluded, *we have to stick together, like it or not, so's each of us can watch each other's back. Damn,* he thought, *we're linked together by trust with those three old women."*

"Trust," Aldo mumbled.

"What?"

Aldo glanced at Rose. "We're tied to those old ladies by the fickle finger of trust."

"Trust?" Rose asked, "Are you suggesting that any one of the five of us is *now* capable of being bound by *trust* to the others?"

"Well, yes," Aldo said, "they seem to be honorable old gals and I certainly trust you. Don't you trust me?"

"Yes, certainly, but just think about this for a moment. They stole half a million bucks and we happily agreed to share it with them."

"But Rose, pumpkin, all five of us are stealing it from practicing low-life criminals!"

"Does that fact make our thievery *acceptable* in your reasoning?"

"Dang straight!" Aldo said.

"How so?"

"I figure stealing from bad-asses is justifiable. We all rationalize our particular points of view, no matter how wrong it may seem to others, don't we? It's human nature."

"But is that *right*?" Rose queried.

"Hey, pumpkin, that's the way it *is.*"

The two old timers sped along in silence trying to catch up with their three accomplices. Aldo and Rose had struggled to keep abreast of the economy their entire lives. Neither had been the happy recipient of a carefully worded will, nor had they been the beneficiary of a windfall of cash or property from relatives. *But that was OK*, they had figured, *they had done alright, all things considered.* Aldo had been too young for the three and a half years of World War II, just right for the four year Korean Conflict, and too old for the thirteen year Viet Nam excursion. Rose had helped pay their living expenses - and minor extravagances - by serving second rate food to her peers in common little locally owned eateries about the Texas Hill Country. Aldo, most of his working life - after his two-year stint in the infantry - painted houses. Mostly the outsides. He didn't have the patience for the precise detail required for inside work. He could have, probably, but he just couldn't bare having to deal with picky homeowners who, for the most part, didn't have empathy for the skills and efforts of hired craftsmen. He'd had to suck up a portion of his previously agreed cost estimate more than once because home owners had changed their minds as to the shade or color they had selected. Somehow the color selection had become - in their minds - *his* decision, not *their* decision. *Oh well, such is life,* he philosophised.

"You know what, Rose? I'm just going to think about the two hundred thousand smackeroos we've fallen into and not dwell on those two dirt bags who're wanting to get back their ill-gotten loot. Even if you think you and I and the three ladies are just as guilty of theft as *they* are."

Rose took a deep breath and said: "Hey, Aldo, it's a done deal. There isn't any going back now. I believe that - in the reality of the minds of those hoodlums - those three old ladies and you and I are the 'bad guys' who stole their loot, and they aren't ever going to give up trying to get it back. Hoodlums don't play by the rules of reason or law."

Aldo drove silently for a few minutes, then said, "I suppose we didn't either in regards to this situation, but so what?"

#

"I see Aldo and Rose now!" Prudence exclaimed as she peered into her giant rear view mirror.

"Are they alone," Marguerite whispered.

"As far as I can tell. I don't see that old Winnebago motor home back there."

"Well thank the heavens above," Louann said. "I wonder what the Chambers did to stop those two hoodlems?"

"Whatever they did is just fine with me," Marguerite said.

"My father used to say: Fighting dirty gets you dirty."

"*This* is not the same."

"Father also used to say: Birds of a feather flock together."

Prudence jerked her head to the side and said: "Shut the hell up!"

Prudence, stared back at the long, open expanse of I-10 between Ozona and El Paso. "Call Rose on the cell phone and ask if we should pull over to the side of the highway."

Marguerite dialed.

"Oh, Rose, honey, are you alright?" she whined into her cell phone.

"I guess Aldo and I are as alright as can be under our cicumstances. How're you ladies holding up?"

"We're in a dither, I suppose. Does Aldo want us to stop along the side of the road?"

"No. Don't stop. Keep on driving, but speed up a bit. We have to get some big mileage between us and those two hoodlums before they get their tires fixed."

"What did you two do to their tires?"

"It doesn't matter what we did. They're gonna be delayed a bit, though, so we have to hurry to El Paso where we can hide amongst the populous."

"What did Rose say?" Prudence impatiently asked Marguerite.

Marguerite closed the cell phone. "She said to hurry to El Paso where we can get off this open highway and hide.'"

"Sounds good to me," Louann murmured.

Prudence sighed audibly. She thought back to the many times that she and her late husband had traversed the five hundred mile I-10 corredor between Kerrville and El Paso. She had enjoyed the lonely drive each and every time. Many of her acquaintaces had complained about the lonesome stretch of highway, but not her. The mountains of northern Mexico loomed off to the south offering a vista that, in her imagination, brought forth imageries of ancient nomadic Americans trekking single file across the plains, and small tenacious bands of Spanish explorers bravely facing the wild unknown. She wondered if each of the distant peaks had been conquered by human beings - or animals other than soaring Eagles or hawks. She had read that Cabeza de Vaca had survived that foreboding, but majestic, wilderness. Humans hadn't overly infected it. Yet. One of her late husband's cynical associates had compared human beings to cancer cells, she reflected. He had stated that he believed: 'humans are, to the earth, as cancer cells are to humans - destroyers.' *Oh well,* she thought, *I'll just allow myself to enjoy what I can as long as I have left. There's nothing that I can personally do to change the course of* mankind*, no matter what any of the pundits expouse. Human nature rules us with an iron fist just the same as the rest of earth's creatures are ruled by their genes.*

"Did you just now sigh?" Louann asked Prudence.

"I don't know. Did I?"

"Yes."

"Well, if I did it'll be the last time. From now on it's on to Las Vegas and let the good times roll!"

"My goodness," Marguerite quipped, "what's gotten into you?"

"Reality!"

IIIIIIIIIIIIIIIII 10 IIIIIIIIIIIIIIIIII

Jesse and Humberto

Humberto gazed out at the blue silhouette of the distant Davis Mountains from the windshield of the Winnebago. It was a typical, blazing hot, late August afternoon, and the Mesquite trees pricking the landscape of western Texas were cringing from the sun - their thorns trying to protect the Mesquite's tiny pale green leaves from the wildlife.

"What're you thinking about?" he asked Jesse, "You're too damned quiet."

"That five-hundred thousand cash in the sleeping bag."

"Yeah, what about it?"

"You'd better be thinking about it harder than me."

"And why's that?"

"Because Turk hired *us,* not *me,* to bring it to him."

Jesse could tell by the look on his face that Humberto was trying to figure a way out of their predicament.

"How much of that money was Turk gonna pay us to

sneak it across the Mexican border for him?" Humberto asked.

Jesse took his right foot off of the gas pedal. The Winnebago began to lose speed.

"Hey, man, what the hell are you doing? Those old women and their buddies are gonna get further away from us."

The Winnebago vibrated as its tires met the shoulder of I-10. Jesse steered the Winnebago to a stop, turned off its engine, and glared into Humberto's eyes. "You listen to me, you dumb turd. Turk hired me - and I hired you - so that makes *you* just as responsible as *me* for that money. We're in this mess together, and don't you try to weasel out of it!"

"Come on, Jesse, just let me off at the next town. I didn't count on three old ladies stealing Turk's money from us."

"Like hell I'm letting you out of this mess. You jumped at the chance to make some easy money," Jesse started the engine, "and you're, by damn, gonna stick with me and help me get Turk's money back to him."

Humberto slumped back into his seat and affected a pout. "What're we going to do if we can't find those old broads?"

"That *ain't* an option," Jesse quipped, "we have to catch them, and that's all there is to it." He shook his head in disbelief as he steered back onto the highway. "No sir, dude, you and me are in this together. And those three old ladies and the two old farts who seem to be helping them as well. At least as far as Turk will be concerned. Hell, man, I figure Turk or someone else will whack *all* of us if we don't get his half a million smackaroos back to him right away. Come to think about it, I reckon they're thinking about whacking all of us whether we get their money back to them or not."

"You think?"

"Damn straight, I think. I was standing outside of one of the cartel's drop houses in San Antonio a few months back when one of the syndicate guys shot a stupid delivery guy in his right knee with a twenty-two caliber pistol 'cause the jerk had tried to cheat him out of one lousy kilo of weed."

Humberto shook his head and affected an expression of wonderment, "Damned thieving three old broads stealing Turk's and our money," he mumbled, "what in the hell were they thinking?"

||||||||||||||||| 11 |||||||||||||||||

Turk and Beto

"Get down lower to the freeway," Beto mumbled to the Mooney's pilot.

The Mooney gradually settled to a lower altitude. Beto focused intently on the sparsely trafficked highway. Turk sat back in his seat and studied the rugged landscape below. It was populated with a smattering of cattle mingling amongst white-tailed deer and oil and gas pumpers. The pumpers reminded him of giant grasshoppers munching the Mesquite trees and cacti. Occasionally the Mooney passed over small, jagged mountains. Many of the peaks served as bases for the lonely towers erected to serve the thousands of cell phones being carried below by the eighteen wheelers, Rvers, and other vehicles headed West toward the Pacific Ocean and East toward the Gulf of Mexico.

The pilot said: "We're as low as I can legally fly."

Beto didn't answer. Turk shrugged.

Condensation trails from commercial airliners

streaked the pale blue sky thousands of feet above them. Whispers of white clouds illuminated by the brilliant Texas sunlight dotted the horizon. The pilot turned back to Turk as if he was going to speak again. Turk glared back and placed his forefinger up to his lips in a gesture for silence. The pilot took a deep breath and resumed his focus on flying. Turk peered down at a sprawling ranch house. There was a large man-made lake in front of the structure. It was surrounded by trees. There was a small island in the middle. The same kind of trees bordered a driveway to I-10. *Someday I'm gonna have a layout like that in Texas,* he mused, *but it sure as hell won't be isolated from the rest of the world like that one.*

"I ain't seen no old Winnebgo motor home yet, Jefe," Beto said.

"They'll be toodling along down there. Just keep watching."

"What if we don't spot them?" Beto shifted his position. "We'll find them because we can get to El Paso flying in this here airplane sooner than they can drive there. If we don't spot them on I-10 before El Paso, we'll turn around and fly over the secondary highways. There's no way we won't be able to see their big-ass motor home from the air. "He leaned forward. "Hey, Pilot, you can land this sucker on one of those lonely roads if you have to, can't you?"

The pilot shook his head from side to side.

Turk grinned. "Sure you can. Me and my buddy, Beto here, will help you make that choice."

"Hey Beto. Take a look at that little mountain down there. It looks just like one of those Egyptian things," Turk exclaimed.

"Pyramid," the pilot mumbled.

"Looks like a giant titty to me," Beto said.

IIIIIIIIIIIIIIIIII 12 IIIIIIIIIIIIIIIII

Rose and Aldo

"Of all the dumb things we've gotten ourselves into this is the dumbest," Aldo said.

"I agree," Rose said.

"Then why are we doing this?"

"Two-hundred thousand tax-free U.S. dollars."

"Oh yeah, I almost forgot."

"Like hell, you did."

"Well maybe, for a moment or two, when I was considering our upcoming demise."

"Think positive."

"You mean like when the Philistines thought: 'Hey, nothing's going to change around here if we just keep doing things the same way.'"

Rose focused her eyes on Aldo's profile. For the first time during their fifty-eight year marriage he seemed genuinely frightened. Only *she* would have been able to recognize that emotion in his demeanor. Others would have thought that he was just being a smart-ass as usual.

"Listen, hon, this journey has begun. Now all we have to do is hide out for a time with the three old ladies until those hoodlums stop hunting us."

"Do you honestly believe that those dope dealers are going to let those old gals - and you and me for crying out loud - get away with filching their half million?"

"Yes. Because there's millions more waiting for them. Every minute that those low-lifes spend looking for us they're actually losing more money."

"Rose, pumpkin, I have to tell you that I wonder whether it's possible for the likes of you and me to actually get along with those three old biddies long enough to pull this off. It may take months…even years, for God's sake."

"I've been thinking about that, Aldo. All we have to do to get along with Louann, Marguerite, and Prudence - and for that matter anyone else - is to just be calm and courteous. And more importantly, *not* express our opinions on *any* subject whatsoever, 'cause nobody gives a hoot about our point of view anyhow. Fifty percent of the time it'll just piss 'em off."

Aldo guffawed, "Yeah, pumpkin, you're surely right about that!"

They were cruising along I-10 watching the rear of the women's motor home and periodically glancing nervously into their own rear view mirrors.

Aldo said: "I've been thinking about us driving on this freeway. We're sitting ducks out here in the open like this. All those hoodlums have to do is begin contacting truckers along this open road. You know, those truck drivers notice everything - except their speed - and they're all in touch with one another. If those hoodlums think about querying the eighteen wheelers they just might locate our motor home and camper."

"What do you think we should do?"

"I was considering turning off I-10 onto one of these state highways and hiding out somewhere for a spell."

Rose reached to the back seat and pulled their Atlas to her lap and began perusing the Texas map. "Darn, there isn't one highway that leads to anywhere that we could hide these two campers, unless we turned off on State Highway 17 at a town called Balmorhea. This map indicates a Texas State Recreation Area there."

"Naw, they might be looking at state parks and such for our two campers."

"Then what's your suggestion?"

After a few moments passed Aldo shrugged his shoulders. "I can't think of anything better. Call the old bidies and tell them to pull off up ahead at that Balmorhea place. We'll stop there and have ourselves a little caucus of sorts. Another shrug. "Who knows, maybe *they'll* have some suggestions."

IIIIIIIIIIIIIIIIII 13 IIIIIIIIIIIIIIIIII

Humberto and Jesse

From his passenger seat in the Winnebago, Humberto read the description in his atlas of the next town on I-10, the colorful village of Balmorhea. "Hey man," he said to Jesse, "This little town up ahead was named for the three dudes who developed it. Balcum, Moore, and Rhea. Balmorhea. I was wondering about a town with a name like that. I figured Balmorhea was an Indian word - or maybe Spanish - you know, like Ozona we passed by a while back."

Humberto snorted: "Ozona ain't a Mexican word, stupid, it's a scientific word that means air. Like when a scientific dude says: 'There's a lot of ozona around the planet'."

Jesse glanced over at Humberto. "You know, Humberto, you oughta read more and enrich yourself. When Turk pays us off we're going to be running with the big dogs, you know, and we'll have to act more educated."

"Hey, I didn't graduate from high school like you, but I almost did. If it hadn't been for old lady Black I would of made it."

"Yeah, right." Humberto looked back at the atlas. "It says here that there's a big-ass spring there called San Solomon Springs and a state recreation area. You suppose they pulled their Rvs over there?"

"Maybe they did. I'll swing through and we can take a look."

It was late afternoon, and the sun's affect on the scene was dramatic. Shadows cascaded across the road from tall trees as the Winnie approached the huge springs. "Gotcha!" Humberto shouted as he pointed excitedly toward the Springs.

"Where?"

"Right over there in that camping area!"

"Yeah, that's them alright. Both campers, side-by-side, just like sittin' ducks." Jesse grinned.

"We got them, man. Pull over next to 'em," Humberto yelled.

"No. Not yet. First let's park this 'ol Winnebago across the camping area and figure out how best we should approach them."

"Yeah. We'll surprise 'em. Catch them off guard. But wait. They might have a gun or something. You know how many old broads are toting guns these days. It's getting to where a guy ain't safe no more."

#

Aldo was seated on the couch. Rose beside him. Prudence had swiveled the driver's seat around facing them. Louann and Marguerite stood next to the kitchen counter. Their eyes exhibited a myopic stare as Rose began to speak. "OK, now, let's all put on our thinking caps and try to figure out our next move."

"I thought that we agreed to drive our campers to that place in Arizona called Quartzsite and lose ourselves among the - what did you call them - Aldo?" Louann sniffed.

"Boondockers."

"Whatever, but I thought that was…"

"It still is our plan," Rose quickly interjected, "but Quartzsite's about eight hundred miles from here," she hunched her shoulders, "and every mile is out on highways that cross the desert. Those dope dealers could spot us real easy out on the open highway."

"How about hanging around here for a few days?" Marguerite suggested. "It seems to be a nice place."

A clunk sound. The motor home shook. Prudence twirled her driver seat back to face the windshield and began to peruse the venue. "Oh my God," she suddenly cried out, "I see both of those hoodlums right now. They're at the door…"

Rose and Aldo jumped from the couch. Louann and Marguerite scuddled forward.

"Our door?" they asked simultaneously.

"Yes!"

"Lock the door!" Marguerite shrieked.

"Start the engine!" Louann hollered.

"Oh, crap" Aldo muttered.

"See what you got us into," Rose said to Aldo.

"Me?" Aldo exclaimed.

"Open the damned door!" Jesse yelled as he began

pounding on the outside of the motor home. "We got big rocks in front and back of the wheels." More pounding. "You can't move forward or backwards!"

"What'll we do now?" Prudence said.

There was a moment of silence, then Rose said: "We'll negotiate with them."

"You mean offer them some of our five-hundred thousand dollars?"

More pounding.

"Hell yes. It's either that or who knows what terrible things those hoodlums will do to us."

Louann, Prudence, and Marguerite turned and stared wide-eyed at Aldo.

"Don't look at *me*."

Rose stepped forward and opened the door. Outside Humberto jumped back a step and hollered: "Don't shoot!

Jesse peeked around the opened motor home door at the RV's five occupants. "You old farts don't have a gun, do you?"

"Heavens no," Marguerite said.

"In that case, we want our money back," Jesse said.

"Do *you* have a gun?" Louann said.

"No, we're just delivery guys - like them pizza delivery dudes - but we're younger and meaner and stronger than you old farts."

Prudence pulled her shoulders back, and with an air of indignation, said: "That's not *your* money anymore. It's *ours* now."

"You sneaky old ladies stole that money from me and Jesse."

"Well, you two got it illegally!"

"Well, so did you!"

"Shut up!" Jesse barked.

"Hey! Everybody calm down here," Aldo said as he stepped forward with the palms of his hands facing upward. "I'm sure that we can resolve this dilemma calmly and fairly if we have a little sit-down together and talk it out."

"Are you crazy?" Jesse said.

"Just hear us out. If you take *all* the half-million from me and these sweet little ol' ladies here, we will be honor-bound to report and identify you to the cops."

"Now *I* think he's crazy," Prudence said to Rose, "don't you?"

"Most of the time."

"You think me and Humberto are gonna let you old codgers rat on *us?* And what the hell do you mean: '*all* the half-million?'"

Aldo shifted his feet to a wider stance, licked his lips, raised his eyebrows, and said: "Look. There isn't one bonafide bit of logic in the world that says all seven of us can't enjoy a share of this ill-gotten money. Wouldn't you feel a tad guilty not sharing this cash with me and my wife - who you can plainly see ain't no rich folks - and these three sweet senior citizen ladies who undoubtedly deserve some relief from a lifetime of duty and service to their families?"

Humberto looked at Jesse. "What the hell is he talking about?"

"He's saying that you and me should split up Turk's half mil with them."

Humberto stared, unbelievingly, back at Jesse. "If we

give any of Turk's money away he'll torture us *before* he whacks us."

"Are you saying all that money belongs to someone named Turk?" Rose said.

"Yeah, lady, and he'll have us all shot dead if we don't get it back to him right away."

"Shut up, Humberto," Jesse barked.

Jesse studied the five tremulant senior citizens. He focused on Aldo. "You little runty old fart. You flattened our tires."

Aldo rubbed the unshaved stubble on his face and grinned. "I thought it was a good idea at the time. Slowed you down a tad, didn't I?"

"I ought to kick your ass for that."

"Please don't," Rose said, ""Cause if you do I'm gonna have to hurt you real bad. He's my little sweet man!"

Jesse glanced back at Humbero. "You're right, dude. These little old-timers are getting downright mean these days. Guess that old TV announcer was right when he wrote that book about the 'greatest generation'."

Humberto shook his head. "What old announcer? What book?"

Jesse shook his head.

Aldo said: "This Turk guy; you're saying that he's a *bad* dude?"

"The baddest."

"When were you supposed to turn the half million over to him?"

"This morning."

"Where?"

"Across the border down in the Valley."

Aldo took a deep breath. "What do you think this bad-ass Turk is thinking right about now?"

"I'll tell you what he's thinking," Rose interjected, "he's thinking that you two fools ran off with his money."

Humberto placed his hand on Jesse's shoulder and began to sniff. "Yeah, Jesse, I bet this little old broad is right," he began blinking rapidly, "and if she's right our asses are in deep shit."

Jesse brushed Humberto's hand off his shoulder and glared at him. "Shut up, man!"

"He's right, though," Marguerite added, "I read an irreverent novel called 'Tit for Tat'," she crossed herself, "and it told about how - even good folks - will go to extremes to get revenge on those who cheated them."

"All of you shut your mouths!" Jesse shouted. "I need to think."

Rose said softly: "Jesse, listen to me: if you take the money back to that Turk fellow *now* you'll be late and he'll never trust you to do whatever it is you do for him again. You'll be through. And if he's as mean as Humberto says he is, well, he may even punish you as well as kick you out of his gang, or whatever it is you're involved in."

"Jesse?" Humberto asked attentively, "What do you think, man?"

Jesse looked at Rose and Aldo. "What's your proposal?"

"We think, maybe, that if we split the money seven ways, each of us will have about seventy-one thousand dollars - give or take - and that's a hell of a lot of money."

"What about Turk?" Humberto asked.

"That's easy," Rose said with a shrug, "all seven of

us will stick together and hide out at Quartzsite in our Rvs."

"Where's that?"

"Arizona. About a hundred thousand RVers cluster about out in the desert after summer's over. We can circle our campers - kind of like the old wagon train drivers used to do - and have a nice little vacation together. That Turk fellow of yours will never locate us out amongst the boondockers. After a while he'll give up looking for us and go on back to his nefarious activities. He'll lose too much money wasting his time trying to locate us."

Humberto turned to Jesse, "Boondockers?"

Rose explained 'boondockers'.

"I think these five old coots are nuts," Jesse mumbled.

Marguerite lifted her chin and peered down at Jesse and Humberto. "You two step up into the motor home and sit down. I'll fix us each a nice cup of Constant Comment and we'll further discuss the pros and cons - no pun intended - of our little stalemate."

"What the hell is 'Constant Comment?" Humberto asked Jesse.

"Tea, dumb ass."

"What have you to lose?" Prudence said.

"Five-hundred thousand grand - and our balls."

"Now if you are going to speak like that we just might not divide the cash with you," Louann said.

"Can you believe this?" Jesse said to Humberto.

Humberto looked up into the motor home at Rose and said: "You got any Kleenex inside there, lady? I gotta blow my nose."

"You mean blot your teary eyes, you knucklehead,"

Jesse muttered. "Come on, let's climb in there and talk this out." He glanced at Prudence. "You got any beer or Tequila in there?"

"Heavens no! But we have some green tea. They say that it's good for your digestion."

"Shit," Jesse mumbled.

"I'm getting hungry," Humberto said, "how about we get out the charcoal and cook up some wieners? I heard all of you old campers carry hot dogs in your RVs."

"We have some in our camper," Rose said with a smile, "They're good ol' Ball Park weenies. Aldo don't like them other fancy ones."

"Christ," Jesse muttered.

‖‖‖‖‖‖‖‖‖‖‖‖‖‖ 14 ‖‖‖‖‖‖‖‖‖‖‖‖‖

Turk and Beto

"Man, I ain't seeing nothing but eighteen-wheelers down there," Beto said to Turk. What if Jesse and Humberto drove off on some other road?"

Turk yawned and scratched his head. "Those other roads don't go anywhere anybody with half a million cash would want to go. Those clowns are down there on I-10, alright. It's the only logical place for them to be running with my money. Parts West: L.A., Vegas, you know, where the action is."

"Oh boy," the pilot mumbled.

"Shut up!" Turk barked at the pilot, "This affair is none of your business. All you're hired to do is fly this airplane where I tell you."

"Maybe we ought to circle over places where campers camp," Beto said.

"There ain't no places to camp down there, man, haven't you been noticing that?"

"I think I see a place up ahead. There's a big old

pecan grove, looks like, and a lake. Hey, yeah, I see some campers down there next to that little ol' burg on the highway."

"Fly low over those campers."

The pilot nodded and decended gradually over Balmorhea and the Springs.

"Tip the wing more," Turk ordered.

"Well would you just look at that?" Beto said.

"Yeah, I see it, too. An old beat-up Winnebago parked next to a huge red, white, and blue motor home and an old pick up with an orange-colored camper on it."

"Yeah, yeah, yeah - and a group of folks sitting around outside. Swing around again, man, so's we can get a closer look."

The pilot nosed the Mooney into a tight circle.

"For crap's sake. Looks like they're having a picnic!"

Turk and Beto knocked their fists together, then began laughing.

"What do you want me to do?" the pilot asked tentavely.

"Find a place close by where you can set this sucker down. Me and Beto have some business to attend to with those happy campers down there."

Beto nudged the pilot and said quietly: "Yeah, man, and I don't think you'll want to join *this* particular picnic party, so land us down close as you can and stay with the plane until we get back to it. If, by damn, you leave without us...well, we know where you live and work."

"Oh boy," the pilot muttered.

#

"What on earth is that airplane doing?" Prudence said as she took a bite of her hot dog and watched the Mooney buzz overhead.

"Probably some local rancher saying 'hi' to his *town* girlfriend," Aldo said.

The seven picnicking conspirators watched the Mooney circle overhead a second time and then fly off to the West. The newly-formed alliance of theives resumed their impromptu party. There was a ambience of relief for the participants of the wiener roast. Their impasse - such as it was - had been quickly and amicably settled. Each party had agreed to the equal division of their stolen cash. All believed, at least for this moment, that they had settled their immediate concerns.

Louann remarked as to the pleasant suroundings of the Springs. Marguerite pointed out - to her new-found friends - the lovely creek beside their Rvs. Humberto openly admired the tall trees providing shade for their repast. Prudence explained to the group that she preferred Kiolbassa brand weiners over the ones they were eating. Jesse pouted. Rose continued to place wiennies on the charcoal grill. And Aldo perused the venue looking for the closest public restroom.

Shrieks of laughter drifted across the campground emanating from San Solomon Springs. Vacationers and scuba divers were frolicking in the frigid waters. Many travellers were amazed to find suited and tanked scuba divers on the plains of West Texas. Crystal Springs had become an icon for divers. There is another surprise, among many, in this vast area of the Edwards Plateau: fresh live shrimp. Ranchers discovered a vast sea of pristine salt water beneath their ranches and pumped it to the surface to shallow ponds so that they could farm fresh shrimp. The ranchers imported shrimp to their West Texas ponds and raised them. "Go figure," Aldo said when Rose told him what she had read about the shrimp farms.

"Hey, all of you listen up," Jesse called out, "soon as we finish our hot dogs let's scram oughta here. I got a feeling that Turk and his top gun, Beto, are hustling their butts to locate me and Humberto. And if they find us, they'll find you too."

Rose was sitting next to Aldo, resting their elbows on a rustic picnic table, looking at the lovely vista about them. The late-afternoon sun was casting an intricate pattern of shadows from the tall trees dominating the Springs. Aldo's left shoulder rested against Rose's right arm. He was aware of her tension.

"Is their something you're not telling us that we should know about?" Rose said to Jesse.

"Only that I know what Turk is capable of, mam, and knowing *that* scares the hell out of me. Radical-minded folks don't seem to analyze *their* perspective on things. They just stubbornly rationalize them. And I reckon Turk has been busy rationalizing the benefits of whacking me and Humberto and anyone else who's screwed him out of his money, on account of he's a radical-thinking hombre for sure."

IIIIIIIIIIIIIIIII 15 IIIIIIIIIIIIIIII

Turk and Beto

The Mooney's pilot circled the outer perimeter of Balmorhea, his eyes searching for a possible landing site. He turned to Turk. "May I speak?"

"What?"

"This Mooney is a high-performance aircraft. I cannot set her down on some narrow, bumpy road. Or field. But I know of an old abandoned seven-thousand foot community airstrip called Mile High just a few minutes from here adjacent to I-10. It's a couple of miles West of the Border Patrol Checkpoint near Sierra Blanca."

"Can't you get us any closer than that?"

"Nope. But the landing strip is within walking distance to I-10."

"So?"

"Well, if I'm hearing you two correctly, that motor home you've been searching for will continue heading West on the freeway. It'll have to drive past Sierra Blanca where I can land. You two can intercept the motor home there."

Beto furrowed his forehead. "What? Run out onto the highway and stop it with our hands?"

The pilot shrugged.

"OK, OK," Turk said, "If that's the best you can do just keep us above that Winnebago. If it rolls back on I-10 follow it and set us down on that abandoned strip. I'll figure something out when we get there."

||||||||||||||||| 16 ||||||||||||||||

Prudence, Louann, Marguerite, Rose, Aldo, Jesse, Humberto, Beto, Turk, Mooney Pilot

Prudence, Marguerite, and Louann peered through the windshield toward the off ramp leading to a rest stop as Prudence slowed the huge motor home to a crawl. A Border Patrol truck was parked just inside the parking area. The Border Patrol Officer nudged his fellow officer with his elbow as he eyed the three elderly ladies staring back at him through the windshield.

"Get a load of this," he mumbled.

"Makes you not want to travel the highways anymore, don't it, what with all these old-timers driving those giant Rvs."

Prudence stopped and opened her side window. "Is it okay to park next to you, officer?"

The officer smiled. "Of course ladies. That is, if you are U.S. citizens?"

"Well, of course we are, officer. Do we *look* like illegals?" Louann said.

The officer grinned. "Well, ladies, have a pleasant stop." He turned to his partner and said: "Those old gals probably have a fortune in contraband or drug money stashed inside that monster."

"Yeah, right." The next officer turned and perused the incoming Winnebago. "Now here comes an 'iffy' one."

Jesse and Humberto pulled to a stop on the other side of the Border Patrol truck. They frowned at the officers.

"Sir, would you please turn off your engine and stand out next to your motor home," the Patrolman called out to them.

"Hey, man, we ain't done nothing," Humberto answered.

"Keep quiet," Jesse said to Humberto as he turned off the engine.

"Bring the sniff-dog," the officer said to his partner.

"Damn," Jesse muttered to Humberto, "you don't have any weed or coke on you, do you?"

"No. Do you?"

"Nope."

"Then we're cool. Just keep your mouth shut an let *me* do the talking."

The first officer stepped from his vehicle and noted Aldo and Rose rolling to a stop nearby in their ancient orange-colored camper. He smiled and waved at them.

"Guess we passed muster," Rose quipped.

Aldo looked at Rose and laughed. "Those fellows do a lot of profiling, hon. This guy just now obviously decided that you and me are too old and broke to do any mischief."

Rose chuckled: "Yeah, well they would've searched us good if it was twenty years back and we were trailing along with the Hill Country Hellers on their choppers."

Aldo affected a nostalgic expression. "We'd of been disappointed if they hadn't."

"We'll just wait here for the Border Patrol fellows to finish harassing Jesse and Humberto. I'll walk over to the gals and tell them to do the same."

Aldo stepped from the camper and looked up. "Hey, isn't that the same airplane with the backward looking tail that buzzed Balmorhea when we were cooking the hot dogs back there?"

Rose glanced upward to the North. "Heck, hon, I don't know; they all look the same to me."

"I believe it is. I've noticed it circling up above several times since we passed through Van Horn. Looks like it's fixin' to land a few miles ahead over by that little old town called Sierra Blanca. Now who on God's earth would want to land out here in this 'no man's' land?"

Rose shrugged. "An Aggie?"

#

Beto kept his eyes on the near vacant stretch of I-10 below. "Yep, Turk, I believe you're right. Looks like those other two campers down there are traveling together with Jesse and Humberto. They just now pulled off the highway into that rest stop."

"Get us down to that Sierra Blanca landing strip now," Turk said to the Mooney's pilot. The pilot rolled his eyes.

"Don't start with an attitude with me, dude," Turk said to the pilot.

"How're we gonna handle this?" Beto asked.

"I don't know, but Jesse and Humberto aren't the smartest assholes on this planet, and dummies like them generally link up with other dummies. 'Familiarity breeds contempt', my momma used to preach to me. It won't be too difficult dealing with those jokers whoever it is that they're in cahoots with down there. They'll get to fussin' with each other over all that cash soon enough."

"Hey, *you* hired *them* to bring *us* the half-a-mil."

"*Shut up,*" Turk said.

"Oh boy," the pilot said to himself.

The pilot circled the deserted Mile High landing strip three times.

"What's the matter? You can land this thing down there, can't you? You said that you could land here when we were over Balmorhea." Beto said.

"I'm checking to see if there's any cattle or debris on the landing strip. The only flyers who've used this strip the last few years were hauling sky-divers."

"Hey, Turk," Beto said, "I just got an idea. We can have this joker fly us all around the country to those stupid sky-diving contests. I bet we could sell a piss-pot full of weed to those dudes who're dumb enough to jump out of an airplane."

"Shut up," Turk said.

"Looks OK," the pilot announced, "so you two sit back and buckle up 'cause we might have a bumpy landing."

"Don't look like there's a heck of a lot of activity over there at Sierra Blanca," Beto said.

"Shut the hell up," Turk mumbled as he tightened his safety harness.

#

Maclovio Maldonaldo watched the Mooney descend onto the Mile High landing strip as he steered his dilapidated nineteen seventy-eight Chevy pickup adjacent to the cracked and weather-beaten tarmac next to the deserted and derelict aircraft hanger. It had become a rare event for an airplane to breach the surface of this lonely and abandoned runway. Maclovio visited the site once a week to confiscate what he could from the old landing field. Every obvious object of any possible use had long since been pilfered by local - and vagabond - scavengers before him, but he searched never-the-less; especially since his grandson had presented him with a used metal detector he had purchased from a pawn shop in El Paso. Just one year prior to this day he had been thrilled to detect a metal object which had lain under the dry, cracked soil since the field had been viable. It was a Zippo cigarette lighter. The previous owner had scratched letters and numbers which spelled 'Kilroy was here - 1943' on its metal covering. He asked everyone he knew, in and about Sierra Blanca, if the object had any special value. Most simply said: "It's a cigarette lighter," and shrugged it off. But Maclovio coveted it and kept it with him at all times. To him it was a reminder that others before him had suffered this desolate landscape. Others who sacrificed so that he and his projected family could suffer here as well. He liked to invision a now-elderly airman who still reminenced about his personal contribution to World War II out on the Texas plains.

Maclovio decided to drive to the edge of the air strip and greet the flyers. He carefully stepped from his pickup and waited patiently for the Mooney to taxi to where he parked.

The pilot cut the engine and opened the cockpit door. "Hey!" he called to Maclovio.

Maclovio smiled and nodded. "Welcome to nowhere, amigos!"

The three occupants disembarked, stretched and perused the venue.

"How far a walk is it to Sierra Blanca, old-timer?" Turk asked.

Maclovio turned and peered toward town. "One mile, maybe, for a local. It will seem like two miles if you're city gringos."

"Jeeze," Beto quipped, "we got hold of a smart-ass out here on the boonies."

The pilot raised his eyebrows at Maclovio and put his forefinger across his lips and slowly shook his head. Maclovio grinned knowingly, turned to Beto and Turk, and said in a polite tone: "What I meant to say, jefe, was that I can give you three gentlemen a free ride into Sierra Blanca if you want to go there. I cannot imagine why you would want to do that, but I'm just a poor hombre eager to welcome visitors to our little village."

"That's more like it," Beto said.

"How's about I give you two-hundred dollars cash for that old truck of yours, instead?" Turk said.

"I love my Chevy," Maclovio said with conviction.

"OK, asshole…three-hundred."

"Sometimes I sleep with her."

"Crap. Give the old fart four-hundred and get the keys," Turk said, "we don't have time to dick around out here!"

Maclovio smiled and dipped his chin, then offered a quick wink to the pilot. "The keys are in the truck," he said to Beto.

Beto pitched four one hundred dollar bills on the ground and followed Turk toward the pick up. "Wait here," he called over his shoulder to the pilot.

The pilot turned to Maclovio. "What's that awful odor?"

"Two hundred and fifty tons of wet basura each week are dumped out here from New York City."

The pilot scrunched his brow and looked at Maclovio. "No shit?"

"Smells like some," Maclovio answered with a nod.

"Damn Yankees," the pilot said with a shake of his head.

#

"Well would you just look at that!" Marguerite shouted as she pointed straight ahead.

"What? What's the matter?" Louann sputtered.

Prudence squinted her eyes forward. "Looks like a couple of nuts in an old junky pickup truck are trying to force Jesse's and Humberto's Winnebago off the highway!"

"My heavens…it's swerving to their side!"

"Look! Look! Look!" Marguerite hollored, "Somebody's pointing something out the truck's window…it's a hand gun. Oh, my heavens, they're going to shoot at Humberto and Jesse!"

"Call Aldo and Rose."

"They're too far ahead to do anything about this," Prudence exclaimed.

"What can we do? Jesse and Humberto are our associates now," Marguerite exclaimed, "we're carrying their share of the money."

"This situation calls for drastic action," Prudence said excitedly as she stomped on the giant motor home's fuel pedal. The powerful diesel rear-engine belched out a blue-gray cloud of exhaust and surged forward. Prudence gritted her teeth. Marguerite murmured: "Sick 'em." Louann, suddenly realizing Prudence's intention, turned and squatted to the floor of the bus and braced her back against the forward television cabinet. The giant RV quickly closed the gap to the rear of the junky pick up truck and rammed it. Prudence steadfastly held her steering wheel with determination as her right foot quivered with strain on the excellerator. The pick up truck's rear bumber slowly flattened against its tailgate. The one working taillight shattered. The bed gradually bent down causing the exhaust pipe to scrape the pavement sending a spray of sparks underneath the two vehicles. Beto dropped his revolver onto I-10 and braced his hands on the dashboard of the pick up. Turk frantically worked the steering wheel in an effort to keep the pick up on the highway.

"Holy crap!" Humberto mouthed as he watched through the Winnebago's windshield at the behemoth motor home shoving the pickup forward, both vehicles accelerating rapidly passing the Winnebago on the left lane.

"That was Beto pointing a gun at us…and Turk driving!" Jesse exclaimed.

"Chihuahua! look at those old gals pushing 'em up the highway," Humberto said.

"Man," Jesse said, "those old broads just saved our rear ends."

The pick up truck gradually veered to the center of I-10 as the motor home tenaciously propelled it forward. Then, in a vortex of dust and debris, Turk and Beto, in sheer panic, were bounced about the pick up's cab as it spun and bounced on the flat surface of the freeway's median.

Prudence managed to keep the motor home on the pavement. Louann and Marguerite, wide-eyed and exhilarated, watched the pick up's demise, then, with admiration and joy, gave each other high-fives and danced about the motor home's interior. Prudence opened her side window and proferred a third finger to the chaotic scene being left behind.

"Holy mackeral!" Aldo said to Rose as he peered into his rear-view mirror at the tumultuous scene unfolding on the highway behind them.

"What?"

"The ladies just rammed the rear of an old pickup truck and pushed it onto the median!"

"What the hell?"

"I don't know…but here they come lickety-split blinking their lights and honking their horn."

The enormous motor home thundered past Aldo's and Rose's little orange camper. Louann and Marguerite were pressed against the right side windows pumping their fists in a victory motion at Aldo and Rose.

"Get the gals on your cell phone and find out what in the devil is going on," Aldo said.

Rose dialed. "What just happened?" she asked Marguerite.

"We just saved Jesse and Humberto!"

"From what?"

"Two men in an old pick up truck were trying to shoot at them with a pistol."

"What two men?"

"We don't know, but Prudence, much to her credit and quick wits, butted them off the highway and saved Jesse and Humberto!"

#

After the pick up stopped spinning and the dust was beginning to settle, Beto, coughing and sputtering, squinted toward Turk. "Are you OK, man?"

"Hell no I'm not OK, fool."

"What happened?"

"What happened? What happened was that big ol' motor home following the Winnebago caught up with us and shoved us off the damned road!"

Beto blubbered dirt from his mouth and wiped his eyes. He looked closer at Turk. Turk was hanging, upside down, from his seat belt. Spittle dripped from his mouth and nostrils. "Hand me a Kleenex," Turk ordered.

"I don't have no Kleenex."

"Then help me undo this seat belt."

․․․․․․․․․․․․․․․․ 17 ․․․․․․․․․․․․․

Pilot, Maclovio, Beto, and Turk

Twilight crept slowly across the plaines to where the pilot and Maclovio sat in wait next to the Mooney for Beto and Turk to return. Maclovio pointed out a lone coyote skulking across the airstrip. The pilot would not have spotted the critter without his partner-in-waiting's alertness to the vagaries of the desert.

"Be dark soon," Maclovio said.

"Yeah."

"It don't get real dark at night out here on the plains during summer."

"Because of the moon?"

"Nada, man, 'cause of the stars."

"Pretty clear, huh?"

"Si. Sometimes you can see seven or eight of them satellites crossing up there."

"What about when the moon is full?"

"Well, that's different. Then it's so bright that you can't see 'em."

"The satellites?"

"Si."

"Many critters out here?"

"Many."

"Rattlenakes?"

"Many. Some slither on the ground. Some walk on two feet."

"Does the odor bother them?"

Maclovio smiled. "The ones who walk on two feet."

"Look over there toward town. I think somebody's coming," the pilot said.

Maclovio focused his eyes into a concentrated stare. "Si. It looks like two hombres on a bicycle"

"Kids?" the pilot said.

"No, man; two *filthy* hombres."

The pilot stood and squinted his eyes toward the approaching bicyclers. "I believe that's Turk and Beto."

Maclovio crossed himself. "My pick up! What did they do with my pick up?"

The bicycle riders rode wobbly up to the Mooney. "Get that airplane warmed up, man, we're in a hurry!" Beto shouted.

"What happened to my truck?"

"Forget about the damned truck, old man."

"What on earth happened to you two?" the pilot said grinning.

"Nothin'," Beto panted, "it ain't none of your business no how, so shut your mouth."

"You two hombres look all banged up and dirty," Maclovio said.

"Yeah, well you don't look so spiffy yourself, old man."

"True, but I ain't all scratched and bruised up."

"Well you will be if you don't shut up and get outa here," Turk said.

Maclovio said: "Can I take the bicycle? It looks like my great grandson's."

Turk turned back to the old Hispanic man and glared.

"I'll accept that look as a 'yes'," Maclovio said. He stooped and righted the bicycle, turned to the pilot and said: "Buenos dias, mi amigo…I'll say a Rosary for you." Then he glanced back at Turk and Beto and spit on the tarmac. "May the buzzards from above do the Mexican Hat Dance on your pelotes."

‖‖‖‖‖‖‖‖‖‖‖‖‖ 18 ‖‖‖‖‖‖‖‖‖‖‖‖‖

Jesse, Humberto, Rose, Aldo, Prudence, Louann, Marguerite

Humberto and Jesse brought seven steaming hot cups of coffee and ten MacDonald's individual fried pies, five cherry and five apple, with them to the red, white, and blue motor home. Humberto served each individual a cup of coffee as Jesse arranged the fried pies on the elegant motor home's granite kitchen counter. "Ya'll can pick out your own pies," he said.

Prudence squinted out at the neon signs across from the MacDonald's truckers' parking area. She was flabbergasted at the swarm of activity in, and around, the fast food stops and enormous fueling stations located on both sides of I-10.

"What are you staring at?" Marguerite said.

"All of the teaming humanity stirring about during the middle of the night way out here near El Paso."

"All those funny looking men and a few of the women are cross-country eighteen-wheeler drivers," Rose said.

"What about those younger ladies over there?" Prudence asked as she pointed to the rear of the truck stop across the street.

"Hookers," Aldo said.

"What do they hook?" Marguerite interjected as she gingerly selected a cherry-flavored fried pie.

"Truckers," Humberto said.

Prudence opened her eyes widely and gasped.

"Oh for heaven's sake, Prudence," Louann said, "get real."

Aldo stood. "Now listen up, folks…we gotta eat up our snacks real quick and skidaddle onward to Quartszite. Those two thugs are most likely already on our tails again and we can't take the luxury of sitting around here on our behinds feeding our faces."

"I'm weary," Prudence whimpered, "this big thing isn't as easy to drive as my nineteen ninety-seven Town Car."

"You have a ninety-seven Lincoln Town Car?" Humberto asked with awe in his tone.

Prudenced nodded.

"Holy moley, mam, how much would you want for it?"

"Shut up, man," Jesse said.

"Yeah, but…"

"Shut the hell up, you buffoon."

Marguerite took a nibble of her fried pie. "You know what, Prudence? I didn't realize what a boring life we were leading at the home before we illogically stole all that money from those dope dealers."

"Me too," Marguerite said. "You realize, don't you, that the perfectly logical people are usually the most boring."

"Remember how shocked we were when that skinny little old grey-haired lady down the hall from Prudence ran off to Alaska with that younger biker fellow?" Louann said, then added: "Well we thought she had lost her mind, but, you know, now I kind of envy her."

"I surely hope that she took along enough talcum powder. I can just imagine how hot her crotch must get in the leather clothes those bikers wear," Marguerite snickered.

"I'm certain we didn't need to hear *that,*" Prudence said, shaking her head.

"OK," Aldo said, "here's what we're gonna do: we'll do a fuel stop in Las Cruces, rest a few minutes, and then head out on across New Mexico. There's a little mountain pass in Arizona with a rest area. The mountains are called the Little Dragoons. They were the stronghold of Chief Cochise for about fifteen years in the eighteen-eighties. Anyway, the pass is called Texas Canyon for some reason. We can hold-up for a few hours and get some shut-eye. Usually there's a whole bunch of truckers and others parked there. Those two hoodlums chasing us won't approach us if they catch up with us 'cause it's too public, plus the eighteen-wheeler drivers will kick their butts if they notice anyone trying to harass these three old gals."

IIIIIIIIIIIIIIIIII 19 IIIIIIIIIIIIIIIIII

Turk, Beto, and Pilot

As the Mooney lifted off the rough, unkept runway Turk asked the pilot for a road map. The pilot, relieved to be in the air again, leaned back and handed a leather packet to the rear seats. Beto selected a map and handed it to Turk. Turk spread the map over his lap and studied it for a moment.

"Tell you what we're gonna do, Pilotman" Turk said, "We're going to fly on ahead and land at El Paso."

The pilot nodded.

"Hell, man," Beto exclaimed, "El Paso's a big-ass city spread all over the desert." He shook his head. "If those crazy old folks, and Jesse and Humberto, get to El Paso we'll lose them for sure."

"They aren't going to stop in El Paso, stupid, except for fuel."

"How do you know that?"

"Think about it: what the hell's in El Paso? Nothing, man, except cowboy boots and Juarez across the border.

And there ain't a human being alive who'd go across that border crossing with a half million cash. No sir, those old foggies are headed west with all the rest."

"But where in the west?"

"Look at this map. We'll set down at the airport in El Paso, rent a car, and drive on I-10 toward Las Cruces, New Mexico. We'll park along side an off ramp and wait for those three Rvs to drive past. Then we'll follow along behind them. Now look at this map again. At Las Cruces they could turn north on I-25 toward Albuquerque - which I doubt - or continue on I-10 toward Tucson, Arizona."

"Why would they go to Tucson?" Beto said.

"Because Tucson is one of the quickest ways to Vegas, or Southern California, man, and that's where half-a-mil will buy the most gratification."

"Gratification?"

"That's right," the pilot interjected.

Turk gave the pilot a hard glance.

"I'm sorry," the pilot murmured.

"We'll drive along behind them until they take an off ramp to one of those big rest stops, again, and nail 'em there."

"Yeah, and then what?"

"You and me will kick some ass, take back the five-hundred thousand they stole from us, and haul our butts back to Nuevo Progresso."

"O boy," the pilot muttered.

|||||||||||||||||| 20 |||||||||||||||||||||

Eduardo Betancourt
Mexico City

Eduardo Betancourt pushed the button to activate the speaker phone on his custom carved desk, turned in his plush, deerskin-upholstered, swivel chair, and gazed out of the huge window facing north from his fortieth story corner office suite. There was a time that the faint outline of the ancient Teotihuacan Aztec Pyramid could be seen from this perspective, but that had been prior to the accumulation of automobile exhaust and industrial smog in the sprawling metropolis of Mexico City.

"What do you mean the money has been stolen?" he spoke slowly.

"Just that, Eduardo."

"Who, in their right mind, would deign to steal money from *us*?" he asked in his Yale-educated English-Spanish accent.

"As far as we can ascertain, the cash was to be delivered

by two couriers to the border town of Nuevo Progresso to a man called Turk. He was the man who organized our South-Central Texas network for us. The couriers never arrived with the cash, so this Turk fellow set out to find them."

Betancourt sat in silence for a few moments, then said: "You know that we cannot allow this to happen. I realize that one lost delivery doesn't mean a hell of a lot in the overall of our operations. But if we allow this to go unpunished our entire syndicate will begin to unravel. We have to rely on uneducated and unprincipled peasant-types to carry on the day-to-day activities, unfortunately, and they must be disciplined properly for their inappropriate behaviors."

"I agree."

"So order *whatever* punishment is called for to stop this breach of our authority. Send a cogent message that all our sindicato will comprehend and fear."

"I understand."

"Bueno. The populations of all the nations with whom we aristocracia collectively are burdened must fully understand that *we,* the elite, are their patrons. That is our destino," Betancourt said as he reverted back to his native accent. "After all, who else would take care of them if it were not for us, the privileged?"

Betancourt turned from his vista and pushed the off button on his desk telephone. *This planet is populated with fornicating peons of all cultures who struggle to mingle with the elegancia. And those who lust for the fantasy of a universal 'middle class' are the most delusional. Why they would allow their misguided thoughts to fester in the belief that we, the patrons, would ever allow that to come to fruition is beyond my comprehension,* he meditated with a thoughtful expression across his face. *It is a burden we, the upper class, must bear. After all, who would do the labor for us? We allow them their plebeian pastimes and their drugs, plus we arrange conflicts to keep them engaged.* He shook his head. *Are those diversions not enough for the boorish masses inundating our planet?*

||||||||||||||||| 21 |||||||||||||||||

Stein's Ghost Town

First, Rose and Aldo in their camper. Then, Jesse and Humberto in their Winnebago. Next, Louann, Marguerite, and Prudence in the lavish motor home. And, unnoticed by all of them, Turk and Beto trailing behind in a rental car from El Paso. If viewed from above I-10 one might consider that the four-vehicle caravan was traveling as a unit. In fact, it was. Turk and Beto had waited on the off ramp of the Interstate Highway between El Paso and Las Cruces across from the odorous cattle feed lots for only one hour prior to witnessing the three Rvers drive past. Turk had immediately pulled onto the highway behind them.

"What now?" Beto asked Turk.

"We'll just follow along until they take an off ramp to one of those rest stops. Then we'll nab 'em."

"What if they don't pull off on an off ramp?"

"They will. They're all old. Old folks have to pee often."

"But don't they have potties in those motor homes?"

"The motor homes do, but those two old farts up front in that pick up truck with the camper on the back don't. And when they pull over the others will too. Those thieving bunch of old-timers are sticking together. I figure that they've decided to split up the money they stole from us."

#

"I'm getting awful nervous, Aldo," Rose said.

"Well, hon, me too. But we got ourselves into this mess with those three old ladies - and now those two hoodlums - and we're honor-bound to see it through."

Rose nodded and stared back at the barren western New Mexico vista. After a few silent moments passed, she said: "I've been thinking about how open and vunerable we are out here on this highway if anyone was looking for us. We'd be easy to spot by those two drug dealers if we stopped anywhere to rest a bit. Especially at one of those rest stops."

"What's your point?"

"Well, I got to thinking about that old ghost town up ahead where we spent a couple of nights last year on our way to Quartzsite."

"What about it?"

"I was thinking that we could easily hide our three Rvs in and amongst those old buildings there for a time."

"Oh, yeah…Stein's Ghost Town."

"Yes. We could hole up there for a couple of days to rest up and re-group, so to speak. I know that I'm weary and you are too. I can tell by the way you keep speeding up and slowing down when there's no reason to. And you can count on those three old gals being tired as well."

"Sounds good to me, Rose. Use the cell phone to tell them what we're thinking."

Rose dialed. "Hey, Prudence. Listen, Aldo and I know of a place up ahead a few miles where we can stop for a couple of days and rest up some. It's an old abandoned town along the side of the highway called Stein's Ghost Town. It used to be a railroad station named after a U.S. Army officer in the early eighteen hundreds."

"We're awfully tired, Rose," Prudence answered, "and that sounds inviting to me. Let me check with Marguerite and Louann."

A moment.

"We're in agreement, Rose. Let's do it."

"Fine. Just follow us down the off ramp when we get to Stein's."

#

"Hey…Turk…where in the hell are they going?"

"Looks like they're heading off I-10 to that little old abandoned town down there."

Turk slowed the rental car and watched the three Rvs veer onto the off ramp. "I bet that they figured that they could hide down there amongst those old buildings. Hell, man, they'll be damned surprised to see us pull up behind them," Turk chuckled.

"Damn straight!" Beto giggled.

Rose studied Stein's Ghost Town as Aldo steered their camper along its virtually deserted main street. Weathered shacks and abandoned one-story store fronts lined the short, dusty main drive. She remembered reading a pamphlet describing Stein's. Cochise and his Indian band of marauders attacked a stage coach on the outskirts of Stein's in April eighteen sixty-one and hung a man named John Giddings and his companion upside down and burned them alive. Twenty years later Southern Pacific built a track through Stein's. The train station had been active through the nineteen forties. Now there were a few squatters and a trickling of curious travellers occupying the smattering of parking spots along the dirt street the ruins bracketed.

"Looks like a ghost or two *could* live here," Aldo muttered.

"Pull on up ahead to that old barn-looking structure," Rose said, "It looks tall enough to hide the gals' big motor home next to it."

Aldo slowly drove the camper over tire ruts and a berm next to the barn, nosed his pick up against a pile of railroad ties, and stopped. "Did I leave enough room for the guys' Winnebago and the gals' motor home?"

Rose struggled from the pick up and shaded her eyes as she peered back. "Yeah, you left plenty of room for them. And it looks like none of us can be spotted from I-10."

Al turned off the engine and set the parking brake as Rose stuck her arm out of her window and motioned for Humberto and Prudence to snuggle their motor homes behind them next to the derelict horse stable.

"Hey!" Rose yelped, "Who's in that car pulling up behind the gals' motor home?"

‖‖‖‖‖‖‖‖‖‖‖‖‖‖ 22 ‖‖‖‖‖‖‖‖‖‖‖‖‖‖

Eduardo Betancourt
Mexico City

Eduardo stood and slowly walked around his eighteenth century hand-carved desk. He stopped near his opulent office's huge window. Placing his hands behind his back, he straightened his shoulders, and studied the sprawling city below. He was proud of his French-Spanish lineage. His aristocratic French ancestors had been run out of Paris by unwashed multitudes much like the teeming hoards below. The royal Spanish branch of his genetic line had, also, been persecuted by the multifold of Spain. Yet, he and his kind, of all the cultures, had survived. *And always will persevere,* he fantasized. *Those few of us who forever prevail - the aristocracies of all races - will continue to direct the course of mankind. The corporation heads, the tribal chiefs, the royals, the doctrinaires, the 'families'. Our endeavors are constant,* he reflected with a sigh, *and require stern measures.*

Betancourt turned to his desk and quickly punched a series of digits on a discard cell phone. "Select your best man and instruct him to erase all who are even remotely involved in the recent disappearance of our cash," he said in a casual manner. And continued, "wherever he can locate them. Order him to retrieve our money and take it to our people in Matamoros." He sat in his chair and discarded the cell phone into a trash-compactor and pushed the crush button. "Estupidos," he muttered to himself.

||||||||||||||||| 23 ||||||||||||||||

Stein's Ghost Town
Rose, Aldo, Prudence, Louann, Marguerite, Humerto, Jesse, Beto, Turk

Turk snugged his rental car against the rear of the red, white, and blue motor home successfully blocking all three Rvs from backing. "Come on, man, let's kick some butt and grab the money and get the hell out of this stupid place."

Beto hopped from his side of the car and trotted along beside the gals' motor home slapping his palm on its side as he approached the door. Inside - Prudence, Louann, and Marguerite - startled by the revererating noise, flinched with concern and fear.

"What in the world…" Prudence exclaimed.

"Mein Gott!" Marguerite shouted.

"Oh, oh, oh…" from Louann.

Turk jogged past Beto to the Winnebago's door,

pounded on it, and shouted: "Humberto! Jesse! Get your butts out here!"

Rose hopped back into the pick up truck yelling to Aldo: "Aldo, it looks like those two thugs Prudence pushed off the highway earlier are back there. They've caught up with us!"

"How'd they do that so fast?"

"I don't know, hon, but they're here!"

"Oh boy," Aldo breathed, "we're in deep doodoo now."

"Well…do something!"

"Do what, Rose?"

"Hell, I don't know, but we gotta do something!"

Aldo shook his head. "We should've known better than to link up with those old larcenous women in the first place."

"It's too late to fret about that now," Rose said as she opened her door, "It's time to begin wheeling and dealing and negotiating."

"You think those thugs are in the mood to *negotiate*? They're acting more like they're in their battle mode," Aldo said as he leaned across Rose and peeked back.

"Wheeling, dealing, dickering, and pow-wowing is most always better than belligerency," Rose shot back. "Get out here with me and let's do some serious reasoning with those two hooligans."

Aldo sighed, rubbed his face vigorously with his hands, and opened his door. "Heaven help us," he mumbled to himself.

Turk and Beto stood, shoulder to shoulder, several feet back from the Winnebago, and watched Humberto and Jesse creep sheepishly from its door. Prudence,

Louann, and Marguerite stepped cautiously down the steps of their motor home as Rose strode purposely - Aldo tagging behind - to where Turk and Beto stood with defiant countenances occupying their expressions.

Rose, Aldo, Prudence, Louann, Marguerite, Jesse, and Humberto stood side-by-side and stared back at Beto and Turk in a mode some might refer to as a 'Mexican Stand-off'.

"Just what the deuce do you two donkeys want from us?" Rose declared.

Turk stepped forward. "We want the five-hundred thousand dollars those two idiots stole from us!" He pointed toward Humberto and Jesse. And if you don't hand it over right this minute we're gonna kick all your butts and take it anyway!"

Humberto sniveled. "*We* didn't steal it…me and Jesse were bringing to *you* when those three old biddies swiped it from *us*." He pointed toward the women.

Turk perused the three ladies. "You gotta be shittin' me," he said.

"It's true, man…those three old broads broke down the door of an old abandoned movie house where we had the loot stashed and stole our - I mean - *your* money. All of it. Me and Jesse have been trying to get it back so's we could take it to you."

Rose, Aldo, Prudence, Louann, and Marguerite twisted simultaneously and gaped at Humberto with disgust.

Beto looked with an incredulous expression at Turk, then burst forth in raucous mirth. "Looks more likely to me that you two dudes have done joined up with those old lady thieves instead of chasing 'em."

Turk looked back at the three women, glanced over at Rose and Aldo, then said: "Holy shit. Now I've heard it all."

Rose took two steps toward Turk. "Now just relax and listen up, young man. We have some talking and proposing to do here."

"Yeah? And just what might that talking and proposing be?" Turk said.

"I'll explain to you two donkeys just what we explained to those two fools there," she pointed toward Jesse and Humberto. "Whoever it was that was supposed to receive that five-hundred thousand in cash is, by now I figure, mighty pissed off that they haven't yet gotten it. Am I correct?"

Turk nodded. "So?"

"Would you surmise that whoever they are they're *badder* than you two clowns?"

Beto's face affected a display of concern. "You old farts in your wildest nightmares can't imagine how baaad those hard-asses down in Mexico City and Colombia can be."

"That's just what I thought," Rose said. "Now assuming that *those* folks are *badder* than you two, and you two are *badder* than these two," she pointed toward Humberto and Jesse, "just picture in your mind's eye what *they're* thinking and planning right now about what to do with the *four* of you." She motioned with her chin toward Beto, then Jesse and Humberto, and then back to Turk.

"Hey, man, she's got a point there," Beto said turning to Turk.

Turk stared at Rose and Aldo for a moment, then

glared at Jesse and Humberto and the ladies. "And now *you* old farts, as well, don't forget. So what's your thinking?" he said to Rose.

"I'm thinking that the nine of us standing out here in this little old ghost town can divy up equal parts of that five-hundred thousand smackeroos and haul our behinds to Las Vegas and parts west and lose ourselves amongst the crazies."

"Yeah, and then what?"

"Parteee!" Marguerite squealed.

"For gracious sakes, Marguerite," Prudence said, "maintain your dignity."

"Yes," Louann said, "calm youself."

Turk roared with laughter. "Listen to me, you old broads, if we split up that half a mil amongst the nine of us that would only amount to…let me figure a few moments…about fifty thousand bucks apiece. Are you willing to risk your life for only fifty thousand dollars?"

"Wait just a minute," Prudence interjected, "we'd each share more than that! You didn't divide properly."

"I factored in some for my expenses."

"What *expenses*?," Rose said, "I already figured it out. It comes to *more* than fifty-five thousand each. You four fellows get the same as all the rest of us. After all, Prudence, Louann, and Marguerite stole it, and Aldo and I helped them escape."

Turk shook his head, walked over to the steps of the big motor home and sat down. "OK folks. Now listen up to the *real* situation here. Let's start with the five-hundred thousand you gals stole from Jesse and Humberto. Roughly figuring, *that* money is the big Jeffe's money in Mexico City and Colombia and, by God, they aren't gonna idly stand back and allow *anybody* to steal it from them." Turk took a deep breath and continued. "Originally there was about seven-hundred fifty thousand cash, give or take a few hundred. Of that, the weed growers in Colombia got around fifty thousand. The Mexican Army brass and various police departments creamed off about fifty thousand. Border authorities on both sides of the Rio Grande pocketed some twenty-five grand to distribute about. And the dealers and street punks in the States will have pocketed some twenty-five big ones, or so, amongst themselves. Having to spread all that those drugs around costs the big Jeffes about one-hundred fifty thousand dollars." Turk raised his eyebrows as he took another deep breath. "That five-hundred thousand you gals swiped from us is the *big Jefe's* share of the pot. Now that leaves - give or take a few bucks - their five-hundred thousand for us to split nine ways. That divides up to about fifty-five thousand dollars each for us…and *zero* for them." Turk cocked his head. "And that's figuring in the absolutely *remote* possibility that the cartel big shots south of the border would *ever* consider allowing *us* nobodies to keep five-hundred thousand dollars of *their* money, which they will absolutely *not* do under any circumstance known to mankind. What they *will* do is hire a biker guy from Brownsville to come find *all* who're involved with stealing *their* money, do bad physical things to them, and take their money back."

"Are you sure all that cash is divied up like that?" Rose asked

Turk shrugged his shoulders. "Well, I'm not so certain about the *actual* amounts everyone gets, but I guarantee you, lady, the Jeffes will be *mightily* pissed off at those who stole *their* piece of the pie."

Beto nodded vigously. "Yeah, man. I've seen 'em have a dude wasted for just holding back one little ol' brick of marijuana."

"I believe you're wrong, lady," Turk said to Rose, "about the cartel honchos *not* forgiving me and Beto for getting their money to them late…even if it is only a few days. They'll be *happy* to finally get their money from us."

"Man, I don't know, Turk…," Beto shook his head… ,"I think the old broad is right. They'll send that bad guy from Brownsville to nail us for sure. You know damn well how those cartel bosses run things. They don't *ever* forgive *any* screw-ups, much less allowing these three old women and their buddies, plus us losers, to snatch their money and keep it."

Turk turned and scanned the desert surrounding Stein's Ghost Town. He watched a smattering of buzzards circling I-10 about a quarter of a mile west. *Buzzards*, he thought. *There's buzzards of all kinds in all places. Me and Beto are buzzards the same as those filthy scavengers up there. So are Humberto and Jesse.* He turned and squinted at the ladies and Aldo and Rose. *I'm not certain whether those old-timers are vultures, too, or just hawks snatchin' what they believe to be some easy money. As for me…I'm sick and tired of being a buzzard who cleans up the left-over* scraps *those dope cartel assholes leave for us.*

"What're you thinking, man," Beto asked.

Rose and Aldo and the ladies stood quietly in place and waited for Turk to speak.

Finally, Rose said: "Hey, Turk…what's it going to be?

Kick our butts and take the money and pray the big Jeffes don't send the Brownsville dude after *you*…or throw in with us and keep the cash and run?"

"It would be tax free," Marguerite said.

"Hush!" Prudence said.

Suddenly Turk grinned. "What the hell," he said, "let's get our butts out of this crummy little burg and haul ass 'west with all the rest' with all that cash!"

There was a brief silence, then cheers led by Marguerite. "Parteee! Parteee! Parteee!"

"Holy moly," Aldo said to Rose, "you pulled us out of another pickle, hon."

"We'll see," Rose sighed.

|||||||||||||||||| 24 ||||||||||||||||||

Kai Ochita
Brownsville, Texas

Kai snapped his cell phone closed and turned to the large rear window of his air conditioned fifth-wheel travel trailer and studied the condensation from the South Texas humidity gathering on the huge rear window. The call had lasted for thirty-two long minutes and necessitated that he write down numerous notations. Then he yawned, stretched, and looked back toward the front bedroom. "Hey!" he called out, "I just got assigned a chore to do, babe, so get up and grab your things."

"Come on, Kai…you said we were gonna hook up the rig and haul it over to South Padre for a couple of days," a sleepy female voice called back.

"Yeah. Well, I didn't know that I was going to get an assignment from the bosses, so haul your buns oughta' here, I have to get going."

"You going to take the fifth wheel?"

"Yes. Hurry up, I need to take a run over to Nuevo Progreso on my Harley to talk to a guy, then ride back and hitch-up and leave right away."

"What about our bike ride to Big Bend with the Ponchos next week?"

"Call Shank and tell him we won't be able to make it. Tell him I'll give him a head's up when I get back."

"What am I, your damned secretary?"

Kai thought a moment. "Yeah, amongst other duties. Now git!"

He stood and walked over to the couch nestled in the RV's slide-out and reached over the back and retrieved a small, highly polished, twenty-two caliber pistol. "OK compadre," he muttered to the small handgun, "time to earn our keep." He replaced the weapon. It was a tool which he had not yet had to resort to as a device to 'convince' his assignees, but because his foreboding stare, menacing demeanor, and excruciating jujitsu holds had always been enough to persuade his targets to instantly comply with whatever his demands happened to be, he had never had to fire the handgun. He'd earned a sharp-shooting medal during his stint in the U.S. Army and he was proficient with firearms, but he disliked shooting them. After earning his master of philosophy degree and completing a stint in the army he had returned to Stanford to earn his PhD. He didn't want to own a gun but felt his current endeavors with the cartel required one, if only for show.

He slipped on a pair of jeans, stepped from his huge rig, and stood braiding his long black hair as he surveyed his diesel tow truck. It looked the same as the majority of eighteen wheeler tractor-trucks that hauled America's commerce over the interstates and byways. He needed the horsepower and braking ability of the four door monster to pull his thirty-eight foot long 'home-on-wheels'. The over-sized fuel tanks he had installed enabled him to drive many hours between fill-ups. Plus, the extra power of the awesome engine afforded him the ability to easily haul his Harley. Kai didn't stay any length of time in any one place. He did prefer the Rio Grande Valley of Texas because it was located almost equal distance between Florida and California, the places where his services were most often required by the syndicate bosses. Besides, he enjoyed the companionship of the girls living along both sides of the Rio Grande. The border women tended to be more compliant.

The comely young woman stepped from the travel trailer. She held an overnight bag in her left hand and a make-up case in her right hand. "Where the hell are you going this time?" she said.

"Can't tell you, babe," he sighed as he continued, "but I'd rather be hauling you and this rig over to South Padre instead."

"Well, why don't you?" She affected a pout as she stared at him. "You sure as hell have enough money to do anything you want."

"Yeah? Why do you think that?"

"'Cause Shank and the Ponchos were talking about you the other night. They said that they believe you have a stash of money in one of those off shore banks."

"They do, huh. Well, those honchos don't know the half of what they're talking about. Besides, if I did have all that money, why in the hell would I be living all over the country in a fifth wheel?"

"They said that you were like a slave, or something, to an international syndicate, and that you couldn't stop whatever it is that you're doin' even if you wanted to. They said that you like living in your rig, anyhow."

Kai stopped braiding his hair and glared at her. "They said that?"

"Yep, they sure did."

"Why don't you just get on home now." He reached into his front pant's pocket and pulled out a roll of paper currency and handed her several denominations. "I'll see you when I see you."

She turned and walked slowly toward her convertible. Then turned back and said: "Hey, be careful, Kai."

Kai watched her drive away. *Damn…I can't even remember her last name. What a hell of a way to have relationships.* He finished braiding his hair, then began the process of putting his awning up. *I'm getting tired of this shit. Maybe it's time to fade away.* He glanced back at his Harley. *Just this one more job.*

Kai Ochita was raised in San Francisco, the only offspring of a couple who had also been born in the multicultural metropolis. He had enjoyed a pleasant middle-class upbringing by parents who were moderately disconcerted that his grandparents had been incarcerated in an internment camp during World War Two. His grandparents had convinced themselves - and their children - that their imprisonment had been 'for their own safety', but the fact that the Protestant Minister - to whom they had quit-deeded their home for the duration of the war - had sold it and pocketed the money just before the end of the conflict thus leaving them virtually homeless, had left a mental scar inside Kai's psyche. He managed to conquer his discontent through the process of achievement in study and physical prowess. Mostly by excelling in the ancient Japanese wrestling art of jujitsu during his undergraduate years at Stanford. After having won several notable matches Kai had been contacted by a stranger who offered him a sizeable amount of cash to locate and 'convince' a citizen of Napa County to return a substantial amount of cash which had been wrongfully sequestered from the stranger. It had been easy money for Kai. *Screw keeping in school to earn a doctorate degree,* Kai reasoned, *I can earn a hundred-fold more income by simply intimidating crooked assholes who think they can screw other crooked assholes and get away with it. Actually, I'm doing society a favor,* he deduced, *even though I am getting paid by criminals.* He allowed his hair to grow to the small of his back, taught himself to never smile, kept in supurb physical condition, and rarely conversed more than absolutely necessary for comprehension. After Kai received his Master of Philosophy Degree, he devoted his full attention to 'retrieving' cash from shady citizens who, in one manner or another, believed that they could bilk professional criminals out of their ill-gotten loot.

During his senior year at the university Kai had written a paper on philosophy in which he proclaimed in part: "Living requires compromise. Therefore all things valuable, as well as insignificant, are fraught with constant negotiation and consequent adjustment." His professor, a nerdy woman who had only known the academia lifestyle, had assigned his paper a 'C' grade. She had scribbled a missive on the margin which read: "Your reasoning is flawed in the sense that true believers in faith, or *their* own particular points of view, must stand firm in their position…no matter how skewed their logic. Because, in my opinion, *compromise connotes defeat and failure*."

Kai had replied to her written criticism with an e-mail to her in which he typed: I do believe that Kim Yong II of North Korea ascribes to your philosophy.

A hunting will I go, Kai thought to himself as he mounted his Harley.

ⅠⅠⅠⅠⅠⅠⅠⅠⅠⅠⅠⅠⅠⅠⅠ 25 ⅠⅠⅠⅠⅠⅠⅠⅠⅠⅠⅠⅠⅠⅠ

Quartzsite, Arizona

"So *this* is the infamous Quartzsite, Arizona?" A wide-eyed Lounn said to Marguerite and Prudence as their four-vehicle caravan approached the bizarre vista from the I-10 freeway crossover bridge on Highway Ninety-five.

"Are all these people out here in this desert *nuts*?" Jesse said to Humberto as he scanned the area and struggled to keep the Winnebago closely behind the gals' motor home.

"Holy moly…would you just look at this mess spread all over hell and back?" Turk mutterd to Beto.

"Are the others still behind us?" Rose asked Aldo.

"I can't see Turk's and Beto's rental car, but I'm sure they're still following us," Rose said, "'cause Prudence said she'd keep an eye out for everyone back there and call us on her cell if anyone came up missing."

"I reckon there's at least five thousand Rvs parked out here on the desert," Beto said.

"Aldo and Rose told me last night that there would be thousands of crazies during the winter," Turk said.

"Thousands? Where do they stay?"

"In their RVs, knuckle head."

"Thousands of people? That must take thousands of Rvs."

"Maybe more than that," Turk said.

"How do they get rid of all their shit?"

"Rose said that big tank trucks called 'honey wagons' drive around amongst the campers and suck out their crap."

"What about water and electricity?"

"She said that tank trucks full of water for sale come around. Most of the campers carry gasoline-powered generators for electricity."

"What do all of these folks *do* out here?'

"She said they go to mineral and rockhound shows inside big tents, stand around flee markets, and mostly just walk around scratching and staring at one another."

"Why?"

"Hell, I don't know, man, they just do. Some folks shiver in cold rivers fly- fishing, other folks sit and sew rags together to make quilts…hell, man, old retired folks do all kinds of shit to keep busy."

Beto rubber-necked as the caravan of four slowly negotiated the heavy traffic. "Hey, look," he pointed, "there's some RV Parks along here."

"Rose and Aldo said that we couldn't hide ourselves good enough in one of those commercial parks. They said we'd have to drive a mile, or so, out into the surrounding desert and find spots to park. They call it boondocking."

"Holy shit," Beto mumbled, "what the hell's happenin' to us?"

Rose told Aldo to keep on driving through the melee until they were a couple of miles up the road toward Parker, Arizona on Highway Ninty-five. Caravaning behind were the gals' humongous motor home, the rickety old Winnebago, and last, the rental car. The occupants of the four vehicles watched, with amazement, the scenerio they slowly drove past. There were Rvs of every description parked closely together on the desert floor. Some were elegant, diesel-powered monsters, brightly painted with flashy designs. Expensive tow vehicles, with matching colors, parked beside their multi-colored awnings. Older model pick up trucks, with campers perched on their beds, nestled amongst them. There were travel trailers, fifth-wheel trailers, and even tent trailers of every description commingling on the dirt. Prudence, Marguerite, and Louann stared - virtually without comprehension - at the tableau. Humberto became speechless. Jesse blinked rapidly. Turk and Beto simultaneously swiveled their heads from left to right in disbelief.

"Would you look at that," Marguerite exclaimed as she pointed toward a large canvas tent, "that sign says it's a café, for heaven sakes!"

"You can't be serious," Louann said.

"She's right," Prudence said, "the sign says it's a café."

"Are we in Hell?" Marguerite gasped.

Behind, in the Winnebago, Humberto scrunched down into his seat. "Hey, man…is *this* the place we're gonna hide?'

Jesse licked his lips. "The sign said 'Quartzsite', so

this must be it." He began to laugh. Then laughed more hardily. Then laughed hysterically.

"Get ahold of yourself, man," Humberto exclaimed.

People walked on the shoulder of the road. Most sported gray hair falling beneath the brims of their head gear. Many of their hats were western styled. Others sported bill caps with slogans from across the United States and Canada. Louann pointed out to Prudence and Marguerite that no one was smiling.

The nine conspirators - for now they were bound together in an unlawful alliance - were not smiling either. All silently - except for Jesse who continued guffawing uncontrollably - squinted at the unbelievable spectacle they were passing.

"There!" Rose said suddenly, pointing to a small, hand-painted, cardboard sign along side the highway.

"What?" Aldo asked.

"Turn off the road here."

"What's here?"

"That little sign. It says: "Nellie's North Forty. One mile. Forty level 40' x 75' spaces. No hook-ups, but privacy and safety."

Aldo began to turn off the highway. "I don't see a road going anywhere."

"There isn't any road, hon, just some tire tracks. Don't you see…it'll be a perfect place for all nine of us to hide out for a bit of time until we can figure out what to do next with all that cash."

Aldo took a deep breath, shifted the pick up into low gear, and followed a feint set of tire tracks across the desert. "Sure hope we don't get bogged down in all this sand."

"Oh, my, lord," Prudence said as she turned off the highway behind Aldo and Rose.

"Stop that giggling and follow 'em," Humberto mumbled to Jesse inside the Winnebago.

"We're doomed to hell," Beto said to Turk as he followed the caravan into the desert toward Nellie's North Forty.

#

Nellie stood beside her ancient Airstream Travel Trailer shading her eyes with a flattened six-bottle beer carton as she studied the gradual approach of the four vehicle parade headed by Aldo and Rose in their orange camper. She pondered the sedan struggling through the desert sand behind the three campers. "What the devil is this rigamarole coming?" she asked herself. *Dang!* she thought, *It's the beginning of the season and, already, the super weirdos are arriving. I suppose those two in that automobile are gonna want to share space with one of those Rvs. Well, we'll see about that. Takes all kinds, I suppose.*

She stepped forward and motioned for the four vehicles to stop by her Airstream. "Hello. My name is Nellie. You folks looking for a safe area to park your rigs?" she called out.

Rose and Aldo studied Nellie for a moment. She seemed out of place out here in the dessert. Her shorts were extremely brief cut-off jeans and the top four buttons of her shirt were undone. The tail of the shirt was tied above her waist exposing her belly button. Her waist-length blonde hair was tied back into a ponytail. Rose speculated Nellie's age to be thirtyish.

"She's a keeper," Aldo muttered.

"Shut up, you horny old fart," Rose whispered.

Aldo offered Nellie a huge smile as he wiggled his fingers in a cutesy wave.

"Yes, young lady," Rose answered from her side of the camper, "we'd like spaces side-by-side, if possible."

"I suppose that could be arranged. Those two fellows in that automobile back there have to pay for a whole space just like the rest of you Rvers here, though."

"That's fair. How much do you charge for a month?"

"Well, being this government land, I can't charge actual rent. What I *do* charge for though, is twenty-five dollars a week or thirty-five for a whole month. Each."

"What's *that* for?"

"It's for my twelve-guage shotgun and my good looks and companionship."

"What?"

"Yes, my shotgun, so I can protect everyone here from all the other loonies staying out there." She pointed towards the Rvs in the distance. "Besides my protection you also get the benefits of my goods looks and sparkling Netherlands personality."

"Holy moly," Aldo mumbled to Rose, "how lucky can we get?"

"Agreed," Rose said to Nellie as she nodded her head. "Show us where you want us to settle."

Nellie turned and perused the empty desert for a moment, then turned back to Rose and said: "Why don't you folks just situate your rigs to form a circle over there?" She pointed. But don't have those two fellows back there in that automobile park near my Airstream. They don't look much like they fit in with our winter desert community out here. Plus I don't want *them* next to *my* trailer."

"I'll have them park their car on the other side of our circle," Rose said.

"Then pull on ahead and get yourselves set-up. When you're settled walk on up to my Airstream, here, and I'll serve us all a welcoming drink and collect your week's money in advance. It'll have to be in cash. Small bills. For each vehicle."

"What kind of drink?" Aldo leaned forward and asked.

"Oranjeboom Premier Lager."

"Never heard of it."

"Doesn't surprise me," Nellie quipped, "Only beer you redneck-type westerners know about is Lone Star, Bud, and Coors, for crying out loud. Oh, I almost forgot, I the second Orangebooms will cost you three dollars a bottle."

Prudence, Marguerite, and Louann stared in disbelief. Jesse and Humberto slumped down in their seats shaking their heads. Jesse continued laughing histerically. Humberto glared at Jesse.

"She's having us form a damned circle just like the old wagon trains use to do!" Jesse stuttered between guffaws.

Nellie stepped back and studied the three Rvs, the sedan, and their occupants. "Verdommt," she muttered under her breath.

‖‖‖‖‖‖‖‖‖‖‖‖‖ 26 ‖‖‖‖‖‖‖‖‖‖‖‖‖

Kai and Junior

Kai steered his Harley slowly across the International Bridge separating Progreso from Nuevo Progreso. He'd been told that this particular border-crossing bridge had at one time been the only stock-owned private international bridge. During the so-called 'Winter Season' in this part of Texas - commonly known as 'The Valley' - this bridge would be teaming with 'Winter Texans', mostly retired folks escaping the boring winters of Kansas, Nebraska, Iowa, the Dakotas, and Central Canada. Most of them stayed for two or three months in travel trailers, motor homes, and rental units. They commonly spent their days relaxing in the relatively mild winter climate of South Texas, taking runs across the border to Nuevo Progreso, Matamoros, and Reynosa - to haggle with the poor Mexican vendors over their goods - or to purchase prescription-free medications of every kind for a fraction of the cost charged north of the Rio Grande. Other favorite trips were taken to South Padre Island to enjoy the seashore and also to the Bird Sanctuary at Benson State Park in Mission. Newest on the list of places to enjoy was the Butterfly Farm in Weslaco.

The crossing was not crowded today. Kai nodded to three familiar Mexican Border Guards as he idled past into Nuevo Progreso. His instructions were to find a person called Junior and persuade him to reveal, if he could, the whereabouts of two fellows known as Turk and Beto. Kai was no stranger with all aspects of the Mexican town. Especially the restaurants, cantinas, and boticas. It was common practice for the street vendors to hassle foreign pedrestrians in an effort to banter price with them over the plethora of items they offered for sale, but not one vendor *ever* accosted Kai as he walked the sidewalks. His demeanor and looks projected danger. He was not the typical Winter Texan.

His instincts directed him to his favorite restaurant. Arturo's. A parking attendant waved him to a spot close to the front entrance of the large cantina. Kai parked his bike and handed the attendant a ten dollar bill. "Watch this Harley with your life, amigo," he instructed the elderly parking guard as he entered the restaurant. The head waiter approached Kai with enthusiasm. "Welcome, Senior Ochita," he effused, "an early lunch?"

Kai smiled. "Not today, Emilio, I'm looking for three fellows."

Emilio smiled. "Please describe them," he looked about the restaurant, "perhaps I can be of service."

"They're called Turk, Junior, and Beto. My suspicion is that the three of them do not tip well - if at all- and that they are generally a pain in-the-ass to serve."

A passing waiter stopped in his tracts, turned to

Amilio and Kai, and said: "Please excuse me for intruding, but I couldn't help but overhear your description of three patrons who regularly come here. I believe that I have served them. I haven't seen the ugly one called Turk, or his companion called Beto, for several days, but the third one called Junior still comes in every evening. He always orders cheese enchiladas." The waiter shook his head. "No imagination."

Kai smiled and handed each - the maitre d' and the waiter - a twenty dollar bill. "Now, my friends, I'd like to know if you can assist me in finding out where this hombre, called Junior, is staying during the day."

"I know where he is staying," the waiter said. "He's renting a room in the rear of the third store up the street from here. I have seen him coming and going from there the last few days. Mr. Gomez, the owner of the store, told me that hombre is a jerk."

Kai handed each another bill and grinned broadly. "Mucho gracias, mi amigos. You have given me a great service."

He turned and walked briskly from the restaurant. Outside, Kai handed the parking attendant another bill. "Continue to watch my Harley. I'll be back shortly."

He strode on the cracked, uneven, sidewalk toward the third store front. He weaved adroitly through the sidewalk vendors and squinting, shuffling, first arriving 'Snowbirds'. Many of the men sported khaki shorts, black socks, and dress shoes. A number of women wore 'sack-type', loose-hanging, dresses; their arms and shoulders sunburned red from the South Texas sun, the Latitude being roughly the same as Key West, Florida to the east and La Paz - on Mexico's Baja Peninsula - to the west.

Kai located the third establishment and peered through the front door. A potporrie of cheap, poorly-constructed but colorful, piñatas, wall decorations, clay pots, straw dolls, and myriad of other souvenir-collector items inundated the small space. He noted a door to the rear of the display room. Kai smiled, then paced quickly to the back and pounded his fist on the rickety door. "Junior…are you there?" he demanded. There was a moment of silence throughout the store as customers and clerks turned and stared at the leather-clad, pony tailed presence. Then, from the other side of the door: "Who wants to know?"

"Someone who'll twist your arms into a Japanese noodle if you don't open up right now!"

"OK…OK, I'm coming."

There was a 'click' sound as the lock was turned. Slowly the door cracked open revealing a disheveled, blearly-eyed, Junior peeking out into Kai's face. "What do you want?"

Kai pushed through the opening. He took Junior's hand and deftly twisted it into an ancient jujitsu hold designed to elicit volumes of truth from the mouths of its victims. "Where are Turk and Beto?" Kai whispered into Junior's ear.

"They flew to San Antonio, rented a car, drove to Kerrville, Texas, chartered an airplane, had the pilot fly them above Interstate 10 toward El Paso where they rented another car and drove toward Arizona," he bellowed quickly.

Kai smiled. "And you know all of this, because?"

"You're gonna break my wrist, dude. You're hurting me."

"I asked you a question, Junior."

"I know this because Turk or Beto call me every time they make a move, man, and that's the truth!"

Kai closed the door with his foot and slowly walked Junior to his unmade bed. "Where's your cell phone?"

"Here, man, on the bed."

Kai reached his free hand to the cell and pocketed it. Then turned to Junior's, now sweating face, glared into his tear-laden eyes, and said in a slow voice: "I'm taking your cell. If you obtain another, or in any other way, contact *anyone* regarding our little meeting here this morning, I will hunt you down like a hungry cheetah chasing a wounded gazelle. Do we have a firm understanding here?"

"*What*…little…meeting?" Junior stammered.

"You know what, Junior? You are smarter than I thought you would be. Now I want to know why your two cohorts are renting cars and chartering an aircraft to fly all over the western parts of the States."

"They're trying to chase down two dudes who didn't show up here with a bunch of cash when they were supposed to."

"What dudes?"

"Humberto and Jesse. They were supposed to deliver a bunch of syndicate money to Turk and Beto and me so's we could pass it on to someone in Matamoros."

"Did this *Humberto* and this *Jesse* think that they could steal that money from Turk and Beto and get away without repercussions?"

"No, man! They said that three old ladies swiped the money from *them* in Kerrville, Texas and ran off in a motor home. They're trying to chase the old broads along I-10 to get it back."

Kai twisted Junior's wrist to a grotesque angle. Junior's eyes closed. Copious tears fell down his scrunched cheeks. "Come on, Junior," Kai whispered, "you can come up with something better than that incomprehensible tale of shit."

"No, man, it's true! I know it sounds ridiculous," sobs, "they call me every day. Three old women from a retirement home stole the half-a-million bucks from Humberto and Jesse!"

Kai let go of Junior's wrist. He sat next to him on the bed. Then he began to chuckle. Then laugh. Then guffaw. "You know what, Junior? You just made my day. I don't think that my life will be complete until - someday, somehow - I get to meet those three elderly ladies, whoever they are. I'd just love to ask them what the *hell* they were thinking. I'll be damned if they don't have more balls than *me*!" Kai's face affected a menacing expression. "Now, Junior, I want you to tell me every - and I mean *every* - little detail regarding what Turk and Beto told you daily on the phone about their search for Humberto, Jesse, and the three gutsy old lady thieves. Where, when, and how."

IIIIIIIIIIIIIIIIII 27 IIIIIIIIIIIIIIIIIII

Nellie's North Forty

Rose stood and watched the men gathering rocks to form a fire pit in the center of the circle of their vehicles so that they could sit outside during the evenings and conference. Prudence, Louann, and Marguerite busied themselves collecting dried up cactus parts and dead brush in and around their cluster of Rvs and Turk's and Beto's rental sedan.

Nellie watched from outside the perimenter of their campsite. "Hey there, ladies," she called, "don't pull up any cactus that's still alive. The verdommt BLM Rangers will fine your butts *big time* if they catch you messing with anything that's still growing!"

"Looks to me as if this desert floor has been picked clean," Marguerite said to Louann."

"You know, Marguerite, we could be back in Kerrville in the card room preparing to play a nice hand of bridge just about now."

Marguerite wiped her brow with her forearm and

peered about the scene. "Yes, but we wouldn't have fifty-five big ones apiece."

Louann frowned as she snapped back: "And just where are we going to spend our fifty-five *big ones,* as you so crudely expressed it, out here?"

Laughing, Marguerite said: "Well, for one thing, we'll be able to pay the honey wagon folks to have a lot of shit sucked from our motor home's sewer tank."

"For gracious sakes, Marguerite, you're beginning to speak like those ruffians we're bound to."

"Why not?" Marguerite answered, "We joined the ranks of the world's misfits when we grabbed up that five-hundred thousand dollars and ran like thieves." she dropped her shoulders and sighed.

"The Good Lord is watching us, you know," sighed Louann.

"Well, we *did* it didn't we? "And now we have to pay the consequences. Besides, Louann, just how many human beings can stand up under close scrutiny from the Lord. Or anyone else, for that matter?"

"Certainly not *us,*" Prudence said as she approached the two. "We can lament or justify all we want, but the truth of the matter is that we stole the money and there's no turning back." She affected an expression of sorrow. "When one profits it's commonly at the expense of others. And the 'others' we profited from aren't going to just shrug and forget about it. "

"But the *others* are *dope smugglers*!" Marguerite justified.

"And *we* are common burglars."

"There's *always* a chance for redemption," Louann quipped as she tilted her head and raised her eyebrows.

"From the Lord, maybe, but not from those international dope dealers," Marguerite said, and added: "I think not."

"Well what on earth are we to do?" Louann half sobbed.

"All nine of us are going to have to have that meeting, Rose spoke about, and come to an understanding of our situation and decipher a way to survive. We have to figure out how we can protect *ourselves* because there's no one else who's going to help us."

"Certainly not law enforcement," Louann murmured, "they'll be after *us* as well as the dope dealers."

Several minutes of silence. Then: "Just standing here is getting us nowhere, so let's pitch in and finish getting set up," Prudence said.

# #

"Now just what do you figure those three old gals are talking about over there?" Jesse said to Humberto, Turk, and Beto as he watched them gathering scraps of dried brush.

The four men peered at the elderly trio.

"Probably trying to figure out how to screw us out of our share of the money!" Humberto blurted with another spasm of mirth.

"Dammit, Humberto, would you stop that laughing at everthing?" Jesse said.

"Yeah, man, it's getting on our nerves. What's so damned funny about this deal, anyway?" Turk asked.

Humberto bent over in another spasm of giggles. "It's hilarious, dude. Three old biddies copped our money. An oddball couple of old farts pitched in to help them. Then the four of us kicked in with them and now the bunch of us are hiding out in this god-awful desert from the syndicate's enforcer."

"You think all of this is *funny*?"

"I reckon I'd just as well die laughing. Dying is most likely what's going to be our outcome of this botched-up deal."

Turks's cell phone viberated out the tune: "It's a Small World."

"That's gotta be Junior calling from Nuevo Progresso. He's the only one who has my number." Turk fished his cell from his pocket. "Hey, Junior. What's up?" Turk listened for a few moments. Expressions of confusion, then anger, then fear, crossed his face.

"Hey, man, what's the matter?" Beto questioned.

Turk snapped his cell off and threw it on the desert floor and stared at it.

"What?" Jesse said.

"Yeah, dude, what's the deal?" Humberto asked.

"Holy shit. We're screwed!" Turk exclaimed.

"How? What did Junior say?" Beto said.

Turk squatted to the desert sand and began rocking back and forward. His eyes clouded with tears. He stammered: "It wasn't *Junior* on the cell."

"Well who the hell was it?"

Turk snuffed: "Some nasty sounding dude sung to me."

"What did he sing?"

"You know that song called: "I'll Be Coming 'Round the Mountain When I
Come?'"

"Yeah. What about it?"

"Well this dude sang *that* melody, but he used different words."

"What words?" Jesse said.

Turk sniffled. "I'll be riding my big Harley when I come…I'll be riding my big Harley when I come…I'll be riding my big Harley, I'll be riding my big Harey, I'll be riding down your off ramp when I come."

"Who would sing something like *that* from Junior's phone?"

"That 'enforcer' dude the syndicate hires to whack people who try to screw them, stupid!"

"You think he got to Junior?" Humberto asked.

Turk looked up to Humberto's face. "*Duh?*"

# #

Rose nudged Aldo's ribs with her elbow. "Get a load of those four assholes over there."

Aldo twisted and watched Turk, Beto, Humberto, and Jesse for a moment. "Looks like they stepped on a big ol' ant bed, or something, the way they're all twisting and stomping."

"Hey, you bozos!" Rose called across the circle, "What's the matter?"

Humberto was hopping about, consumed with mirth. "We're all gonna die!" he bellowed back.

Rose looked at Aldo. "That's funny?"

Aldo shook his head as he said: "You realize, don't you Rose, that those fellows are as slow-witted as nails. There's no telling what's gotten into them."

#

"Verdommt," Nellie said to herself shaking her head as she watched her new neighbors, "those Texans are all cuckoo. I'm glad I have my shotgun handy."

#

Aldo, Rose, the three women and four men, situated themselves closely around the small campfire in the center of their circled campers. Aldo stood and pitched a dried cactus pod into the flames. He glanced about at the forlorn group. "Listen up, folks. It's not helping us to sit around out here in the boonies just moping and scratching." He sucked into his lungs a breath of the fresh evening desert air and continued: "If you fellows truly believe that we're all in harm's way from some 'enforcer' dude the dope syndicate honchos have sent to punish us - or whatever - then we have to figure out how to permanently avoid him, or let him find us and confront him." Aldo shook his head slowly from side to side. "So…what's it gonna be? Run scared or stand up to him somehow?"

"Yeah," Rose said.

"Run scared!" Humberto shouted, then rolled to the desert floor holding his ribs in convulsions of laughter.

Everyone watched Humberto writhing in the sand.

"You know, girls," Louann said, "we're going to have to shoot that silly nincompoop."

Marguerite nodded affirmatively.

"We don't have a gun," Prudence said.

"Nellie does."

"Shut the hell up!" Turk hollered at Humberto. Then turned to the others. "You have no *real* idea of the shit we're in."

Aldo straightened to his full height of five feet six inches. "Listen ace, Rose and I hung out with the Hill Country Hellers biker club for a lot of years. It's not as though we don't have a few tricks up our sleeves, you know."

Humberto exclaimed: "Hill Country Hellers?" Then floundered about in the dirt in another spasm of mirth. "I've seen some of those old Hill Country Hellers," he guffawed. Then: "*Oooooo…*that syndicate enforcer dude is really gonna be *scarred* of you old has-beens!"

"Laugh and make fun all you want, dummy," Rose said, "but us old-timers know a thing or two about taking care of ourselves."

"What're you thinking, Rose," Turk said, "getting together with the three old broads there," pointing toward Prudence, Marguerite, and Louann, "and that little runt of a husband of yours, and giving a lecture on '*good behavior'* to that enforcer who's hunting us down to do 'who knows what' to us?"

"Screw you," Prudence interjected, "you and your bozo friends think that you are *soooo* tough. Well, I'll tell you what, mister, you haven't seen anything till you rile up a bunch of us old farts. Tom Brockaw calls us the 'Greatest Generation'. We survived the Great Depression,

World War Two, and watching movies starring Ronald Coleman. You call back to that cell phone of Junior's and tell that enforcer fellow to *'bring it on!'*.

Humbero stopped giggling and looked up at Prudence. "Who's Ronald Coleman?"

"Shut the hell up, Humberto," Louann said in a tone of disgust. Then muttered: "Nincompoop."

28

Kai Ochita

Kai pulled his fifth wheel down the I-10 off ramp into Sierra Blanca and stopped on the side of the main drag. "Hey, buddy, I heard that there's an old landing strip near here? Can you tell me where it's located?" he asked a filthy, bewhiskered pedestrian with a huge back pack being followed by a skinny mixed-breed dog. The dog stopped, but didn't bother to look up into Kai's truck.

The pedestrian hesitated a moment, as if he was straining his brain to come into focus, then pointed toward the northwest. "Yonder," he replied.

Kai dug into his pocket and produced a couple of bills and pitched them from his cab. "Get your dog some food and water, man," he said. Then shifted and slowly turned onto a dirt-covered asphalt road leading to that direction.

After slowly negotiating his RV a few hundred yards over the deteriorating roadway Kai spotted the dilapidated landing strip's hanger. He noted an old Hispanic man sitting next to a bicycle in the shade of the structure as he approached. As Kai pulled his fifth wheel next to the derelict hanger, the old fellow stood and nodded to him. He greeted Kai with a broad smile. "Buenos dias, amigo," he said to Kai after the obnoxious sound of Kai's diesel engine quieted.

"Hey," Kai answered.

Kai stepped down from the enormous cab and looked about the area. "What happened out here?"

"Nothing."

"Nothing?"

"Not sense the military abandoned this landing strip after the war."

"Which war?"

"World War Two."

Kai studied the forelorn landscape for a few minutes, then said: "I was told that I might find a fellow named Maclovio out here."

"Si, that's me. I'm Maclovio. Maclovio Maldonado."

Kai smiled. "How'd you like to earn an easy twenty dollar bill, Senior Maldonado?"

Maclovio grinned. "Those two jackasses and their friendly pilot flew out of here headed for El Paso a couple of days ago," he said.

Kai laughed. "Now how'd you know that I was going to ask you about *those* jackasses?"

Maclovio chuckled as he held his hand out, palm upward, to Kai. "They had lots of money like you, but they didn't act like no Bill Gates or Warren Buffet, so I figured that *they* estola that money from someone else."

Kai handed Maclovio a twenty dollar bill, then reached into his pants and proffered a second twenty.

"Nada," Maclovia said, "Twenty is plenty."

"Take it, my friend, you just made my day."

"Mucho gracias." He turned his head and frowned. "Those bastardos wrecked my pick up truck."

Kai furrowed his brow. "Did they pay you for it?"

"Just four hundred dollars."

"What was it worth?"

"I loved my pick up. To me it was worth two times four hundred."

Kai reached back into his pocket and pulled out a roll of currency. He counted out four one hundred dollar bills. "Here, friend, take this. You've more than earned it as far as I'm concerned. You've saved me a lot of time." He glanced at the bicycle next to Maclovio. "Ride that bicycle in to town and buy another pick up. Eight hundred dollars should cover your cost."

Maclovio grinned broadly. "Thank you, senor. I wish you luck in catching those bastardos. Oh, senor," he quickly added, "do not hurt the pilot. *He* is a *good* hombre."

"What makes you think that I'd harm those two assholes"

Maclovio grinned. "Oh, I don't know. The look in your eyes and the large amount of money in your pockets?"

׀׀׀׀׀׀׀׀׀׀׀׀׀׀׀׀׀׀ 29 ׀׀׀׀׀׀׀׀׀׀׀׀׀׀׀׀׀׀

Nellie's North Forty

Nellie sat under her aging Airstream's awning sipping a warm Oranjeboom lager as she studied the uncommon coterie seated around their fire pit in the center of their RV circle. *Mien Gott, what a mishmash of humanity those folks are. I best join them and find out what they're up to.* She stood and stretched her back, squared her shoulders, and called out to the group. "Hey! You people want your Oranjeboom lager now?"

The bickering about the bonfire ceased momentarily as the assemblage peered back at her.

"Well," Nellie said, "do you want your beer or not?"

Aldo stood and called back: "Rose and I would, for sure."

The four guys nodded in unison. The three women were silent.

"OK, then. A couple of you fellows get over here and help me tote it to your fire ring."

"Is it cold?" Louann asked.

Nellie jammed her fists to her hips and called back: "Of course not. No self-respecting lager drinker takes Oranjeboom cold. Only you spoiled Americans drink chilled beer."

Humberto and Jesse walked to Nellie's Airstream and picked up several six packs of the lager. "Warm beer tastes like peepee," Humberto whispered to Jesse.

Jesse shrugged. "I wouldn't know, hombre, I ain't never tasted whiz."

Humberto and Jesse distributed the beer. Silence for a moment as each of the gathering sipped their lager.

Then: "Doesn't taste like beer to me," Prudence said. "It tastes like bitter orange juice."

"Why Prudence. I didn't know that you had ever tasted beer, being proper and all, like you are," Louann said.

"I wasn't *always* proper, dear. I attended Baylor, you know, but I did go out with a fellow from UT in Austin once."

"*Oh my*," Marguerite giggled knowingly.

"I went out with a student from A and M," Louann quipped.

"You didn't!"

"Just *once*," she added with a snort.

"Why just once?" Marguerite asked.

"Must you ask?" Louann said.

There was a few minutes of silence as the assembly cautiously sampled the warm lager. They eyed one another testily as each swallow made its way down their throats. Finally, Rose stood and spoke in a firm and commanding voice. "Alright folks, we have to get down to our business at hand! I'm not going to sit here and review our little debacle over and over, 'cause time is our enemy. Aldo's and my take on what we should do here is this: the first thing we should consider is deciding on our strategy in regards to *negotiation* with that enforcer dude you fellows seem to believe is coming to do harm to us and take back the money."

"Negotiate?" Jesse scoffed. "There ain't going to be no *negotiating* with the enforcer, lady. Don't you get it? We're screwing with the syndicate. Stealing their money. Dishonoring them. Them jackals don't *negotiate* with their *mommas* much less a bunch of stupid folks like us who're ripping them off!"

Prudence raised her hand. "*You* and your cohorts were associated with those jackals - as you so aptly referred to them - and *you* negotiated with *us*."

"Yeah, but we're just the errand boys and go-fers for them. It ain't like we're *them*."

"There's a difference?" Marguerite asked.

"I'm afraid you'll soon be finding that out," Jesse huffed.

More contemplation. The mournful lament of a coyote punctuated the silence framing the tense scene. Louann and Marguerite peered into the lovely sky canvassing overhead They studied the millions of stars. Prudence slowly shook her head. The four fellows focused on the embers in the firepit. Rose looked at Aldo and shrugged her shoulders. Aldo took a deep breath. "The way Rose and I figure is: trying to make a deal of some sort to avoid mayhem is worth our effort, if and when, that scary dude catches up with us. If that doesn't work… well, then we'll see."

"We'll see what?" Turk asked, "The Pearly Gates?"

"How 'bout the "Gates of Hell?" Humberto whimpered.

Nellie walked slowly around the fire pit as she studied the faces of the group. "May I ask a guestion of you folks?"

Silence.

"Just what in the *hell* have you crazy-acting ninnyhammers been up to?"

"We stole five hundred thousand dollars from a nefarious association of international dope smugglers," Marguerite whispered with a sigh, "and just this afternoon we learned that they are sending a really bad-ass dude to find us and take it back. And," she whispered, "he may be planning to kick our butts. Or worse!"

Louann glared at Marguerite. "Watch your language, Marguerite."

Marguerite proffered Louann her third finger.

Prudence scoffed. "Oh, come now. You two behave yourselves."

Silence.

"Are you *serious* about stealing *money* and a *bad-ass* dude coming *here?*" Nellie asked with widened eyes.

"'Fraid so," Aldo said.

|||||||||||||||||| 30 ||||||||||||||||||

Mexico City
Eduardo Betancourt

"Has the man from Brownsville found those couriers with our money?" Eduardo Betancourt asked with a calm voice.

"Not as yet, sir," a nervous reply from Eduardo's cell phone.

"What is the delay?"

"Our enforcer, Ochita, reported that he located one of our bag men in a little border town called Nuevo Pregresso. The fellow told Ochita that our money was stolen from the original two couriers while they were in Kerrville, Texas."

"How in the hell did they manage to let that happen?" Betancourt asked, again in a calm tone.

"It happened."

"Well, then, does *anyone* have a notion as to the identidy of the thieves?"

"Yes sir. Three elderly women from a retirement center."

Betancourt leaned forward and squared his elbows on his desk. He was silent for several moments. Then he leaned back and swiveled his chair so that he could look out into the vast metropolis of Mexico City. "Repeat, please," he said.

"Sir, our man in Nuevo Progresso told our enforcer, Ochita, that three old ladies who live in a retirement center in Kerrville, Texas somehow learned where our two couriers had secreted the five hundred thousand dollars for overnight safe-keeping. The three women broke into the hiding place and stole our money. Then they ran off in a large RV."

"What in the hell is an RV?"

"In this instance, a big motor home."

Betancourt watched a city bus negotiating the traffic forty stories below. "I'm seated in my office more than five hundred feet above the traffic on Paseo de Reforma and I am watching a city bus. I believe that I could spot that same bus from an airplane flying at five thousand feet. How hard could it be to locate the three thieving old women in such a vehicle?"

"Sir, our man is on their trail, but there is another concern."

"What other concern?"

"Well, sir, I don't quite understand what the devil is going on with this situation, but our man reported that two of our original couriers joined forces with the three elderly women and are running away with *them* and our money.

Betancourt's parents had migrated to Mexico City

from Colombia when he was five years of age. He'd enjoyed a privileged childhood, unaware - until he was fifteen years old - that the considerable wealth of his grandparents and, subsequently, his parents had been generated by the growing and selling of marijuana to the enormous market north of Mexico. He was tutored at home until his fifteenth year. Then sent to a private military boarding school in San Antonio, Texas. His father wanted three disciplines for Eduardo to conquer while attending the military school: fluency in the English language, orderliness, and discipline. Eduardo had mastered all three. Especially discipline.

"What about our three couriers who were waiting to receive our money in Nuevo Progresso?" Eduardo asked in an almost inaudible voice.

"It is my understanding that two of the couriers set out to find the first two couriers. They located them with the old women off the Interstate 10 at a place called Stein's Ghost Town near the Texas/New Mexico border."

"And?"

"Well, sir, we believe that *they* joined up with the old women as well."

Eduardo took a deep breath, exhaled slowly. "Stein's Ghost Town?," he said.

"Sir?"

"Nothing."

"Well, sir, we just have to wait until Kai Ochita catches up with the bunch of them."

"No," Eduardo said, "this situation is too consequential for us to let our enforcer find them on his own. If our syndiate associates learn of this breach of our organization it will undermind my control *my* phase of the operation, much less make *me* the laughing stock of our competitors as well as the authorities who pay to allow our business to flourish. Three old women stealing our money and running off with our couriers: *that* is ludicrous. I will not let that happen. You may be under the assumption that *I*, Eduardo Betancourt, am the head of this illicit dope-smuggling cartel, but you would be incorrect. There are always others - higher up the ladder - who are the bosses. No one ever knows for certain who those people are. Even *I* don't know. But I suspect that they are U.S. citizens in the highest order of their government. Why else would it be so easy to smuggle tons of illegal narcotics daily across the border year after year?" Eduardo shook his head. "It's delusional to think otherwise." He shuddered as he thought: *They're shadows of the devil.*

Eduardo snapped his cell phone closed and punched a button on his desk. "Book two seats on the next available flight to Stein's Ghost Town."

"*Sir?*" his secretary asked.

"Just look up Stein's Ghost Town - wherever the hell that is in New Mexico - and get me two first class tickets to the nearest city!"

Eduardo punched the intercom closed and opened his cell phone and dialed. "What's the cell number of that Kai Ochita?" He listened a moment, then punched in the number. After four rings Kai answered. "What?" Kai said.

"Eduardo Betancourt, here. My associate and I are flying to the nearest city to that place called 'Stein's Ghost Town'. I'll call you as soon as we know exactly where and when we will land. I expect you to meet us at that airport. I'm going to take charge of this absurd situation regarding the theft of the syndicate's money. Keep your cell phone handy."

Kai said: "Mr. Betancourt…I'm taking care of this business. There's no need for you to come here."

"Oh, I believe there *is* a need for me to take charge, Ochita. It seems that several of our delivery-boy assholes, and now, you…what in the hell *are* you anyway…a damned Chinaman or a Jap…have managed to let three elderly women abscond with five hundred thousand dollars of the sydicate's money." After a brief interlude of silence, he added: "Do you understand me?"

"Oh, I understand you, Mr. Betancourt, loud and clear."

"Expect my call."

Betancourt slammed the cell phone into his drawer and turned to stare at the busy city streets below. *Tres abuelas…mi Dios!*

A light on Betancourt's intercom blinked. He leaned forward and pushed it's button. "What?", he barked.

"Sir, the nearest airport to Stein's Ghost Town is Tucson, Arizona. Shall I book two first class tickets?"

"Yes, on the first possible flight."

#

Kai slowly closed his cell phone as he reflected on his exchange with Eduardo Betancourt. He turned his head slightly to his left and studied the blue-gray outline of the Dragoon Mountain Range in the distance. He had driven across I-10 many times. Each time he marveled at the vistas the route offered. Miles of clear blue skies laced with contrasting white clouds. Distant mountains carving exotic designs on the horizons in every direction. This portion of the I-10 corridor is often referred to as: Al Entrada de la Pacifica. He especially enjoyed the vast openess of the scenario, his imagination flooded with visions of ancient Indian tribes slowly migrating to their next encampment, content to live a serene life of free movement and independence. Other tribes the world over had experienced those same joys in the distant past. *Such a shame,* he thought, *that humans have lost their serenity during the eon.* His thoughts returned to Eduardo Betancourt and this current endeavor. Then, to the turn his life had taken after his first encounter with the low-life individual, back in the Bay Area, who had paid him generously to intimidate others. He cogitated back to Betancourt's insulting comment about his ethnicity. *My ancestors would be shamed by my association with this illicit syndicate.*

|||||||||||||||||| 31 ||||||||||||||||||

Louann

Louann backed away from the squatting and standing group around the make-shift fire pit and slowly tilted her head forward. *For heaven's sake. What on this earth have I gotten myself into?* she asked herself. Turning, she scanned the scenario about the circle of campers. *My momma and poppa are probably looking down at me and shaking their heads.* Scenes of her early life floated through Louann's thoughts. Her first recollection was one of a solemn scene in which she was a five-year old standing beside her mini-desk. Her father was looking down at her as her mother handed her an ornate black and gold embossed bible. Her father had his normally serious expression across his face. It was her fifth birthday. She had hoped for a blue tricycle. Another, later, remembrance streamed before her mind's eye: Walking on stage, for the first time, before an audience. It was during a high school play: 'Bell, Book, and Candle'. She remembered that she had altered one of the words her character spoke. The word 'darn' had been part of the dialogue she was to speak and her mother had strenuously objected to that bit of profanity, so she had been instructed - no, ordered - by her mother, to substitute the word 'pity' in its place. The drama teacher - who had received her teaching degree from the University of Texas the previous year - was outraged by the word-substitution of the script and confronted her after the play. At the end of the semester the drama teacher was shocked to learn that she had not been offered a contract for the next school term. The accusation against her: she had directed a student to use 'profanity' during a school-sponsored drama production. Louann's mother was a member of the school board that year. Louann thought of the dating offers that she had turned down during her school years. Her parents didn't approve of youngsters who were not affiliated - or not active - in the youth group sponsored by their congregation. She often wondered how different her life would have been had her parents embraced living differently. Then, later, after marriage, her devoted husband had been employed thirty-one years in the same division of one company. They had attended the same church in the same town during that thirty-one year span of time. She had never met - much less talked to - one other human being who was not similar to her in thought or dress. She had been told that all movies were lewd and offensive, so she didn't attend them. Not even 'The Wizard of Oz'. She never ventured into the lesser - or 'poor' - neighborhoods of her town so she wasn't intellectually aware of how those citizens lived, nor did she speculate regarding their life's situation. She was taught that no person should be poor, for every individual on earth - regardless of the situation they had been born into - had only to 'pull themselves up by their bootstraps' and pray to become self-sufficient and self-reliant. After all, she mused, all of her acquaintances were. Louann, for the first time, took a speculative look at her new-found associates. Then she actually listened to them. Suddenly she had an epiphany: *God, my life has been boring! Is this capitulation, I'm now experiencing, a reaction to my self-enforced, narrow-minded, and blinded existence - or simply an 'awakening' to the 'real world'?* She couldn't decide. But, somehow, she was beginning to feel more alive now than in any previous period of her life.

Louann turned abruptly to the klatch bantering about the fire pit. "Screw it!" she shouted, "I agree with Aldo and Rose. We should wait here until that drug cartel enforcer man finds us. We'll endeavor to reason with him. And if *that* doesn't work…well, we'll just have to defend ourselves as best we can!" She thrust her balled-tight right fist toward the group: "That half-a-million dollars dope money might as well be *ours* than *theirs,* dammit! *We* got ahold of it just as illegally as *they* did!"

Sudden silence as the others turned to stare back at Louann.

"Holy shit," Humberto mumbled as he rolled in the desert sand bellowing with laughter.

׀׀׀׀׀׀׀׀׀׀׀׀׀׀ 32 ׀׀׀׀׀׀׀׀׀׀׀׀׀׀׀

Humberto and Jesse

Jesse turned to Humberto. "If you don't stop that stupid laughing at things that aren't funny I'm gonna smash your nose clean into the back of your skull!"

Humberto sat up and wiped his eyes as he peered back at Jesse, then snuffled a few times and rolled back onto the desert floor and stopped laughing. He reminenced back to the first time he and Jesse had fought. It was during their middle school days. He had ruffled Jesse's hair one time more than Jesse would tolerate and Jesse had turned and punched him hard twice in his ribs. They wrestled around on the ground a minute or two until they were both exhausted. Then began to laugh. The two had been buddies since grade school and a playful shot to each other's side had been a common practice. But these blows were serious ones. They had hurt him to the point where tears streamed from his eyes. He remembered the shocked reality of his best buddy striking him in anger. The only other times that he had received angry blows were those delivered to him by his parents. Their anger had been delivered to him with verbal assaults. No one laughed after those encounters, however. *I didn't deserve that,* Humberto thought. *I tried to be good, I really did. But things were harder for me than they were for my brother and sister. Shit, almost every high school teacher had taught classes for my brother and sister before me.* "Your brother didn't have any problems with this material, Humberto. If you would just apply yourself and not be such a smart-aleck you could do better. And not one of us teachers considers your crude sayings as clever." Words of that nature were often spoken to him.

He'd managed to received his high school diploma in spite of dyslexia, but that didn't make it easier for him to get a job, so he joined the United States Army. The enlistment sergeant had told him that he could learn a useful trade in which to earn a living after the army - or better yet - make the army his career, plus he'd receive a cash bonus for enlisting. That sounded swell, so he joined. He figured that enlisting would be a good deal for him, all things considered.

Humberto returned from the Middle East three years later with an oblique view of life. He didn't re-enlist. Folks back home treated him better than they had greeted his dad and uncle years earlier when they returned from Viet Nam. He didn't remember anyone being outright joyful or appreciative of his service, either. Just mildly gratulate. He'd learned to shoot a rifle and multiple other skills, but that didn't qualify him for any of the available above-minimum wage jobs in the Rio Grande Valley of Texas. So he drifted about for a couple of years doing 'handy' work in the packing sheds - packing canalopes and watermelons alongside 'wetbacks' - as the local anglos called the illegal Mexican workers and seasonal crop laborers.

Then one evening, in Nuevo Progresso, Mexico, by happenstance, he met Jesse. Jesse was driving a nice-looking used Ford 150 pickup truck, wearing two-toned leather 'cowboy' boots, and a broad smile. Jesse up-dated Humberto on his life to date by telling him that he had gone to Mexico immediately after leaving high school. Jesse said that he learned that he had migrated illegally from Mexico to the States with his family when he was four years of age. Two months prior to his graduation his father had been picked up by the authorities and sent back to Mexico. Jesse reluctantly followed his parents back to Mexico to help them cope.

"Hey, man, what're you up to nowadays?" Humberto asked Jesse.

"Nothing much, buddy, except making some easy money delivering stuff across the border for some scary dudes over here."

"What stuff?"

"Oh, just *stuff* from the States they want me to sneak across the border to Nuevo Progresso."

"Marijuana and shit like that?"

Jesse laughed as he said: "No, man. No one smuggles dope *to* Mexico - just dope *from* Mexico."

"What *stuff*, then?" Humberto asked with a puzzled expression.

"*Dollars,* dummy. Someone has to take all that dope cash back to the cartel dudes."

Humberto laughed and punched Jesse's shoulder.

"you mean to tell me that some drug cartel honcho trusts *you* to deliver money across the border to *him*?"

"Shit yes, man. I do it every couple of weeks. I'm an American citizen and have a passport. It's easy to go back and forth across the border. He pays me good, too. Shoot, man, the cash I sneak across is just peanuts and change to them. It's mostly loose bills from the street pushers - but it does mount up."

Humberto stepped back and perused Jesse. "Well, I gotta say that you're lookin' fine, buddy."

Jesse asked: "What's up with *you*? I heard that you'd joined the army, man."

"Yeah, I sure did. Spent two tours in Iraq."

"You OK?"

Humberto looked down at his feet, then glanced past Jesse's shoulder. "Yeah, I guess. I've been working the packing sheds. I don't make a hell of a lot of dough, but it's a pay check."

"*Packing* sheds? With *obreros?*"

"Hey, Jesse, those people work like hell for what little they earn."

"I didn't mean any disrespect, man. But that's peon shit. Can't you do any better than *that*?"

Humberto shook his head. "I've been sort of mixed-up since leaving Iraq."

Jesse stepped back and sized-up Humberto. "Tell you what, buddy, I think that you can do *better* than that. I'll give you an intro to one of the guys I deliver for. Forget this packin' shed crap."

"I don't know, Jesse, what you're doing sounds iffy to me. What happens if you don't get the dollars to those dudes?"

Jesse grinned as he made an exaggerated motion across his neck with his hand. "No mas cabeza, hombre."

Humberto studied Jesse for a few moments. "What you're doing is dangerous, man. You're gonna get your ass in deep shit."

Jesse laughed hardily as he draped his arm around Humberto's shoulder. "Hey, buddy, it ain't nowhere as extreme as the crap you were dealing with over there in Iraq."

"Sure, but that was for a cause."

"Whose cause, man?"

Humberto stared back into Jesse's eyes. "*Our* cause."

"You want to talk *cause*? Huh? I'll tell you what *cause* is: *cause* is making some money so's you can live decent. Wear some nice clothes. Drive yourself around in some cool wheels. Be able to take a nice chick out dining and dancing. Having friends. Getting along with everyone." Jesse smirked as he continued: "Tell you what, Humberto, we'll take a run over to the Texas University campus at Edinburg and meet up with some of those sophomore chicks who're studying philosophy and stuff like that and discuss how '*cause*' figures in with low wages and rich share-holders."

"What in the hell are you talking about, Jesse?"

"Forget it, Humberto. Let's just focus on *us* for a moment. You and me and getting *our* piece of the pie. We'll make that *our* cause. OK?"

Humberto turned and perused the main drag of Nuevo Progresso. It was truly a pitiful sight. There were sand bags clustered haphazardly on the side of the intersection of the main thoroughfare. Boys in Mexican Army uniforms, brandishing rifles, loitered about laughing and playing 'grab ass'. "How come the Federales are watching the streets, man? They're scaring off the Winter Texans."

"Cartels. The dope cartels are taking over the border towns and the Mexican Federales are trying to stop them." Jesse laughed as he said: "Fat chance."

"Why do you say that?"

"Shit, half the border on both sides is getting paid off with cartel money. How in the hell do you think hundreds of tons of grass and coke gets across the border every month?"

"Just like *you* are getting paid off?" Humberto asked.

"Hell yes, man, except that I actually perform a service for the cartel." Jesse shrugged, "Most all the others get paid just to turn their backs."

Humberto took a deep breath. "Just like the Middle East," he muttered. His features took on a pensive expression. After a long pause he said: "You know what, Jesse…what the hell…introduce me to your cartel dope dealers."

ⅠⅠⅠⅠⅠⅠⅠⅠⅠⅠⅠⅠⅠⅠ 33 ⅠⅠⅠⅠⅠⅠⅠⅠⅠⅠⅠⅠⅠⅠ

Aldo and Rose

Aldo peered into the campfire while Jesse chastised Humberto. He glanced to his right, where Rose stood, as he contemplated her. Rose looked back into his eyes and shrugged her small shoulders in a gesture of frustration. Oftentimes Rose's take on the situations they had managed to muddle through during their fifty-seven short years of their mostly colorful marriage had amazed him. He adored her every single second of those years. *Can't help myself in regards to that little gal,* he reflected. *She never complained about having to work to supplement our income.* He respected her opinions, even in regard to watching Judge Judy during the day and The Hallmark Channel when the sun set. And she had worked hard all those years in little mom and pop cafes before her legs and feet began to ache so badly from waiting tables and having to put up with assholes who considered their crude behavior to be clever. And receiving meager tips because they figured that *less* than minimum wage for the waitresses was enough for her services. *Love my little Rose,* Aldo thought.

Aldo side-stepped closer to Rose and slid his arm around her waist. "Come on, pumpkin, let's scoot back a bit so just the two of us can re-analyze the predicament we're all faced with here."

Rose nodded and backed several feet. "What, hon?" she asked.

"Well, we told the gang *our* opinion and they didn't shoot it down right away. Even old prudish Prudence seemed to approve of our suggestion."

Rose smiled. *My little ol' man is something else,* she thought. *He'd been a real busy worker for the first twenty-five years in spite of being so short, but all those years of painting houses had taken their toll. He'd had to use a ladder, or step stool, for every stroke of his brush. That just darn near wore out his little ol' body. This just may be our last chance to live the 'good life' for a spell.*

"So…help me out here. Is it *really* a smart thing to confront this dope syndicate enforcer who's looking for us?" Aldo asked Rose.

"Aldo honey, we don't have but two choices: keep running, or face up to whoever's after us."

Aldo Chambers had always considered that he had been particularly blessed to have met and married Rose. He had grown up in a smallish South Texas town where his short stature had been a hindrance. Every girl remotely close to his age had been several inches taller than he. Except for Rose. *Bless Rose's heart,* he constantly thought, *she opted for me rather than any of the taller guys. And not because she felt sorry for me - or that she, too, was short - but because she actually thought that I was OK. And contrary to every other local girl's opinion: humorous. Go figure. Oh, well,* he often sighed to himself, *I usually brush my teeth - what's left of them - every day, and don't fart under the sheets if I can help it.*

"Ok, then, let's scoot back over to the group and convince all the rest of us to confront that enforcer, if and when, he catches up with us," Aldo said with resolution.

"*That's* my guy," Rose said with gusto, "Sick 'em partner!"

Aldo called over to Humberto. "Get up off the ground! We've gotta make some decisions *now* that'll effect all us. And you and Jesse have to be a part of it."

Humberto slowly got to his feet. "Whatever, man."

Jesse nodded. "Well, I reckon Aldo's right. We've screwed ourselves big time with the cartel assholes, that's for sure. Ain't no future *there* for *us* anymore."

|||||||||||||||||| 34 ||||||||||||||||||

Turk and Beto

Beto glanced sideways at Turk. Turk seemed mesmerized by the camp fire. "What are you thinking, Turk?"

"I'm trying to figure out how in the hell you and me got ourselves locked in to this stupid situation." Turk leaned forward and picked up a branch of dried brush and pitched it further into the center of the fire. *I thought that I'd gotten away from harm's way when my parents moved to Mexico City from Turkey when I was twelve years old. Now, here I am, 'back in deep shit,' as the Americans say, when they've screwed up.* "I just don't know what to think, man. You and me…we were sittin' pretty, you know, making some easy money delivering cash across to Mexico. Then those three old ladies snatched the money from Humberto and Jesse and suddenly we've joined up with them and the others and we're all running like scared rabbits."

Beto shrugged as he answered: "Shit happens, man."

"Well, we sure as hell stepped in it *this* time, buddy."

Turk looked up at the millions of stars overhead. He began to ruminate about his life. Back in Turkey, his father and mother had been bookstore-librarians and teachers in their village. One morning - when Turk was twelve years of age - two young men dressed in black suits stepped into the small bookstore-library and left a book. The book, it turned out, was a condensed version of the history of Budism. Turks's father had been busy in the rear of the small establishment and hadn't noticed the manual lying on the front counter. An Islamic fundamentalist practitioner entered the front entrance and noticed the book. Consequently Turk and his parents had to flee Turkey in fear of their well being. They ended their flight in Mexico City where Turk lived with his parents until his eighteenth birthday. Finding work in Mexico was difficult, so he contacted a 'coyote' - a smuggler of people to the United States - and subsequently ended his illicit journey in the Rio Grande Valley of Texas. There he survived by a miscellaneous series of jobs. Mostly smuggling drugs from Mexico and cash back to Mexico. Turk didn't particulary relish his 'occupation', but it paid him relatively well considering that he had no 'in demand' skills, except for his gift for languages and his talent for passing to and fro across the United States/Mexican border. He had, by necessity, become a 'loner' with the exception of his association with Beto, who he had befriended in the small neighboring town of Progresso on the Texas side of the border. Beto was his age and the thing the two young men had in common was an aversion to field labor and being poor. Together they figured a way to slip both ways across the border -

unnoticed and unchallenged - by the border authorities. Thus their usefullness for the drug cartels.

Turk had grown through his pre-teen years in Turkey accustomed to living in close quarters with his extended family and neighorhood friends. And in Mexico City he had become accustomed to the 'barrio' style of life which entailed close association with neighborhood friends and acquaintances. He sorely missed the camaraderie of both of those lifestyles.

Beto's claim to fame was his ability to catch a football. Before he dropped out of high school during the football season of his eleventh grade, he had gained some local notoriety in his small Texas border town as the Fighting Red Ant's football team's leading receiver. But his grades didn't hold up. He was dropped from the squad. He stopped attending classes, thus joining the lonely and aimless life of those who do not conform - or belong to - the various groups of humans who make up the whole of 'acceptable' society.

||||||||||||||||| 35 |||||||||||||||||

Prudence and Marguerite

What on earth would my friends and kinfolk back home think if they saw me now? Prudence thought to herself as she perused the fire pit encircled by her fellow conspirators. She had been reared by her parents on their small farm several miles from the county seat. Their neighbors had grown corn and a few farm animals just as her family had. Every member of their mid-western farm-owner acquaintances had viewed life much the same way as she did. Hard work: she could drive all of the farm machinery. Honesty. Pureness of thought and action. Correctness. Faith. Law abiding. Patriotic. Yet she found herself in her golden years, after a life of propriety - except for playing the card game called bridge - out in the middle of the Arizona desert huddled around a camp fire with fellow thieves contemplating a showdown with an illicit dope cartel's enforcer. *Please, dear Lord, don't allow my parents in heaven to view me now,* Prudence silently prayed.

She glanced at Marguerite. Marguerite looked back.

The two women simultaneously raised their brows in a silent recognition of their mutual plight. Marguerite had grown to adulthood in in Germany imbued with the same values as Prudence. Each were silently acknowledging to one another the same guilt for the activities in which they had voluntarily participated with Louann and the others for the last few mind-boggling days. Marguerite sidled next to Prudence. "What are you thinking, dear?" she whispered.

"I think we're all going to hell in a hand basket. At least that's what my dear old departed grandpa would be saying if he knew what we've been up to the last few days."

Marguerite nervously licked her lips. "My opa would be saying the same thing."

The two women stood leaning against each other for a few moments. Then Prudence straightened her shoulders, and with an air of resoluteness, stated: "Well, Marguerite, there's no turning back. We have become part and parcel of a gang of thieves. We've made our beds and now we're just going to have to sleep in them! If we have to stand up to that enforcer…well, so be it!"

Marguerite proffered a grand smile and said: "Oh, Prudence, I was praying you'd say something of that nature. I'm of German heritage, you know. Sic 'em!"

The two hugged briefly, then turned to join the others around the camp fire.

IIIIIIIIIIIIIIIIIII 36 IIIIIIIIIIIIIIIIIII

Kai Ochita

Kai eased his foot off of the gas padal of his huge deisel-powered truck and fifth-wheel travel trailer as he approached the sprawling greater Quartzsite area of western Arizona. Interstate 10, at this point, was built much higher than the surrounding Sonoran plain, because of the mostly loose sand and silt covering the dusty steppe, thus enabling him to have an unobstructed vista covering several square miles in every direction.

Prime season for the hundreds of thousands 'boondockers' - winter snowbirds who RV to the area - begins in earnest during late fall every year. Yet, hundreds of travel trailers, motor homes, and campers were already scattered, dotting the horizon, to and fro across the desert.

Kai had stopped at virtually every service station along I-10 west from Sierra Blanca, Texas through Tucson and Phoenix, Arizona probing for the three camping vehicles and the sedan carrying his prey who had absconded with the cartel's five hundred thousand dollars. Knowing fuel was the one absolute necessity the three elderly women, the pickup camper, and the four cartel deserters required for their escape, Kai deducted that gasoline stops were the key to their trail. This endeavor wasn't difficult because the highly uncommon alliance of three senior ladies with four questionable looking younger men and a seedy looking elderly married couple was memorable to all who had sold gas to them. Kai had learned from a cashier - who worked in the last service station in which he had inquired about the three Rvs - that she had remembered overhearing two of the described campers talking about Quartzsite. It had taken time, effort - and a bit of frustration - for Kai to tract them west across I-10. Especially since Eduardo Betancourt, the cartel honcho, had insinuated himself into the search. Kai received cell phone calls from Betancourt every three hours. This was not only aggravating for him but insulting as well. He had successfully accomplished every single assignment since aligning himself with the illicit operations of the Mexican drug cartel and he didn't appreciated Betancourt's interferance. Kai was also brooding over the crude remarks Betancourt had sarcastically said to him during the first call he received from him. *"What the hell are you, a damned Chinaman or Jap?"* Kai remembered Betancourt asking him this insulting question during that initial call.

Betancourt and his bodyguard had flown to Phoenix, per Betancourt's secretary's suggestion, and waited, irritably and impatiently - in a motel close to the Sky Harbor International Airport - for Kai to find and confirm the location of the three Rvs.

Kai pulled slowly down the Exit 19 Off Ramp onto Main Avenue of Quartzsite and executed a sharp right turn onto Sherriff Road and eased his fifth-wheel off to the shoulder. He sat in the truck's cab for several minutes analyzing the situation. *If they decided to stop in this Quartzsite managerie of campers I would have a hell of a time finding them. There are literally hundreds of vehicles scattered for miles around. Many of them look the same,* he reflected. *What's the quickest way to see if they've parked out here somewhere?* As he sat pondering his next move, he heard a small gasoline engine laboring overhead. He looked upward from his cab and spotted a small ultra-lite aircraft slowly passing about three hundred feet above his rig. It was towing a banner advertising: 'Will's and Buck's Flea Market - Millions of Everything!'. Kai stepped from his truck and hailed a nearby pedrestrian. "Excuse me, sir. Would you happen to know where that little kite-plane up there lands?" The fellow glanced up, then peered back at Kai. The deeply sun-weathered man tilted back his 'cowboy' hat, spit on the road, and said: "Now just why in the world would a Jap like you want to know about that there flimsy little old toy airplane up there? You cain't bomb Pearl Harbor with it."

Kai stared back at the man. He was wearing sweat-stained camouflage hunting apparel and dust-laden, broken down, combat boots. His hatband sported a small Confederate flag. A patch sewn to his shoulder read: 'From my cold, dead, hand!'.

"Tell you what, you annoying piece of redneck trash: I promise you I won't rip off your stupid hat and shove it down your throat if you answer me in a polite and civil manner. Otherwise, just walk away."

The pedestrian took two steps back and squinted into Kai's eyes. "You're just full of yourself, ain't you?"

"Yes, as a matter of fact I am. At least that's what my drill sergeant in boot camp use to tell me."

"*You* was in the *U. S. of A.* Army?"

"Yes, I was," Kai answered. "Desert Storm."

"Well, my daddy was in the army out in the Pacific during WW II fighting Japs."

"That's admirable. Which branch of the armed forces did you serve?" Kai asked.

"Me? Well, I was between wars. But I would've served."

"Yeah, right," Kai said.

"Yes indeed, I would've been 'Johnny on the spot'."

"I'll ask you one more time: do you know where that ultra-lite's landing area is located?"

Pointing straight ahead the man said: "That-a-way about a mile and a half."

Kai nodded. "Thank you. I wouldn't have actually jammed your hat down your throat, but I thought you could benefit from a little lesson in civility just now."

"Oh?" the pedestrian asked as he backed another two steps. "And what lesson is that?"

"You never know who the hell you're speaking to: a nice, pleasant, stranger - or a guy such as me who's a Special Services veteran and can cause you so much pain that you wouldn't be able to describe it adequately to the 911 operator." Kai nodded and continued politely: "Thank you for directing me to that ultra-lite's landing spot," then turned and entered his truck's cab.

The pedestrian shook his head as he cogitated: *Jeez,*

everyone's so danged sensitive nowadays. Dammed uptight politically correct hardnoses.

#

Kai pulled his rig next to the small clearing for the ultra-lite landing field. There were several small flying machines parked randomly around two large 'hauler' fifth-wheel trailers. A sagging canvas awning - held with nylon ropes and metal poles - shaded a dozen men sitting in folding camp chairs watching him park. He climbed from his truck's cab and greeted the onlookers. "Gentlemen!" Kai called out as he affected an imploring expression, "Would it be possible for me to buy a ride above Quartzsite with one of you pilots?"

"Yep," one of the men answered as he stood, "we charge passengers the same hourly rate that we charge merchants to pull their advertising banners."

"Great!" Kai answered with a broad smile. "This is my first visit to the Quartzsite area," he looked about, "and it's a fascinating place to behold. I'd like to see it all from above to help me decide where I would like to park my rig."

"You interested in boondocking or a regular hookup park with facilities and all?"

"I don't know. Which is best in your opinion?"

The pilot looked back toward his companions. "Some of us pay for hookups and some of us boondock." He shrugged, "I reckon it's a matter of money, mostly. You can stay out a ways for a couple of weeks for free. After that you gotta move to another spot or go and pay the public servants twenty-five dollars for long-term camping.

Or, if you want to, you can pay the government folks out yonder one hundred and forty dollars for long-term camping and hang out for up to seven months."

"I'd just like to boondock for a few days to check out the area."

"It's up to you, fellow. Just step over here to this card table and sign this release form and pay me for as many hours as you want - up to one hour at a time - of actual flying time. We accept cash only. These fellows here will watch your rig for you while we're up there."

"Thanks," Kai said, and walked to the table and signed the form.

"Ain't you going to ask me how much it'll cost?"

"Nope," Kai answered as he pulled a large roll of bills from his pocket. "How come all these folks are out here in the middle of the desert?" Kai asked the ultra-lite pilot.

"Well, it's like this: Quartzsite's known for mild winter weather, plus it's the location of several giant mineral shows. In February, hundreds of thousands of folks show up to visit the annual Pow Wow rock and mineral exhibits, plus winter 'snowbirds' and Social Security retirees come out here to bask in the sun and shop for bargains at the 'flea' markets." He laughed, then continued: "During the season you'll find more Rvers out around here, at the same time, than anywhere else on the face of old mother earth."

Kai laughed as he replied: "This part of the desert should be covered with an enormous circus tent."

"Well, it would take one hell of a tent, for sure," the pilot answered with a grin. "Some call this part of the desert: 'Tacky Town'," he added with a chuckle.

"I can't imagine why," Kai replied grinning.

#

Kai marveled at the scenerio below as the pilot guided the ultra-lite in widening circles above the Quartzsite complex. There were numerous 'flea market' sites being set up randomly across the area. He watched a caravan of brand new motor homes slowly snaking into a huge vacant lot being guided by sales personel who hoped to peddle them to retired citizens who would be convinced to trade in their current RV and sign up for a long-time loan to cover the remaining cost of their existing camper plus the addition of the new motor home.

"In three or four years from now you can trade for another brand new motor home and take out another loan - as you're now doing - and continue paying virtually the same monthly payments," the salespersons would explain enthusiastically, "and continue your 'full-timer' RV lifestyle in a brand new motor home without additional financial concerns."

"We can afford the monthly payments, but we'd never live long enough to fully pay off such a loan!" the elderly retiree's wife would oftentimes exclaim.

The salesperson would then effect a sly expression, and wink, as he answered: "Who cares? We'll let the loan folks worry about that."

Kai watched several 'honey wagon' septic tank trucks winding their way through the maze of Rvs searching for campers who were 'boondocking'. The 'honey wagon' drivers were soliciting the Rvers to dump their 'black water' holding tanks into the septic truck's tank for a fee. There were other tank trucks patrolling the desert. Those drivers sold fresh water to the campers.

Large - four and five-hundred thousand dollar - diesel motor homes nestled amongst groupings of pick up trucks laboring to support camper backs. There were forty-plus year old silver Airstream travel trailers - those were the only make that would stay viable for that long - mingling with later model Rvs. Tents sheltered the less affluent Quartzsite affectionados. Motorcycles dotted the landscape along with two and three wheeled bicycles. Kai spotted numerous golf carts and ATVs moving about. *Looks like ants scurrying about,* he thought.

"Some sight to behold, isn't it?" the pilot called to Kai.

"It reminds me of a saying my father once said," Kai answered. He said to me: "*Human beings* are to the earth as *cancer cells* are to a human."

The pilot nodded in agrrement. "Spot an area you'd like to park your rig?"

"Not yet. Just keep on flying in wider circles."

"It's your money."

Kai concentrated on trying to spot three Rvs and a sedan clustered together: a large diesel-pusher motor home, an older model Winnebago, a pickup truck with an orange-colored camper back, and a late model sedan. After thirty minutes winging above the desert his eyes focused on such a grouping. He patted the pilot's shoulder. "Can you circle over this area a couple of times?"

The pilot brought the ultra-lite around in a tight turn and traversed the area several times. Kai watched three senior women gesturing as they spoke to two younger men. A short man stood on a footstool bending under the pickup's raised hood. An orange-colored camper perched on the truck's bed. A man stood beside a sedan - on the outer side - urinating onto the desert sand. *This has got to be the thieves of the cartel's cash,* he concluded.

"Hey, pilot," he announced, "I've seen all that I want to see right now. Please take me back to my rig."

The pilot nodded and swung the tiny aircraft in a tight turn and headed back toward the landing field. "Spot an area you'd like to park?"

"I sure did, and it looked like there's a group of campers situated in a circle around a fire pit I'd love to meet."

As soon as the ultra-lite landed Kai called Betancourt. "Fly to Tucson, Arizona and wait there until I call. I'll soon have the old gal's exact location."

ꡛꡛꡛꡛꡛꡛꡛꡛꡛꡛꡛꡛ 37 ꡛꡛꡛꡛꡛꡛꡛꡛꡛꡛꡛꡛꡛ

Nellie

Nellie turned from the gathering and strode back to her Airstream. She mused silently: *My special year - since I moved to the States, at least - I've had to adjust and adapt to the bizarre ways of the so-called winter visitors. I moved out here in the Arizona desert boonies to write my doctorial thesis on the peculiar phenomenon of American recreational vehicle full-timers. Now this: a bad man coming to my North Forty RV outdoor study laboratory to cause trouble for a bunch of crazy Texans. I think they're all cockoos.* She took a deep breath of the hot desert air and sighed loudly. *Guess I'd better get my shotgun handy. Mien Gott! I was considered a sophisticated intellect back in the Netherlands. What would my friends and family think if they saw me now?* She reached inside her Airstream, grabbed her twelve-gauge pump-action shotgun, checked for shells in its chamber, then strode with a purposeful demeanor to her stash of beer in her Airstream. *That bad dude will have me to deal with when he arrives to cause harm to my Rvers.*

₁₁₁₁₁₁₁₁₁₁₁₁₁₁₁ 38 ₁₁₁₁₁₁₁₁₁₁₁₁₁₁

Kai, Nellie, and the Group

Kai slowly eased his fifth wheel off Highway ninety-five onto the barely discernable path marked by a small roadside sign indicating 'Nellie's North Forty'. As his rig ponderously approached one enormous motor home circled with several lesser campers, a tall, shapely, determined acting female - attired in tight-fitting cut-off jeans - stepped from her ancient Airstream travel trailer cradling a twelve-guage shotgun across her bosom clutching a bottle of beer in her right hand.

Wow!, Kai thought.

"You can stop right where you are and turn off that confounded, obnoxiously loud, diesel engine so's we can talk without shouting!" Nellie called out.

Kai stopped and cut his engine. "Hey, I saw your sign back there next to the highway and figured that I'd like to park my rig for a few days in this area."

Nellie approached Kai's cab and peered up into his

eyes. "I'm Nellie," she said, "and I don't allow just *anybody* to boondock on *my* North Forty."

Kai laughed as he replied: "Oh yeah, it's my understanding that most of this area out this way is government land."

Nellie lowered her shotgun. "Well, I'll tell you what, stranger, this particular forty acres of government land is under *my* care for *this* season."

"You've convinced me? How come it's under *your* care?"

"'Cause my shotgun says so."

"I wonder what the government folks would say about that?" Kai chuckled.

"I didn't ask 'em."

"So you just arbitrarily parceled off a piece of this desert and claimed it for yourself?"

"Yep. I keep *my* forty acres clean and secure for *my* winter visitors. And for that - and the honor of enjoying my scintillating personality - I charge twenty-five dollars a week…in advance."

"Well that sounds fine to me. May I park on your North Forty for one week?"

"Depends."

"On what?"

"You telling me who you are and where you're from."

"My name's Kai Ochita and I'm from all over. I'm a 'full timer'."

"You look too young to be a full-timer."

"I'm just lucky, I guess."

"I noticed that your rig has Texas plates."

"I belong to Escapees."

"Livingston's your home base, huh?"

"Yep, once in a while."

"Are you law-abiding?"

"Most of the time."

"Better be if you intend to park your rig here. Hand me thirty dollars and park over there next to that circle of campers."

"You said twenty-five dollars."

"I'm adding five dollars for you."

"How come?"

"Your stupid ponytail."

"What about it?"

"It tends to irritate me."

#

Kai backed his fifth wheel between Jesse's and Humberto's Winnebago and the rental sedan Turk and Beto were sharing.

"Hey, man!" Humberto yelled, "This here camp circle is private!"

Kai stepped down from his truck and affected an expression of dismay. "I'm sorry, I didn't realize you folks were camping together." He looked around as he continued apologizing. "Looks so cozy and inviting the way all of you are parked around this fire pit together. I just figured it would be okay to join you, but , if…"

Prudence stepped from her motor home and called out across the circle: "Hey guys. He looks and sounds like a nice and polite young man to Louann and Marguerite and me…let him park his rig with us if he wants to!"

Humberto turned and glanced at Jesse. Jesse shrugged.

"It's okay to park with you, then?" Kai asked.

"The ladies said it would be O.K.," Humberto answered.

"Thank you, mam," Kai called to Prudence, "you're as sweet as a Ruby Red Grapefruit from the Rio Grande Valley of Texas!"

Humberto turned to Jesse and mumbled: "Another bullshitter."

Kai quickly set about unhooking and leveling his rig. Aldo, Rose, Prudence, Marguerite, Louann, Turk, Beto, Humberto, Jesse, and Nellie gathered to watch Kai go about his routine of securing his rig."

Kai smiled broadly at his audience each time he walked around his fifth wheel. When he finished setting-up, he said to his on-lookers: "I sure do appreciate you nice folks letting me join your circle out here. Your camp reminds me of the friendly western pioneer folk who circled their wagons for safety and companionship back in the old days."

"Isn't he a nice young man?" Marguerite said.

"He has a ponytail hanging down his back," Louann whispered.

"So does Richard Branson."

"Who?"

"Branson. The smiling millionaire who owns an airline and a bunch of other enterprises. He's *hot*."

Kai stretched his back and said: "Tell you what, friends, I have a freezer loaded with frozen filet mignons from Omaha Steaks in my rig. How about me treating all of you to a steak-fry later this evening?"

"I'll bring the beer!" Nellie added.

"We have napkins and silverware, and card tables!" Marguerite added.

"Aldo and I'll provide the beans!" Rose shouted.

All turned and stared at Turk and the other three fellows.

Turk looked back at Beto. Beto grinned and said: "We'll play loud music from our car's CD player."

Humberto giggled. "I'll dance!"

Jesse rubbed his belly. "I'll eat!"

Nellie brandished her shotgun above her head and exclaimed: "I'll stand watch and guard us from the bully who's coming to harm you folks!"

Kai held up his hands motioning for silence. When everyone quieted, he asked: "Hey, wait a minute. What's *that* all about, Nellie?"

"What?"

"Some bully coming to hurt these people?"

Nellie arched her back as she replied: "These good people tell me that some sort of *enforcer* from a dope syndicate is coming to do bad things to them."

Kai turned slowly as he looked at each individual. "Well, that's just *not* right. Good and decent folks - such as you guys obviously are - shouldn't be harassed by some cartel bully. Tell you what: count on me to join you good people in whatever disagreement you may have fallen into with those cartel criminals."

The group collectively cheered Kai as he high-fived each of the fellows and hugged the ladies.

#

"I found them," Kai said quietly to Eduardo Betancourt over his cell phone.

"Well, it's about time!" Betancourt quipped, "where in the hell are you?"

"I'm near Yuma, Arizona, but before I reveal my precise location to you I have to finalize a few details which will insure the return of your five-hundred thousand dollars in a safe and secure manner."

"What details?"

"There are nine people here - no, possibly ten, or eleven, maybe - who may be splitting the half-million. I need a day to work out the details of getting all of that cash together at the same time," Kai smiled to himself as he continued, "so just stay put for another twenty-four hours, Mr. Betancourt. I'll call and fill you in on my location and plan as soon as I set things up here."

"Dammit you coolie, or whatever you are, tell me right this minute where you are or…"

"Or what, Mr. Betancourt?"

"Oh shit, just do your *thing* and call me tomorrow!"

"I'll do that, but until you receive my next call I suggest that you fly to Yuma, Arizona and wait there."

"I'm flying to Tucson. Can I get a flight to Yuma?"

"There's a commercial airport there. You may have to book on a commuter plane."

Kai clicked his cell phone closed and turned to the large rear window in the back of his fifth wheel and studied the group as they busied themselves preparing for the evening's steak fry. The four fellows were gathering and pitching branches of dried-out desert brush on the fire pit and tidying up the area. They were laughing and 'horsing' around as they worked. Rose and Aldo busied themselves assisting the three women as they arranged three charcoal burners near the center of the circle of RVs beside the fire pit. Aldo and Rose were wrestling with a large sack of charcoal briskets. Nellie stood guard on the perimeter of the site, her shotgun at the ready. He smiled to himself as he slowly shook his head. *What a mishmash of colorful characters,* he mused, *they seem to be genuine folks caught up in a bad circumstance that's way over their heads. I think that I'm beginning to identify with this group of crazies.*

Kai walked to his kitchen area, opened his freezer, and extracted eleven frozen steaks and took them outside to one of the four folding-tables from the Rvs Aldo and Rose were setting up. "These will thaw in this heat in time to cook for our dinner," he said to Rose.

"Want Aldo and me to cook 'em?" Rose asked.

"Thanks, but I'll fix them," Kai said, "charcoaling steaks is one of my specialties."

"What other *specialties* do you have, Kai?" Aldo asked.

Kai cocked his head and thought for a moment. "I suppose one could say: 'arranging things'.

‖‖‖‖‖‖‖‖‖‖‖ 39 ‖‖‖‖‖‖‖‖‖‖‖‖‖

Betancourt

Eduardo Betancourt pocketed his cell phone and turned to his bodyguard. "That damned enforcer is getting to be too much of a smartass for my taste. When he hands over the money I want you to eliminate him. We can always find another enforcer who'll give me proper respect."

The bodyguard nodded. "What now, Mr. Betancourt?"

"We fly to Yuma, Arizona wait there until that Kai Ochita asshole calls us tomorrow, then we'll meet him and you can take care of the nasty clean-up after we receive the money. I do not want any of those thieves, or anyone else, to think they could get away with their short-lived escapade of stealing our money, or anything else from our cartel."

"Yuma?"

"Si."

"How many will be there?"

"Ochita said there are nine of them. Maybe eleven."

"*Nine or eleven?*"

"Yes, but don't worry about the number. Four of them are our flunky courier assholes and the others are three old women and an elderly couple." He sneered, "We can handle that bunch of losers or any other freaks they may have added to their stupid little gang of thieves."

‖‖‖‖‖‖‖‖‖‖‖ 40 ‖‖‖‖‖‖‖‖‖‖‖‖

The Group

Aldo and Kai served a filet mignon to each as the group queued before the charcoalers. Rose spooned pork and beans. Nellie passed out warm bottles of Orangeboom lager and Heineken beer. Humberto took his bottle from Nellie's hand and grimaced.

"Get accustomed to warm beer, Humberto, we're out in the boonies here. Ice is expensive," Nellie said with a huff.

"Yeah, what about the refrigerator in your trailer?"

"Propane is more expensive than ice out here, dumbkoff."

Nellie took her plate of food to the edge of the circle so that she could be the sentinel while everyone enjoyed their steak and beans.

The desert was beginning to cool slightly as the sky began to show its array of stars. There was a moderate breeze wafting through the group's camping circle as each of the campers completed their fare and began to situate themselves around Kai. Everyone of the group quietly perused Kai.

"*What?*" Kai said to the group.

"We've been speculating about you," Prudence said.

"Yes sir, Mr. Kai Ochita, we've been discussing you all afternoon," Aldo added.

Kai laughed as he asked: "And just what exactly would you folks like to know about me?"

"Well, the first thing is," Louann said, "how is it that a nice young man, such as yourself, is driving about the country in such an expensive RV set-up and not having to work for a living? The fellows figured that you inherited a lot of money. Aldo and Rose think that you're receiving some kind of government entitlement for a disability or something, and the girls and I believe that you are a movie actor between jobs."

Kai chortled: "Now just why would you ladies think that I was in the movies?"

Marguerite giggled and she stuttered forth: "Because you are so handsome and have such a marvelous physique…and have a lot of free time to squander."

"Jesus," Turk mumbled to Beto.

"Marguerite's right," Prudence interjected, "Kai is a lovely young man…and so polite and gentle…and obviously educated."

Humberto leaned forward and pantomimed placing his fingers down his throat. "I think I'm gonna puke."

"Shut up, you," Rose said to Humberto, "Kai is all those things, and more. Just look at how perfectly groomed he is," she waved her hand about, "out here in this isolated desert, yet."

"Sounds *gay* to me," Beto whispered to Turk, "he's

just too good looking. Hell, I bet he don't even have to turn his underwear inside out after the first day."

"Well, thank you, I think. But you are *all* off the mark." Kai smiled as he said in a quiet, gentle tone: "Actually, I'm that enforcer guy who was sent to take back the dope cartel's five-hundred thousand dollars you stole from them."

There was a moment of total silence as the group stared, wide-eyed, back at Kai.

"May I have another Heineken?" Marguerite said cheerfully.

Louann turned to Marguerite and punched her on her shoulder. "Didn't you hear what Kai just *said*?"

Marguerite giggled. "Kai is just playing a little joke on us, dear. How could a lovely young man, such as he, be a meanie?"

The group, in perfect unison, turned and stared at Marguerite.

Humberto began to giggle. Then laugh. Then guffaw as he rolled back onto the desert sand.

"I had a notion that Kai was to good to be true," Aldo muttered to Rose.

Moments drug by as the group stared at Kai and Kai smiled back. Finally, Rose spoke up: "Well, what's it going to be Mr. Kai Ochita? War? Or what?"

Just at that precise moment Nellie appeared from the darkness of the perimenter of the campfire behind Kai, her shotgun held to her shoulder pointing to the back of his head. "You folks want me to blow his head off, or take him prisoner?" she said in a quiet voice.

Kai slowly raised his hands above his shoulders, a smile remained across his features.

"I reckon it's time for you to wipe that smile off your face," Aldo said with a nervous voice, "'cause Nellie's got you square in the sights of her twelve-guage shotgun."

Still smiling, Kai said: "I slipped over to her Airstream and took the shells out of her shotgun while she was carrying the beer over here this afternoon. As a matter of fact, I confiscated *all* of her amunition from her truck and rig as well."

"Whop him on his head, Nellie!" Marguerite shouted.

Kai laughed as he turned to Nellie and said: "Please lower your weapon, Nellie. I have a proposition to discuss with you people that I've been considering all afternoon."

"Put the gun down, Nellie," Rose said, "and let's hear what Mr. Kai Ochita has to say." Then she turned to Humberto and shouted: "Shut up that laughing, Humberto, and straighten up! We need to hear what Kai has to say. He can't be the *only* one hunting us, you know!"

Nellie laid her gun against the nearest card table. "I had the jump on him," she muttered.

Kai stood and faced the group. "It's true that I've been an enforcer for the cartel and other nefarious individuals for a period of time," he said as his features changed to a sincere expression, and I *have* been on your trail the last few days. But I've been considering a serious life-style change lately. And recent exchanges between the cartel honcho and I, plus meeting *you* folks, has led me to make a major decision this afternoon." He nodded his head," Meeting *you* characters has been a catalyst for me to change my ways."

"What's a catalyst?" Beto whispered to Turk.

Turk glared back at Beto as he placed his finger across his lips.

"What's on your mind, young man?" Prudence asked with a nervous quiver to her voice.

Kai took a deep breath. "Well, I was studying each of you - as best I could - this afternoon, and trying to figure out how the group of you and I could work together to establish an honorable and peaceful lifestyle for each of us. I've watched all of you. Every one of you seems to be footloose, so to speak, and sort of drifting through the days virtually purposeless, except for Nellie. When I slipped into her Airstream to confiscate her shotgun shells I noticed that she's in the process of writing a doctorial thesis. You three lovely ladies, I believe, decided to steal the cartel's cash because you felt that you were existing without purpose. Bored. Restless. Playing bridge, for God's sake - not that that's a *bad* thing. And you four guys," he pointed toward Turk, Beto, Jesse, and Humberto, "you fellows aren't on-tract to any purposeful destination, except perhaps, getting your heads blown off by some low-life in the dope trade.

Kai walked over and placed his arms over Aldo's and Rose's shoulders. "And you two lovebirds: you volunteered to assist these wonderful three ladies with their, self-induced, perplexing predicament. You didn't have to. They were strangers to you. But you did. And I do *not* believe your kindness had everything to do with the money involved." He turned to Nellie. "And Nellie: writing about North American gypsies who are searching for some sort of decent existence out here in the boondocks." He looked back to the fellows. "I'll wager that not one of you guys has health insurance, or for that matter, have been paying into Social Security, or saving money for your old age." Kai shook his head as he continued: "The divided shares of that half-a-million cash you're stealing from the cartel will disappear from each of you like butterflies in the wind before you realize it, and then all of you will be in the same boat as you were when all of this ridiculous escapade began: living aimlessly."

All of the group sat silently staring into the flames of the dwindling campfire. Kai turned back and picked up a couple of weathered branches and pitched them onto the dwindling flames.

"What's on your mind, Kai?" Rose asked in a tentative tone.

"I have some ideas for all of us, but there are a few more details I need to work out tonight before I broach it to you. Let's all retire to our RVs for the rest of the evening and in the morning, when we're rested and fresh, I'll tell you what I'm contemplating and we can discuss it." He turned to face Nellie. "Oh, and Nellie," he handed her a paper bag, "here are your shotgun shells."

Each member of the group silently looked into the flames of the campfire as they reflected on Kai's comments. Aldo glanced at Rose and raised his eyebrows. Rose shrugged her shoulders back at him. Humberto's facial expression slowly transformed from a silly grin to one of pensiveness. The other three fellows shuffled the toes of their shoes in the desert's sand. The three ladies continued to stare into the firepit.

After several minutes of total silence, Louann asked: "What's so bad about playing bridge?"

#

Prudence, Louann, and Marguerite busied themselves serving freshly brewed coffee in styrofoam cups to the group as they, one-by-one, shuffled from their campers to the still-smoldering fire pit. The brilliant morning sun had begun its ascent over the desert's RV-freckled surface. Each member of the group accepted their coffee and stood about the burned out embers sipping their morning booster. No one acknowledged another, except to side-step to allow room for all to gather closely together preparing to hear Kai reveal his thoughts. The greater Quartzsite locale was virtually devoid of the sounds of its human conglomeration during this early hour giving the solemn gathering a sense of foreboding.

Kai stepped from his fifth-wheel and greeted all with a cheerful: "Good morning, potential partners!" His happy greeting was acknowledged with slight nods, except for Marguerite, who waved heartily back as she answered with a giggling: "Come fetch your hot coffee, dear!"

Kai walked briskly to the gathering and accepted his cup. "OK potential partners, let's get the ball rolling right now. We do not have the luxury of time-to-spare for executing my plans." He looked intently into the eyes of each person. "That is, of course, if you agree with me." He glanced over his shoulder: "Where's Nellie?"

"I'm up here on top of the ladies' motor home keeping watch!"

"Come on down and join us, Nellie. I think that you should be part of my proposal, too."

"Why *me*?" Nellie asked.

"Because your thesis will fit in perfectly with my plan."

Nellie shouldered her shotgun and climbed down the chromed ladder attached to the rear of the motor home.

"We're listening," Rose said.

"First thing that we have to do is neutralize our - now common - threat."

"What's that?" Aldo asked.

"A man named Eduardo Betancourt and his notoriously bad-ass bodyguard. They are currently in Phoenix waiting for my call to tell them that I'm ready for them to come and assist me in regaining the money you stole from them and punishing you for stealing it."

Turk shook his head vigorously, "You wouldn't do *that*, would you?"

"Yes," Kai nodded, "because having *them* come to *us* is the only way that we can neutralize them."

"Hey! I may be guilty of delivering money and shit for those cartel guys, but I ain't into killing folks, and I don't think any of the rest of us are, either!" Jesse said as he perused the others.

All nodded agreement.

"When I used the term 'neutralize' I wasn't referring to 'killing'.

"Then what *were* you referring to?"

"This," Kai said with a smug expression crossing his face, "The bunch of us setting them up be arrested and incarcerated by the authorities."

"Now just how in the world could *we* do *that*?" Louann said.

"Now bare with me until I finish explaining

everything. Then we can, together, work out the kinks as we spot them."

Everyone pivoted their heads back and forth looking at each other.

"OK, so let us hear your thinking," Rose said after a moment of contemplation.

"Anyone care for a second cup of coffee?" Marguerite chirped.

"For heaven's sake, Marguerite," Prudence whispered.

"*What?*" Marguerite whispered back with raised eyebrows. We are *civil*, aren't we?"

Kai continued, "The first thing that I'm proposing is this: you three ladies," he nodded toward Prudence, Marguerite, and Louann, "Take a couple of thousand dollars from the cartel's money you have stashed in your motor home, take Humbero with you and drive back to the border next to Algodones, Mexico - that's about one hundred and twenty miles from here - park in the large parking lot on the U.S. run by the Quechan Indian Tribe, unhook your Volkswagen, and the four of you drive it across the border crossing into Algodones, and spend the cash for marijuana."

"Oh…my…God!" Prudence exclaimed.

"Then bring the marijuana back here to Nellie's North Forty." Kai held his hands up for silence. "Humberto will purchase the marijuana. He'll tell you how to smuggle it back through the customs inspectors." Kai raised his eyebrows, "I honestly believe that - of our little association here - you three sweet-looking ladies are the only ones who will be able to safely smuggle the marijuana across that border point."

"Won't we need passports, or something, to get back across the border?" Louann asked.

"Sure, but don't you ladies have passports?" Kai asked.

"I do," Marguerite said, "but Prudence and Louann don't."

"Then you two will need your driver's license and birth certificates," Kai said to them.

"We have those," Prudence said.

"Now why would you two be carrying around your birth certificates?" Aldo asked.

"In the event that we venture off to the *Great Beyond* while we're 'on the road',"

Prudence answered with a wistful smile.

"Yeah, but what about that dope-sniffing dog with the Border Patrol out there on Highway Ninety-Five at that check point between Yuma and Quartzsite? I ain't never seen such a dedicated-to-his-job critter as that dog when they stopped us there a couple of days ago," Aldo quipped." He turned his head, "That dog was one serious dude!"

Kai nodded. "I've thought about that. I have several empty Omaha Steaks shipping boxes." He looked at the gals, "You ladies can take those boxes with you. When you drive the VW back to your motor home in the Quechan parking lot with the marijuana you can insert it into a couple of those boxes, slip in some moth balls, wrap the boxes with duck tape, slip the boxes into ziplock bags, and secure them in the your motor home's freezer."

"Hell," Aldo said, "*that* dog out on the highway check point will *still* sniff it out."

"Not if the ladies are wearing the same enormous

amount of perfume they usually splash on themselves," Humberto said. "That sniffer dog won't be able to smell a skunk after he pokes his head inside that motor home and gets a whiff of *that* plus the mothballs."

"But first, how will we girls manage to smuggle the marijuana through the custom check point at the Algodones border crossing?" Prudence asked Kai.

Kai turned to Jesse and raised his eyebrows with a questioning expression.

Jesse grinned and glanced at Humberto, then back to Prudence. "Well, *one* sure way to do that - especially for three old sweet and innocent looking ladies like you and Marguerite and Louann riding in a Volkswagen bug, for cryin' out loud - is this: now pay attention, ladies, 'cause this will take some serious acting on your part, not to mention the disgusting things you'll be doing."

Marguerite giggled and said: "Oh, this is getting exciting!"

"*What* 'disgusting things?" Prudence asked.

Humberto's facial expression became focused; serious. "We'll, I'll take a crap into a ziplock bag and put that bag in the back seat of the Volkswagen. The four of us will take it across the border in the VW. I know how to locate and buy the marijuana. After I buy the marijuana, I'll give it to you three gals. You'll will drive it back to the border crossing. I'll walk back across to the Quechan parking lot and meet you at the motor home. When the custom agent pokes his head into the VW to question you…and you've shown him your passport and all…one of you - I suggest Marguerite - will be in the back seat pretending to be sick with 'Montezuma's Revenge' - you know - *serious* doo-doo. At that exact moment Marguerite will open the ziplock bag back there to let out the smell of my 'business'."

Humberto guffawed as he watched the facial contortions of the gathering.

"That's…just…gross!" Nellie exclaimed.

"Exactly what the Border Patrol dudes will think," Jesse replied with a grin.   "And Marguerite, can you make a loud farting sound with your mouth?" Humberto asked.

"I do not know, Humberto, I've never attempted such a disgusting thing."

"Oh, heck. Well then, I can teach you how to do that." He grinned, "I do it all the time."

"I wouldn't doubt that for one second," Prudence snorted.

"And I'll guarantee you folks that the border guard will not - I repeat, *not* - be interested in further inspection of you ladies or, especially, the interior of *that* Volkswagen." Humberto chuckled as he continued, "And all the while that's going on Prudence and Louann will be pretending to become hysterical. You know, crying and whimpering and all, just to add to the bad-ass scene."

"Are you certain that will work?" Rose asked.

"Worked for my momma and my aunt and my grandma back at Nuevo Progreso a couple of times," Jesse said, "when they smuggled across a couple of my cousins under serapes in the back seat of their car."

Humberto began to giggle. "I know that you three gals can do *your* part in convincing those Border Patrol Inspectors to back away from your Volkswagen."

"OK," Rose pointedly asked Kai, "then what do we

do with the marijuana once the gals and Humberto get back here to Nellie's with it?"

Kai grinned. "Here is the devilish part," he said with a chuckle. "We take the stash of marijuana from the ladies' motor home's freezer. Then we have Rose and Aldo drive their camper - leading the three ladies in their motor home with the balance of the cash - north on Highway Ninety-five to Parker, Arizona. That's about fifty miles from here."

"Hey!" Jesse exclaimed, "what about those of us left behind here at Nellie's?"

Kai lowered his chin and focused on the group's eyes. "Just allow me to finish explaining the details. Now here's where our little *sting* will become critical: as soon as the gals and Rose and Aldo leave Nellie's for Parker, I'm going to call Betancourt and his thug and tell them that I'm here in Quartzsite at Nellie's North Forty. I'll tell them to rent a car and how to find Nellie's. I'll suggest that they get here quickly because the folks who stole their money are planning to drive north with it soon."

Nellie asked: "So how's that going to figure in our scheme?"

"Yeah," Turk added, "and what about me and Beto and the rest of us?"

"We'll wait for Betancourt here at Nellie's. Jesse and Humberto will hide here and stay out of sight while Turk and Beto and Nellie I convince Betancourt and his bodyguard that the three old ladies, Rose and Aldo, and Humberto and Jesse who have the money and are escaping with it."

"Whoa, there!" Humberto interjected, Then they'll come looking for the gals and me and Jesse."

"Of course they will," Kai chuckled, "but Turk and Beto and Nellie and I are going to set up Betancourt and his buddy for a big-ass rude awakening when they drive toward Parker looking for you guys."

"Oh, what fun and games!" Marguerite shouted.

Louann fluttered her hands. "Go on, go on," she repeated excitedly.

Prudence leaned forward with a gleam in her eyes as she licked her lips.

Aldo turned to Rose, raised his eyebrows, and whispered: "See that? I always told you that the American Indian men turned their prisoners over to their *women* to do the torturing."

Rose grinned. "And don't you ever forget that, hon."

||||||||||||||||||| 41 |||||||||||||||||||||

Rose, Aldo, Marguerite, Louann, Prudence

Rose was driving. "Are the gals still following us? She asked Aldo.

Aldo leaned forward and squinted into his rearview mirror. "Yep, they're still back there." He continued to stare outward toward the desert mountains in the distance. "You know, Rose, we've been driving for about eleven hundred miles since we left Kerrville, and except for El Paso and Tucson and a smattering of little towns, we haven't had any traffic to speak of. Those pioneer folks who wagon-trained out this way must have wondered what in the hell they got themselves into a few days after they shouted: 'Westward ho!'"

"Yeah, hon, and I'm wondering the same dang thing right this moment. What're *we* planning to do when we get to Parker, for heaven's sake?"

Aldo cleared his throat. "Well, I've been considering that. Kai told us to figure somewhere to park for a few days - when we get there - until he and the others do their 'thing' and then they'll catch up with us. I saw a pamphlet back there at Quartzsite, you know, one of those advertising flyers. It said that there's an RV resort across the Colorado River from Parker that'll give Rvers a free three-day stay. It's called: Colorado River Park. CRP for short. There was an asterisk under the free offer, though."

"Ain't nothing for free, Aldo. What's their catch?"

"Well, it seems that in order to have a *free* visit you have to attend a sales pitch in their sales office."

Rose drove silently for a few moments. "That doesn't seem so bad. You don't *have* to buy, do you?"

"I guess not. What can they do if you *don't* buy into their RV resort?" Aldo laughed.

"OK, let's lead the three ladies to CRP and wait there for three days until Kai and the boys us."

"Sounds good to me. I'll call the gals and tell them the plan."

#

Prudence steered the huge motor home north on Highway Ninety-five behind Rose and Aldo as she bantered excitedly with Louann and Marguerite. "Did you two notice the sparkle in Nellie's eyes when we invited her to join up with us at Parker?"

"Oh, yes," Marguerite chirped, "Nellie was especially invigorated when Kai explained to her that she would share in our stolen half a million dollars."

"Money talks," Louann quipped.

"I don't think Nellie's eyes brightened because of the money."

"You are right. I, too, have noticed the way Nellie and Kai look at one another."

Prudence's cell phone chimed. She opened it and listened for a few seconds, then said: "Sounds good to me," and snapped it closed.

"What?" Louann asked.

"It was Aldo. He said that we're going to an RV park across the river from Parker. We can stay there free for three nights if we agree to sit in on a sales pitch."

"There's a river out here in this dried-up desert?" Marguerite asked.

"That's what Aldo said. He told me that it used to flow all the way from the Rocky Mountains in Colorado to the Mexican border in Arizona where it peters out."

"Peters out? Why?"

"Aldo said that the Californians use up all of the water in the river."

"Oh."

"Look," Louann said as she pointed from her seat, "what's that?"

Prudence peered ahead. "I think that it's some poor souls camping out in the boonies. Look, there are some others."

"Imagine that," Louann said, "how do they stand this heat?"

"They have gasoline generators that run their appliances and air conditioners,"

"Oh, this is all *sooo* exciting!" Marguerite exclaimed.

"Just think," Louann said, "a few days ago we three girls were bickering about bridge and lunch at the retirement home, taking naps, watching Regis and Kelly and Days of Our Lives…and just look at us *now*."

"Yes," Prudence answered, "running away from a dope cartel boss from whom we stole five hundred thousand dollars. Consorting with dope dealers. Racing across a desert in a fancy motor home. And meeting all sorts of strange people…"

"…and drinking beer and eating filet mignon out in the middle of Quartzsite, Arizona," Marguerite interrupted with a giggle.

"And what about that Kai person," Louann added, "he's a *dude*."

"Did you notice how Nellie looks at Kai?" Marguerite squealed. "I think she's hot for his bod!"

"Who isn't?" Louann said with a throaty rasp as she rolled her eyes. I'd like to braid his pony tail."

There was a pause in the conversation.

"We're not the same ladies that we were last week, are we?" Prudence said.

The three were silent for several minutes as they perused the desert scenery flowing past the motor home. Each contemplated their sudden change of lifestyle.

"You know, this desert has a calming sort of feeling about it, Louann said."

"Yes it does," Prudence answered, "if one disregards the fact that we're running from a illegal narcotics cartel boss."

Louann and Marguerite nodded in the affirmative.

‖‖‖‖‖‖‖‖‖‖‖‖‖‖ 42 ‖‖‖‖‖‖‖‖‖‖‖‖‖‖‖

Kai, Nellie, Turk, Beto, Jesse, Humberto

Kai stood next to the smoldering fire pit sizing up Nellie, Turk, Beto, Humberto, and Jesse. They waited quietly for him to speak. Finally, Nellie asked: "So?"

Turk said: "Yeah, Kai, this plan of yours better be good or all of our gooses are cooked *real* good."

Beto, Jesse and Humberto nodded.

Kai smiled. "I think you guys will like my scheme." He laughed, "And I truly believe that you'll get a real boot out of executing it."

"OK, so enlighten us further," Nellie said.

Kai squatted to the desert floor, picked up a dried cactus leaf, and began sketching in the sand. "Here we are now at Nellie's North Forty. And this down here is Yuma. And this up here is Parker." He looked up into the faces of his audience. "Now this X here is the beginning of the Indian Tribal Nations next to Parker. Are you with me so far?"

"The Indians have a nation?" Humberto asked.

Three nods. A puzzled expression from Humberto. "I'll explain it to Humberto later," Jesse said to Humberto.

"What I'm going to do is phone Betancourt and his goon - who'll be waiting my call at the Yuma airport - and tell them to rent a car and drive up here," he touched the X indicating Nellie's North Forty. Rose and Aldo and the ladies will be up *here* somewhere waiting for us." He touched the X in the sand indicating Parker.

"Yeah, but what if those three gals and old Rose and Aldo keep on going and don't wait for us" Jesse asked, "they have all the money with them, remember?"

"Come on, Jesse, don't you trust those ladies?" Kai answered with raised eyebrows, "Remember, all three of them are prudishians."

"What country is *that*?" Beto answered, "I ain't never heard of it."

"It's not a country, "Kai said, "it's a condition."

"Condition? You mean like a sickness?"

Kai laughed as he answered: "Well, some folks I know would call it a sickness. But no, it's being prudish. You know, like those people you meet who are always serious, don't joke around, or do not understand innuendo, and are forever politically correct."

"What the heck is *innuendo?"*

"Satiric wit."

"What?"

"Forget it," Beto, "I was just trying to say that those ladies have spent a lifetime of innocence. They're basically honest and pure of heart."

"Yeah, well they stole half a million bucks from *us*," Jesse said with a sneer, "that don't sound *innocent* and *honest* and *pure of heart* to *me*."

"Well, Jesse," Kai answered, "I understand your point. But I believe one's ideological principles hold true - as far as honesty among acquaintances is concerned - whenever a strong bond of friendship has been established." He smiled, "And I sincerely believe that, strangely, *our* odd little consortium of eleven misfits are in the process of establishing that bond of true friendship and trust."

"What's all that mean?" Humberto asked.

"It means that we're becoming a bizarre gang of thieves who're beginning to like each other," Nellie answered with a serious expression crossing her features, "and that we should start trusting each other."

Several moments of silence. Then Kai continued. "OK, the ladies, and Rose and Aldo, will be in Parker waiting for us to phone them while the rest of us are distracting Betancourt and his man - after they arrive here - by telling him that the old folks are driving their motor home with the cartel's money to the Parker Strip Riverside Casino to gamble with it," he pointed to Jesse and Humberto, "you two will sneak into Betancourt's rental car and hide the marijuana Humberto bought in Algodones - along with Nellie's sawed-off shotgun - underneath their back seat."

"Are you nuts?" Jesse said. "How're Humberto and I going to stash those things in their rental car without them knowing it?"

"Turk, Beto, and Nellie and I will keep them occupied and away from their car."

"Now just how're you gonna do that?"

"Trust me," Kai said in a deadly serious tone, "I guarantee you that Betancout's and his companion's full interests will be directed elsewhere from their rental car while Humberto and Jesse are hiding those two items inside."

"I, for one, believe," Nellie said. She thrust a 'thumbs up' gesture toward Kai as she affected a giant smile.

"How're those two gonna do that?" Turk asked.

"First, they're going to park their Winnebago across Nellie's drive from the highway which will prevent Betancourt from driving up to where we are. Next they're going to saw off her shotgun's barrel. Then they're going to hide inside the 'Winnie'. When Betancourt drives in he'll have to park behind the 'Winnie' and walk up here to where we are. That's when Humberto and Jesse will place the shotgun and marijuana under the back seat of Betancourt's automobile while I tell Betancourt and his goon some cock-and-bull story about the three old gals and the two old-timers driving off to a casino to gamble with the five-hundred thousand bucks. Betancourt and his cohart will race off toward Parker to intercept the ladies. The six of us will tail along behind them." He nodded toward Jesse and Humberto. "You two will follow - well behind - in the Winnebago. Turk and Beto will follow in their rental car and Nellie and I will bring up the rear in my truck and fifth-wheel."

"Then what?" Turk repeated.

"This is the good part," Kai said. "I'm going to have Nellie get on my cell phone - as all of us follow Betancourt north - and call the Indian Nation Tribal Council Police Department - it's this side of Parker at Poston, Arizona - and report what she thinks is a crime. I'll have her tell them that she witnessed two men drive off from Quartzsite on Highway Ninety-Five with a sawed-off twelve-gauge shotgun and a suspicious package she witnessed them hiding under the back seat of their car as she was buying gas in a filling station. Nellie will give the officers the car's description and license plate number. She'll tell them that she saw the two men drive off a few minutes before her call. Then I'll have Nellie call the Parker Police Department and tell them the same story."

"*My* shotgun? Sawed *off?*" Nellie exclaimed.

"We'll buy you a new one, Nellie," Kai said with a chuckle. "We need to saw off eighteen inches of the barrel of your shotgun so Jesse and Humberto can easily secret it under the car's rear seat. Law enforcement agencies tend to get really excited when they find a sawed-off twelve-gauge shotgun hidden beneath a seat next to a suspicious package inside a vehicle."

Silence. Then: "Me and Jesse are sure happy we're on *your* side, Kai," Humberto mumbled as he slowly shook his head.

||||||||||||||| 43 ||||||||||||||||

Aldo, Rose Prudence, Luann, Marguerite

Rose slowed the camper to a crawl as Aldo searched the atlas for the bridge crossing the Colorado River at Parker.

"Just drive straight on through Parker. The bridge is up ahead," he mumbled to Rose."

"The ladies are right behind us," Rose said.

"Look there at that sign. It says this little ol' town is a hundred years old."

"Looks like it, too," Rose said.

"I kinda like this place, though," Aldo said, "it's wide open and friendly looking."

"I don't know, Aldo, I've noticed some strange-looking folks walking along beside the road."

"Hey, pumpkin, have you looked at you and me in the mirror lately?"

Rose offered Aldo her third finger. "There's the bridge. It sure does look narrow," she said, "hope it doesn't freak out Prudence back there following us."

Aldo chuckled as he answered: "I don't think so. Those three old gals have been beginning to be real street smart the last few days."

Aldo studied the map. "This road dead-ends on the California side of the bridge. Then we have to turn right on the road that goes to Parker Dam."

The two vehicles turned and slowly negotiated the narrow river road. Hard-packed sand and dirt hills hugged both sides of the stretch intermittently offering the five seniors colorful vistas of the Colorado River on their right side and the rugged Whipple Mountains in the distance to their left. The contrast of the silvery-blue waters of the river and the rugged desert shouldering it was mesmerizing. The two RVs were snaking along beside the Parker Strip; a river-lake formed by two dams sixteen miles apart. They passed multi-million dollar estates - entwined with lesser 'week-ender' abodes - and several mobile home parks. Many had boat docks on the chrystal clear water.

The origin of the Colorado River lies thousands of feet of elevation in the Rocky Mountains of Colorado. Melted snow, lesser rivers, and streams feed its drop from the high country thus adding to the pureness of the water as it drifts through Lake Powell, pummels its way through the spectacular Grand Canyon to Lake Mead, then winds south to Lake Havasu before dropping into the Parker Strip. From Parker it flows south to the Mexican border.

Residents and vacationers enjoy the Parker Strip river-lake year around. During the intense heat of the summer months Californians and Arizonians - mostly - play long and hard on the Parker Strip. They bring boats of all shapes and power to pull one another up and down the Strip on water skis as well as a myriad of other floating devices. And party joyfully when the sun sets

The mild winter season attracts retired 'winter visitors' from the northwest: Canadians, North and South Dakotans, Montanans, Idahoans, Oregonians, and others who endeavor to escape the damp and chill of their winters. These 'visitors' are more sedate than the younger westerners. Bocce Ball, standing and gossiping in the heated swimming pools, pitching washers, napping, and retiring early in the evening, are their 'sports'. And, of course, the several Colorado River Indian Tribe gambling casinos are of year-round interest for both classes of the self-called 'Colorado River Rats'.

Rose slowly approached the entrance to the Colorado River Park recreational vehicle resort. An enormous sign welcomed all visitors for a three-day stay. There was a tiny asterisk after the offer. It indicated below, in small print, that a visit to the sales office would be required.

"Well, we're going for their deal. I'm getting weary from all the stress and travel of the last few days, not to mention how worn out our three old ladies must be."

#

Prudence followed Rose and Aldo into the RV park. They completed the checking-in procedure and drove slowly through the park to their assigned parking area. The resort had numerous vacant RV spaces because the summer season was ending and the winter visitors had not begun their southward trek. After parking and hooking into the electrical and water connections and attaching their sewer hoses, the five fugitives reconnoitered in Prudence's motor home where the two air conditioners could keep them comfortable.

"Well, here we are. What's our next adventure?" Marguerite asked the assembly.

"We park ourselves here until Kai calls us and explains our next move," Aldo said with a shrug.

Just then, there was a tap, tap, tap, on the motor home's door. All five simultaneously executed a nervous jerk. Aldo struggled from the couch and peered out of the window. "Oh, thank heavens. It's just a little determined looking woman who drove up in a golf cart. I reckon she's come to tell us when we have to go to the sales office and listen to their propaganda."

"Tell her to go away," Louann quipped.

"Can't," Rose said. "We agreed to listen to their sales proposition when we checked in."

"Come on, Marguerite, you and I will go to the sales office and listen to their offers and then come on back and take a nap. It shouldn't take more than a few minutes," Rose said.

"OK. Tell her we're on our way," Marguerite quipped.

#

Aldo, Louann, and Prudence settled back on the couch and the plush swivel chair to wait for Rose and Marguerite to return from the CRP sales office.

"I suspect that Marguerite and Rose will be in that sales office for a good long while," Aldo said.

"I'll fix us hot tea while we wait," Prudence said.

"I'll settle for a beer," Aldo said.

The three waited in silence while the water was heating. Aldo yawned as he scratched his chest. Louann busied herself cleaning her bifocals. Prudence handed Aldo a bottle of beer, then stared at the tea kettle. Suddenly there was knocking on the motor home's door.

"What the devil?" Aldo said.

"Who is it," Louann asked.

Prudence peered outside the motor home. "It's Rose and Marguerite," Prudence said. She opened the door and looked down at the two. "What on earth happened? Why are you back so soon?"

Rose stomped up the steps into the motor home. Marguerite followed.

"Well?" Prudence asked.

Rose shook her head as she exhibited a disgusted expression across her features. "Ask Marguerite."

The four turned to Marguerite. She shrugged her shoulders as she said: "That feisty sales woman asked us to come in and sit in a cigarette-smoke-filled room. I told her that we didn't intend to sit down in that smelly little office until she, first off, told us how long this meeting would take and how much would it cost to join." Marguerite smirked. "Well, she proceeded to tell us that the sales conference would take at least two hours and the membership costs are, at the minimum, ten thousand dollars plus a yearly fee. Well, I looked right back at her and said: Out *here*? That's ridiculous!"

"What was her reply?" Prudence asked.

Rose took a deep breath and said: "She told us to leave immediately. That we couldn't even park overnight."

Aldo guffawed as he asked: "What was your reply to that?"

Marguerite backed her shoulders and stood tall. "I told her to *kiss my ass*!"

Prudence and Louann turned to Rose, both wide-eyed. Prudence exclaimed: "Marguerite! What has gotten into you speaking language like that?"

There was a silent pause. Aldo began laughing.

"I've been liberated from my sheltered past!" Marguerite proclaimed.

"Louann thrust forward her fist with a 'thumbs up' gesture.

"Holy moley," Rose said.

"Well, I guess that we should begin unhooking everthing and hitch-up again to go find another place to camp," Aldo said with a weary sigh after a few moments of silence.

"I'll tell you what, ladies," Rose said nodding her head, "wherever we end up camping the next couple of days it's gotta have electrical hook-ups on account of the heat out here in this desert at this time of the year. Aldo and I darn near had heat stroke the last several days. We don't have a generator *or* an air conditioning unit in our camper."

"This motor home has a generator and *two* air conditioners," Prudence said. She shrugged. "It's big enough for all five of us to wait in - and sleep in, as well - wherever we end up while we wait for Kai's call."

‖‖‖‖‖‖‖‖‖‖‖‖‖ 44 ‖‖‖‖‖‖‖‖‖‖‖‖‖

Betancourt, Bodyguard, Kai, Turk, Beto, Humberto, Jesse

Betancourt and his body guard turned their rental car carefully off Highway Ninety onto the tracks next to Nellie's little North Forty sign.

"Mi Dios," the bodyguard mumbled as his eyes scanned the area. "These gente must be disparatado staying out here."

"They're crazy, alright. First for believing that they could steal our cartel's money, and second, thinking that they could keep it," Betancourt growled.

The bodyguard pointed forward. "Aqui! Ahead is the ugly silver trailer and the big truck and fifth-wheel trailer Ochita told you to look for."

"There's an old-looking motor home parked across our path. It looks as if someone got it stuck in the sand on this stupid one-lane road leading to that Nellie's North

Forty," Betancourt answered. "Stay alert," he snarled, "I don't trust that Kai Ochita."

The bodyguard tilted his head as he spoke: "Look on the other side of the old motor home, Mr. Betancourt. There are *three* hombres and a hot-looking gal watching us."

"Now listen to me," Betancourt said, "I'm paying you a lot of money to protect me and enforce the cartel's orders, so get ready to earn your pay."

"I can handle three hombres and a woman, but one of those hombres is Kai Ochita. I can see his pony-tail I've heard others tell about."

"Yeah, well I've heard some bad things about *you*, so get ready to do your thing."

#

Kai, Nellie, Turk, and Beto stood next to Nellie's old Airstream travel trailer and watched

Betancourt drive slowly toward them. Betancourt stopped next to the stranded motor home. Kai motioned in a gesture to convey to Betancourt that he acknowledged him and to exit the automobile and walk around the stranded Winnebago. Turk and Beto stood rigidly beside Kai, their expressions frozen into masks of concern.

"Mr. Betancourt, I presume," Kai called forth as Betancourt and the bodyguard walked cautiously toward them.

"So you're the Kai Ochita I've been speaking to over my cell phone so often these last few days," Betancourt said as he nodded slightly.

Kai turned and motioned to his companions. "This

lady is Nellie. These two fellows are your former curriers, Turk and Beto. We've been tracking down the three women and two old-timers who stole your money from your other two curriers, Jesse and Humberto."

"And where are Jesse and Humberto?" Betancourt asked.

"They sneaked away from us early this morning. We have no idea where they are."

"I see," Betancourt said with a nod, "and just where are the syndicate's five-hundred thousand dollars and the five old-timers who took it?"

"They drove out of here about thirty minutes ago heading for an Indian gambling casino near to Parker, Arizona. It's about fifty miles north of us on the highway you just turned off of." The bodyguard stepped casually from Betancourt's side and began a slow walk to the rear of Kai and his cohorts. Kai's eyes followed the man's progress as he strolled. Kai continued speaking. "I didn't stop the old-timers from driving off because a couple of Park Rangers were here checking up on Nellie's camping arrangements," he waved his hand toward the smoldering campfire circle, "and I didn't want to cause a scene while the old gals were driving away."

"So, that is why you decided *not* to detain them?" Betancourt quipped.

"Well, Mr. Betancourt," Kai continued to prevaricate with raised eyebrows, "the Rangers stayed here a few minutes chatting with Nellie. I had already called you to come to this location," Kai shrugged, "so I just thought that it would be prudent to let the old-timers drive off and for us to wait here until you arrived. We knew where they were headed, so I just let them go." Kai shrugged.

"I figured that, together, we could follow the old folks to the Indian casino and nail them there in the casino's parking lot."

Betancourt twisted his head back to his bodyguard and said: "Back off. We'll settle this matter later. Let's get back to our car and drive to that casino."

The bodyguard turned and began walking toward their car. He had failed to notice that Kai's feet were planted solidly in the sand and that Kai was secreting his small twenty-two caliber hand-gun next to his hip.

#

Jesse and Humberto had slipped from their Winnebago immediately after Betancourt and his companion walked past toward Kai, Nellie, Turk and Beto. Humberto carried Nellie's shotgun across his chest as he sneaked toward Betancourt's automobile. He and Jesse had completed sawing off most of the gun's barrel moments before Betancourt's arrival. Jesse followed toting the package of marijuana Humberto had purchased earlier in Algodones. As an added incentive - for whichever police authority would first approach Betancourt and his partner as they drove into Parker because of Nellie's cell phone tips - Kai had instructed Jesse to include one thousand dollars cash, from the monies the gals had stolen, next to the package of pot.

The two quickly opened a rear door of Betancourt's rental car and secreted the three items underneath its back seat, snickered quietly, and scurried back into their Winnebago.

ⅢⅢⅢⅢⅢⅢⅢⅢⅢ 45 ⅢⅢⅢⅢⅢⅢⅢⅢⅢⅢ

Aldo, Rose, Prudence, Louann, Marguerite

"Prudence, you and the girls follow Aldo and me. We'll drive out of this dumb RV resort and find another place near Parker to settle for a couple of days," Rose said as she and Aldo climbed from the motor home and walked toward their camper.

"OK, you two," Prudence said to Louann and Marguerite, "now is just as good a time as any to teach you how to undo the sewer hose, water hose, and electrical cord."

The three ladies stepped from the interior of the motor home and walked around the rear to the 'hook-up' side.

"Marguerite. You pull the electric cord from that meter box and feed it into it's cabinet. Louann, you stoop down there," she pointed to the motor home's sewer connectors, "and pull that little handle to the right of the sewer hose. Then, after you hear the tank drain out, undo the sewer hose connection. First put on those rubber gloves on the ground next to the sewer hose." Prudence turned and walked several steps toward the water faucet attachment then turned suddenly back to Louann as Louann squatted next to the motor sewer connection. "Don't undo the hose first, Louann!" Prudence hollered. Prudence was a split second too late with her warning. Louann had dutifully slipped the rubber gloves on her hands and wrenched the sewer hose from the motor home and jerked open the little handle. Sewage - or 'black water' RVers refer to it - spewed forth from the motor home's septic tank. Louann lept backward with a well-executed tarantella dance step as she shouted: "*Phew! Phew! Phew!*"

Black water - which had been accumulating in the septic tank from the moment the girls had parked it at Nellie's North Forty three days previously - continued to splatter onto the desert floor. Aldo and Rose turned from the door of their camper and stared, wide-eyed, at the senario taking place beside the motor home. The sales lady from the RV resort grasped the left side of her chest as she watched the scene from the sales office window. Marguerite bounded with giant back-steps away from the RV site with an expression of disgust emanating from her eyes. Three elderly men standing across the road wearing white shorts, black socks, and black dress shoes - who had been discussing the merits of warming-up their diesel engines for at least forty-five minutes prior to placing their transmissions in gear - gasped with outrage.

"Hey, you! You're not allowed to dump on the ground!" one of the old men shouted.

Prudence turned toward him and shouted back: "Shut the hell up, you old northerner!"

Aldo turned to Rose and said: "The RV park workers are running over there to the gals' motor home and pitching a fit. Let's get inside our camper and pretend that we didn't see or hear anything."

#

Rose turned the camper onto the road heading back toward Parker. "Maybe we should drive back over to the Arizona side of the river and park in the casino's parking lot."

"Sounds good to me," Aldo said. He glanced into his rear-view mirror. "The gals are about a hundred yards behind us. Three old men are still shuffling behind the girls' motor home shaking their fists and shouting."

Rose shook her head. "You know, Aldo, I figured that you and I had experienced some unusual things when we bummed around with the Hill Country Heller Biker Club all those years, but this bunch we're linked to now takes the cake."

"Look across the river," Aldo said, "there's the Indian casino."

"We'll drive over there. This pamphlet indicates that they have a public RV park next door."

#

After locating the RV park next to the casino and completing the process of checking in and parking the motor home and camper side-by-side, Aldo and Rose knocked and entered the ladies' motor home. Prudence, Louann, and Marguerite were sprawled about on the couch and lounge chairs.

"OK, girls," Rose announced, "make room for Aldo and me." She fanned her face, "It's getting too dad-gummed hot for us to sit in our camper."

"Prudence has both air conditioners turned on full blast," Marguerite said, "so make yourselves comfortable."

"We're going to have to sleep in here, too," Rose said, "'cause it sure doesn't cool down around these parts at nighttime."

Rose and Aldo turned the motor home's two large front seats around facing toward the interior of the coach. "We can adjust these seats and sleep here," Aldo said.

The five fugitives relaxed and dozed off. They were exhausted. Their mission had now been relegated to waiting for Kai's cell-phone call.

|||||||||||||||| 46 ||||||||||||||||

Betancourt, Bodyguard

Betancourt instructed his companion to drive. He closed his eyes and contemplated his situation as they sped toward Parker on Highway Ninety-Five. For more than two decades Betancourt had lived a life of privilege and wealth in his villa near Mexico city. This 'good life' had been guaranteed for him and his family - as well as his fellow drug collaborators - due to the Americans' insatiable appetite for marijuana and cocaine. He and his associates had worked diligently to build up an illicit drug distribution cartel that was the envy of every legitimate international marketing system. But now their labors were beginning to unravel. The authorities from north and south of the border were not the problem. The fabric of his cartel was tearing apart from competition from another budding syndicate from the northern Mexico border states. And now this: even old ladies were stealing his cartel's profits. *What in the hell is happening to the natural order of things?* he mused.

"What are we going to do when we catch up with the old women?" Betancourt's bodyguard asked.

"Retreive our money."

"Then what?"

"*You* are going to make an example out of them."

"Such as?"

"That is *your* expertise. I don't want to know about the things you do."

During the past two years Betancourt's organization had been in a viscious killing war with their rival cartel as well as the Mexican Federales. Much of the Mexican-United States border was becoming a battle zone. Lawlessness was rampant. Kidnappings. Murder. Rape. And the United States government - curiously - was reacting to all of this by building a fence along the border. Then, out of nowhere, three old women had joined his 'enemies'. Betancourt's implausible reaction to elderly ladies stealing an infitesonal bit of the syndicate's money was a puzzlement to his bodyguard. *Why waste time and energy on such an insignificant thing?* the bodyguard was pondering as they sped toward Parker. He decided that recent problems were causing his boss to lose his perspective. But such questions were not his to ask, so he ceased his speculations and concentrated on the road to Parker.

#

The Colorado River Indian Tribes Chief of Police leaned back in his chair as his dispatcher relayed the jist of his just-completed telephone conversation.

"Say again," he said to his officer.

"Sir, I just finished a call from a woman who reported that she witnessed two Hispanic - or Indian - looking men hiding a sawed-off shotgun, a suspicious package, and a large amount of cash under the back seat of their car."

"Where?"

"In a gas station at Quartzsite. She stated that the two men gassed-up and headed north on ninety-five toward Parker."

"Did she say how long ago?"

"A couple of minutes."

"Did she give you a description of their car?"

"Yes sir. The model, year, color, and license plate number."

"The informant described the two men as Indian?"

"She said that she thought the two men were Hispanic or Indian."

"If they're driving the legal speed limit they should arrive at the ninety-five/seventy-two intersection in about twenty-five minutes. We'll try to intercept them at that location. I'll give the Parker PD a call in case we don't get there in time or miss them. You get on the radio. Contact Officer Thomas and give him the info. I'll call Billy and tell him to meet Thomas and us at the intersection with his dope-sniffing dog for back-up."

#

Kai followed a mile behind Betancourt's car in his truck and fifth wheel. Nellie sat forward in the passenger seat and peered intently ahead in an effort to keep Betancourt and his companion in her sight. Jesse and Humberto tagged along in their Winnebago about a quarter of a mile behind. Turk and Beto trailed in their rental car at the rear of the caravan.

"Think the Indian Tribal Police will respond to our cell phone 'tip' in time to stop Betancourt's car before they get to Parker?" Nellie said to Kai.

"I did some checking around Quartzsite before we left. From what I've heard about those tribal policemen, they take extreme measures to make sure that their tribal citizens toe-the-mark in regard to obeying the laws. If they suspect that one of their Mohaves, Hopis, Navajos, or Chemehuevis is inside that automobile hauling an illegal gun and marijuana, they'll snatch them up and haul their butts straight to their own Colorado River Indian Tribal Court. The word is that the CRIT Police and their Tribal Court deal with their arrestees a whole lot more swiftly and directly than other police departments."

"But Betancourt isn't one of them."

"Well," Kai chuckled, "Betancourt is Hispanic and his bodyguard *looks* like an Indian. That'll be enough to motivate the CRIT officers when they stop Betancourt's car. They'll find your sawed-off shotgun next to the marijuana and cash and, then, it won't make a bit of difference whether or not Betancourt and his man are Indian or not."

"What's our plan when we see the officers stop Betancourt?"

"We'll pull over to the shoulder of the road and watch from a distance to make certain Betancourt and his buddy are arrested. Then we'll call Aldo and Rose to find out where they and the three ladies are waiting for us."

Nellie narrowed her eyes and stared intently at Kai's profile. "Then what?"

Kai glanced at Nellie: "Have you ever thought about *really* being in business, Nellie? You know, such as being part owner of a *genuinely legitimate* first class RV resort with all the trimmings?"

Nellie turned and studied the passing desert scenery. She spotted a lonely 'boondooker's' motor home perched atop a cacti-laden hillock. Then, in her mind's eye, she visualized an oasis in the same location. Palm trees, standing tall, casting shadows across an enormous imaginary adobe-shingled clubhouse. A large swimming pool - sporting a cascading waterfall - shouldering the clubhouse. RV's, of all kinds, parked beneath shaded - brightly colored - canopies encircling a gigantic pavilion featuring multiple peaked tops with pendants flagging from tall poles. Smiling and laughing Rvers were playing bocce ball and lounging in the swimming pool. Several men, holding coffee cups, stood next to their idling diesel-engine vehicles.

"Yes," she replied, but I'm writing my thesis now, and…"

"It would be a business that would allow you to continue your writing."

Nellie smiled at Kai. "Yes, I'd love that."

"Me, too," Kai murmured.

|||||||||||||||||||| 47 ||||||||||||||||||||

Colorado River Indian Tribal Police

The CRIT Police Chief clicked the 'on' button of his hand-held patrol car's police radio and said: "Officer Thomas, have you spotted the suspects' automobile?"

"Yes sir," came an instant reply. The target vehicle is headed north toward us here at the ninety-five/seventy-two intersection. There are two adult males in the front seat. They're slowing to a stop."

"Hit all of your lights and use your outside speaker and order them to pull off the road and stop. Keep them there until Thomas arrives for back-up and Billy shows up with his narcotics dog. I should be there in a minute or two."

"Yes, sir."

#

"Look, Kai. There's a patrol car flashing for Betancourt's car to stop!" Nellie exclaimed as she pointed ahead.

Kai grinned. "Right on the button. Now all we have to

do is pull over to the shoulder of the road and watch Betancourt and his man get arrested and hauled off to the Colorado River Indian Tribal Court."

Kai pulled his rig off to the side of Highway Ninety-five and waited. Behind him the Winnebago and the rental car followed and stopped. Turk, Beto, Jesse, and Humberto exited their vehicles and trotted forward to Kai's rig. Huge grins dominated their expressions as they stood next to Kai's cab and watched the scenario unfold a forth-a-mile ahead.

Two more patrol cars raced to the intersection where Officer Thomas had stopped Betancourt's automobile. Three officers and a leashed German Shepherd cautiously approached Betancourt's car. The officers held their right hands on their holstered service pistols. Suddenly the Shepherd became visibly agitated. Betancourt and his bodyguard exited their vehicle as the officers drew their guns. Nellie laughed hardily as she watched Betancourt, intermittently, raise his hands, then wave his arms in a perturbed manner, then reach for his identification. The bodyguard stood in a stolid manner seemingly ignoring Betancourt's behavior. One of the officers opened a rear door of the car and leaned inside. The German Shepherd became virtually spastic as the officer backed away from the car holding Nellie's sawed-off shotgun and two packages.

The six observers watched as Betancourt flailed his arms. They could see that he was shouting. Officer Thomas, a native Colorado River Indian Tribe citizen, who stood an estimated six feet three inches tall and appeared to weigh close to three hundred pounds, picked up Betancourt by his shirt and held him at arm's length as Betancourt flailed his arms and thrashed his legs about.

"That is one really *big* policeman," Humberto murmured to the observers.

Then, as the officer began to shake Betancourt as if he was a rag doll, the bodyguard broke away from the scene and sprinted off toward the desert. Officer Billy leaned over and unleashed the German Shepherd, who joyfully attacked the bodyguard before he had run twenty yards. Kai, and his entourage cheered and high-fived one another.

Kai turned to his cohorts and said: "Well, that takes care of one of our major obstacles, at least for the time being," then opened his cell phone and dialed. "Where are you guys?" he asked when Rose answered.

ⅢⅢⅢⅢⅢⅢⅢⅢⅢ 48 ⅢⅢⅢⅢⅢⅢⅢⅢⅢ

The Partners

"OK, then it's agreed," Kai nodded as he looked back into the serious expressions of Rose, Aldo, Prudence, Louann, Marguerite, Turk, Beto, Jesse, Humberto, and Nellie, "hence forth we'll refer to our alliance as: 'The Partners'."

All bobbed their heads in the affirmative.

"So," Rose said, "just *what* do you propose that our quirky little *partnership* should do with our half-million dollars of stolen dope money - give or take a few bucks?"

Kai took a deep breath. "First, I want you to keep open minds regarding my proposition. I know that it will sound a bit far fetched, at first, but just hear me out."

The partners nodded.

Kai peered out of the large windows of the motor home as he spread his arms. "*This* RV resort is supposed to be 'First Class'. Isn't that what their brochure indicates?"

All nodded.

"And that so called first class RV resort you guys got chased out of a couple of days ago was described as 'Five Star', am I correct?"

All nodded.

"Now, let me ask all of you a question."

All nodded.

"Do you consider these two RV parks to be 'First Class' and 'Five Star'?"

All shook their heads in pronounced negativity.

"Do you believe that *really* nice RV parks are scarce here in the western states?"

"I do," Prudence answered, "my late husband and I visited many of them when we full-timed it, and believe me, there are few *really* nice RV parks available, especially for the space rentals they charge."

"Now, I'm going to ask all of you another question. And this is an important one: had each of you been satisfied and comfortable with your personal lifestyles before we met each other recently?"

Each partner looked down toward their feet as they considered Kai's query.

After a few moments of silence passed, Kai asked: "Well?"

Rose spoke first. "Aldo and I had been doing alright, I guess. We got to knock about in our camper a couple of months each year, and eat pretty good."

"I've been doing OK, I suppose," Nellie mumbled, "but I suspect that I could be getting more written on my paper than I have been lately."

"What about you?" Kai said as he looked at the fellows.

"I guess we've been getting by - as well as can be expected - for guys like us."

Nellie leaned forward. "OK, Kai, let us ask *you* the same question."

Kai smiled. "Fair enough. I've been fortunate to earn - and save - a lot of money. I haven't been proud of how I came by all of my earnings, but I have saved it so that I could, one day, break away from my past endeavors and earn my way in a legitimate business."

"OK, then, we're all a little restless with our respective situations," Prudence said, "so explain your proposal to us."

Kai laughed as he shook his head and shrugged his shoulders, "I've been thinking that the eleven of us - working together - could honestly, I believe, pool our resources and build and manage a truly first class RV resort."

Stunned silence.

"Are you crazy?" Nellie quipped. "That would take more money than the half million the gals stole." She glanced about, "and I bet there's not more than a couple of thousand bucks scattered amonst the rest of us seated here in this motor home other than that stolen cash."

"*I* can match the half million we have stashed here in the motor home," Kai said. "That would give us a million dollars cold cash to invest in building a first class RV resort."

The silence was awkward as the group glanced from one to the other in a state of stupor.

"I understand that my proposal sounds a bit far-fetched, but I've lived in RV resorts around the southwest for the past three years and I believe that I have a pretty good take on how one could be run properly - plus earning a profit."

"But there are eleven partners, here," Aldo said, "how're we gonna share the take?"

"By establishing a legitimate corporation."

"How do we do that?" Louann asked.

"*I'll* be fifty percent in partnership with the ten of *you*. Our corporation will pay me a management salary to be decided by you, the stockholders. Nellie and Rose could be the office-managers and receive appropriate wages, and you guys can split up the maintainance duties and such and be paid accordingly. We'll all live in nice Rvs inside the resort. At the end of each year we can all share bonuses from any profits we garner."

"But where would we locate the RV park?" Marguerite asked.

"Remember that little old abandoned railroad ghost town you stopped in for a day back in New Mexico?"

"Yes," Marguerite answered, "Stein's Ghost Town. I thought that it was simply charming."

"I stopped there, too, when I was tracking you folks," Kai said, "and I did some checking around regarding the place. I believe that Stein's location, adjacent to Interstate Ten on the border of New Mexico/Arizona, would be a perfect 'winter visitor' RV resort during the winter months and a great location for Rvers during spring, summer, and fall."

"It's way out in the boonies, man," Turk said.

"Not really," Kai answered. "It's only about fifteen minutes from Lordsburg, New Mexico where there are merchants and medical facilities and such. And Wilcox, Arizona's only about a fifty mile freeway drive. Plus it's only an easy two-hour drive to Tucson, Arizona. The scenery is spectacular with its mountain and desert vistas. Rvers will love it. It's a genuine abandoned village except for one couple who own it and live there. It has a fascinating history. Land is relatively inexpensive in, and around, the village, and the climate is amicable for recreational vehicle aficionados."

"Mind you, Kai, not one of us you are speaking to here," she fluttered her hands, "has the foggeist notion as to how much money would be required to purchase, or lease, the land - much less construct - such a resort," Prudence said.

"Together we can figure it out," Kai said with growing enthusiasm in his demeanor. "There are real estate brokers, lawyers, and contractors who specialize in this kind of endeavor. They'll set us on the right track."

"But would a million dollars be enough?" Louann asked.

"Yes, it would. And if we needed more capital there are banks that would be delighted to lend it to us. Hell, they'd be jumping to lend money to a legitimate corporation that wanted to start a million dollar project if the corporation already had a million debt-free cash on hand."

"Wow!" Marguerite exclaimed, "I haven't had *this* much excitement since I…" she stopped suddenly and blushed."

"Since you what?" Prudence asked.

"Oh, Prudence," Marguerite whispered with a demure expression, "I don't think that you would understand, much less approve."

"Be mindful of the fact that Kai is proposing that all

of us Partners will be buying ourselves *jobs*," Prudence quipped. "We ladies haven't held jobs in years, you know," she directed her comments to Marguerite, Louann, and Rose.

"Are you saying that being married *isn't* work?" Rose quipped.

"Of course it is, dear," Prudence turned and peered over her spectacles toward Aldo, "we have all observed Rose's continuing chore?"

"Hey! Hey! Hey!" Aldo exclaimed, "Why're you looking at *me?*"

Rose leaned across to Aldo and patted his knee. "Don't pay any heed to Prudence, Hon, I think you're worth it."

Aldo turned to Prudence and stuck his tongue out at her.

"What about *us* guys?" Beto asked. "We ain't used to holding down regular jobs."

Kai smiled toward the fellows. "Each of you have job skills that *you* don't even know that you posess. Take Turk, for instance. He's a natural born boss, I've noticed. He'd be a great supervisor. He'd be excellent as the general manager for the up-keep of the facilities and park streets. And Humberto - he's a 'people' person. He'd be perfect as the clubhouse manager. You know, keeping the clubhouse and swimming pool clean and all. Take Jesse: Jesse has the makings of a superb kitchen and snack-bar manager. I visualize Beto as the landscape and grounds supervisor."

"What about us?" Louann said as she indicated Prudence and Marguerite.

"Prudence, you would be a sensational social hostess

for our guests. You'd be great as a party and event planner. Louann, you'd manage the reservation desk and check-ins. I've observed how pleasant your personality is for meeting and dealing with people.

"And what would *I* do?" Marguerite said, as she squiggled excitedly on the couch.

"I'm still pondering *your* role," Kai grinned, "but I'm certain that you'll be much appreciated for whatever it might be." Kai pondered a moment, "Perhaps our RV resort's emissary or 'greeter'."

Marguerite giggled as she bobbed her head to and fro and clapped her hands.

"I could help manage the office and be the security person," Nellie said as she raised her hand.

"And Aldo could be the 'handyman' and fixer-upper," Rose said with excitement building in her voice.

"Yeah, and Rose is real good at cooking and maintaining a snack-bar and that sort of stuff," Aldo added.

"So, what's *your* job gonna be?" Turk asked Kai.

Kai turned and stared out of the motor home's front windshield for several minutes as the Partners waited patiently for his reply. He was reluctant to give them his answer, for they had begun to join his enthusiasm for their proposed project, and he didn't want to squash their burgeoning excitement. He studied the miserable dirt streets - in and about the RV resort in which they were temporary parked - as he watched an elderly couple attempt, with difficulty, to back their pick up truck into the stingy parking space allotted next to their travel trailer. *Jesus,* Kai thought to himself, *and those two retirees pay forty bucks a day for this?*

He slowly rotated to face the Partners. "I must tell you that I sincerely want to follow through with this RV resort proposal. I believe that we, together, can make it worth our efforts both for profit and our own personal satisfaction. Plus, of course, our mutual safety. But I feel obligated to explain to you that we are not home-free in regard to Betancourt and the Mexican dope cartel. You see, we may have eliminated Betancourt and his goon, but their fingers of the cartel will certainly reach out from their prison cells to grasp us by our throats to revenge the fact that we stole half-a-million dollars from them and were responsible for the incarceration of one of their honchos and his 'soldier'." Kai studied the attentive group. "Betancourt is absolutely certain to figure out that it was *us* who set him up."

He took a deep breath. "Now is the time for any one of you who wish to back away from our project. No one will judge you if you do. Certainly not me. But I do believe that not any one of us will be exempt from the cartel's revenge. Even if we split up and go our own ways they *will* find each one of us sooner or later. I *do* think, however, that if we stick together - as I've been proposing - we can better protect ourselves from retribution from the dope syndicate goons. The number one reason that I thought of this RV resort proposition located out in the middle of the desert is simply this: if we band together we will have the best possible chance for survival. We'll be located out in one of the most isolated parts of the American west. There's only two highways to Stein's Ghost Town. Only one off ramp. There's no landing strip. Only two people live there as of this moment. No police department to contend with. We can watch one another's back twenty-four seven."

Humberto stood and said: "I'm scared of those cartel dudes.

"It took me only four days to find you guys for the cartel," Kai answered, "so you *should* be afraid." Then Kai looked at Turk. "Now, Turk, you asked me what *my* job in our proposed RV corporation will be. Well, I'll be *our enforcer*. I've done the cartel's nasty jobs for a while now and I know how they operate. And I'm not especially proud to say this, but I was considered their best enforcer. I plan to call on my expertise to protect all of *us,* the Partners." The Partners sat in stolid silence for several moments. Not one glance iminated from the assembly for a few moments. Then, one-by-one, heads begin to nod.

"What will we call it?" Marguerite chirped.

"I know," Nellie said with excitement in her voice: "Stein's Ghost Town North Forty RV Retreat!"

Everyone sat back in their seats and clapped.

"OK, Partners, we're in agreement, so let's caravan back to Stein's Ghost Town tomorrow morning and get to work on the planning and construction of a brand new first class RV resort," Kai said as he grinned at the assemblage.

Suddenly Marguerite jumped from her seat and exclaimed: "Holy scheisse! Isn't this just the most exciting thing that's ever happened, or *what*?"

|||||||||||||||||| 49 ||||||||||||||||||||

Six Months Later
Stein's Ghost Town North Forty RV Retreat

"Good afternoon, Partners, it's been a hectic six months since we inaugurated the construction on our brand new RV resort," Kai announced to the group seated in the sparkling new dinning hall of Stein's Ghost Town North Forty RV Retreat. "I've called this meeting of you shareholders to celebrate the culmination of - oftentimes - a frustrating and difficult six months of thought, work, and effort in the creation of our first class RV resort." He glanced at each of the Partners as he continued: "We've had our differences in regard to the planning, design, and layout of our wonderful North Forty, but we persevered in regard to our final goal. Rose's initial idea of establishing a 'Think Tank' amongst ourselves to facilitate our dream park worked to our advantage in completing the project in record time and under budget. Our corporation had to borrow in order to complete the construction of the park, but our initial capital investment was more than sufficient to secure that loan. Tomorrow is the grand opening of our joint commercial adventure. Join me in wishing ourselves success, happiness - and above all - a safe enclave from our dope cartel enemies. We haven't, as yet, been threatened by the syndicate's enforcers, but we cannot assume that they have forgotten about the money we stole from them and that we were responsible for Betancourt's and his goon's imprisonment. So, we must continue to be vigilant as we begin our new entrepreneurial lifestyle. So, here's to the success of Stein's Ghost Town North Forty RV Retreat! Hear! Hear!"

Nellie stood first. "Beer is in order!" she exclaimed.

Marguerite, Prudence, and Louann jumped from their chairs and embraced.

Rose and Aldo leaned together and hugged.

Turk, Beto, Jesse, and Humberto grinned broadly and high-fived one another.

"I knew that we could pull this off, my friends," Kai exclaimed, "Now let's start living the good life out here in this beautiful RV resort in the shadow of the lovely Peloncillo Mountain Range of this grand New Mexico desert!"

Nellie turned to the kitchen area of the clubhouse as she called to the fellows: "Come help me parcel out the Oranjeboom Lager and beer, you bozos!"

Kai strolled to the huge front window of the clubhouse and perused its view of the RV park. The streets - as well as every RV parking space - were paved. Roofed shelters shaded each RV parking spot. All locations had been freshly landscaped with native desert foliage. He studied the large wagon wheel-shaped swimming pool - flanked by two cactus-shaped spas - adjoining the clubhouse. Roofed shuffle board courts extended from the large patio facing two flat-topped mountains adjacent to the RV resort.

Thoughts of the area's colorful past flooded Kai's musings. He had checked out Stein's Ghost Town on his laptop when he stopped there during his search for the three ladies and the four ex-cartel couriers. Excerpts from: 'Stein's Ghost Town', a Larry and Linda Link Site brochure, had garnered his interest. He read about the U.S. Army officer, Captain Enoch Stein - the first 'white man' to sign a treaty with the Mimbres Apache Indian tribe. The village was a stop for the Birch stage line for a short period. Later, the Butterfield Overland Stage Company took over the route. In 1861 Cochise led his warriors on an ambush of a stage coach near Stein's. Two travelers were killed during the attack. Three others - including the traffic manager of the Butterfield Texas route who resided in San Antonio - were taken alive and hung by their feet and burned to death. During subsequent years, Black Jack Ketchum and other horse thieves and express robbers terrorized the stage stopover. By the early 1880s Southern Pacific Railroad laid tracks through the village. After World War Two the railroad work station at Stein's was closed and the town quickly died off. *Now Stein's Ghost Town is coming back to life*, Kai thought, *just as The Partners are.*

||||||||||||||||| 50 |||||||||||||||||||

The Cartel's Enforcers

"Senor Betancourt is furious," Miguel grumbled. "We have to find those three old women and those four jerks or we'll be in serious trouble with the Betancourts and the other cartel bosses."

"What about Kai Ochita? Are the Betancourts still ranting about him?"

"Especially him."

"Listen to me, Betancourt's in a federal prison for a helluva long time. Why should we have to take orders from *him*? He's not a player anymore."

"The hell he's not…his crazy-ass son took his place in the cartel and he wants revenge, man. Listen to me: that son-of-a-Betancourt is insane when it comes to getting vengeance for his ol' man being set-up by Ochita and those crazy old ladies.

"Damn! Don't we have enough crap to put up with already? Those syndicate gangs along the Texas border are taking the dope trade away from us. *Those* hombres are the ones we should be hunting down and whacking, not old women and stupid delivery jerks. Besides, I've heard too many stories about Ochita. I *don't* want to mess with him."

"I don't either, but we don't have any wiggle room about this. The Betancourts want *us* to take care of Ochita and his buddies. If we don't find them and settle the Betancourts' beef with them *we'll* be on their short list, and man, that's definitely a place we *don't* want to be. Not for *you*…or *me*…or our families back in Juarez."

Miguel licked his lips several times as he thought about Otilia's comment. "OK," he said after several minutes, "I agree." He took a deep breath and sighed audibly. "So let's get going with this stupid assignment."

"Fine," she said, "our first step is to trace their movements from that desert town called Parker on the Colorado River. That's where they set-up Betancourt and his man."

"Betancourt's son told our lawyer that he heard that Ochita and the bunch were caravanning in Rvs back toward New Mexico on I-10 several months ago."

"How'd the lawyer know that?"

"Hell, I don't know. The syndicate has dealers in every truck stop in the United States. I suppose one - or more - of our dealers happened to notice that bunch of characters in a gas station, or something." He smirked as he continued: "You gotta admit, seeing *that* caravan trailing into the truck stops would be an unforgettable sight."

"Alright. The first thing we should do is start getting in touch with our truck stop dope dealers along I-10. Then we'll have an idea of where the caravan stopped or turned off. We'll check out which off ramp is nearby and follow that trail."

"We have to decide how we're going to take them out when we find them."

"We won't know until we stake out their location, so we better take all of our weapons."

"Our sniper rifles, too?"

"You bet, if they are hiding out together somewhere in the boonies - that's what I'd do if I were them - the two of us could sit back and take them out one-by-one before they could figure out what the hell was happening."

"How are we going to hide all of our weapons in a sedan or truck? "We'll be passing through Border Patrol check stops and state-line checks, you know."

"We could rent a motor home and pretend we're a retired RV couple. The check-point jerks don't pay a helluva lot of attention to those old farts, plus we'll have a ton of room in the rig to stash everything we might need."

"Hey, that's a great idea. If they're still altogether in their rigs we could park near them and pretend we're full-timing it just like they are. Ochita doesn't know us. I seriously doubt that he'd expect that a man and woman traveling in a motor home would be doing a hit job for the cartel. This is going to be easier than I first thought it would be."

ⅠⅠⅠⅠⅠⅠⅠⅠⅠⅠⅠⅠⅠ 51 ⅠⅠⅠⅠⅠⅠⅠⅠⅠⅠⅠⅠⅠ

Stein's Ghost Town North Forty RV Retreat

Turk drove his golf cart next to Kai's Harley and beeped its horn a couple of times. "Hey, Kai, that idea of yours to give the first three day's space rent free to the Rvers passing by on I-10 was great. Every dang one of them who spots our sign out on the highway is pulling onto off ramp number three to stay with us at least *one* night!"

"It's human nature, Turk," Kai laughed in return, "offer something free to retirees and they'll even forget about their arthritis for a time."

"Well, your promotion is working. Fifty percent of our spaces have been occupied since you put up the sign when we opened for business last week. All of them seem to like our RV retreat. Some are going to stay a while and many others say they intend to come back."

Kai smiled and gunned his Harley a couple of times before he drove into Stein's. He rode his bike around the quaint little ghost town and back to the RV park several times every day and night. He was diligently on the alert for any sign of suspicious-looking characters who may have been sent by the cartel. He knew that he was depending on his ability to profile - an act of which he disaproved because of the constant profiling others performed in regard to him; doo-rag, ponytail, riding a 'chopped' Harley. But profiling was *his* first line of defense against The Partners' common enemy; the cartel. During the period of time Kai was engaged as an enforcer for the cartel he didn't resort to disguises or subtrafuge. His demeanor, plus his reputation for intelligence, sufficed to induce whatever respose was required for his services. He had never met - nor did he care to meet - the other cartel enforcers. Kai understood that he was not like them. He didn't kill, or torture. He simply intimidated, and because of his understanding of human nature, that worked for his purposes. He fervently hoped that he would be able to spot other enforcers should they appear. *Six months and counting*, he thought, *so far, so good.*

The most gratifying feelings Kai had been experiencing since The Partners had formed their corporation was that of purpose. Purpose for him and The Partners. The three ladies bustled about their repective jobs chattering and laughing. The four fellows were obviously happily engaged with their chores. And Rose and Aldo scurried to and fro concentrating on their assignments. Nellie was making progress with her studies and thesis. The corporation was beginning to serve its purpose in regard to every aspect. Even the RV guests seemed to be happy with their stay in the resort. There were a few 'wrinkles' to be ironed out, but, all-in-all, life was good at Stein's Ghost Town North Forty RV Retreat. The men played pool, stood outside their rigs scratching and discussing diesel engines, walked their wives' dusty little dogs, and complained about fuel prices. The ladies played bridge daily in the clubhouse, took shopping runs to Tucson, and stood immobile in the extra warm water of the pool telling each other about their grandchildren.

Rose and Aldo enjoyed visiting the many surrounding 'land of enchantment' historical sites. The ladies visited the surrounding towns, haunted the shopping centers of Tucson, and played bridge with the guests. Turk, Beto, Jesse, and Humberto took 'rest and recreational' runs to nearby border towns, Tucson, and Phoenix. As for Kai: he loved it all.

#

The large diesel-engined motor home coasted smoothly down off ramp number three leading to Stein's Ghost Town. Miguel and Otilia studied the layout of the village.

"There it is," Otilia said as she pointed.

"That's it, alright," Miguel muttered.

Miguel steered the motor home slowly past the abandoned rustic adobe and rough-cut lumber buildings toward the Stein's Ghost Town North Forty RV Retreat situated about a quarter of a mile away on the mountain side of town. As he approached the entrance to the RV resort, Otilia abruptly leaned forward in her seat and peered intently into the right rearview mirror. "There's a guy following us on one of those fancied-up motorcycles."

"What's he look like?" Miguel asked.

"He looks oriental. He has a ponytail."

"Damn," Miguel muttered. "An oriental with a ponytail riding a bike…that's got to be Kai Ochita."

"What're we going to do?"

"Act like typical retired Rvers. Assume an expression of confusion and offer a silly grin. I'm gonna slow to a near stop so's he'll have to drive past us."

The motor home barely moved along the dirt main street of Stein's. Kai pulled beside its left side and smiled up at Migue and nodded. Miguel smiled down as he lowered his side window. "Hi there! Is that the RV park up ahead that's offering three nights for free?"

"It sure is," Kai answered.

"Well, good. We think that we might just take them up on their generous three night offer."

"I'm staying there, myself. Just follow me to the office. They'll be pleased to check you in and give each of you a big piece of Rose's homemade 'Better-Than-Sex' cake."

"Sounds good to me, friend. Lead on."

Otilia watched Kai accelerate toward the park. "You sounded just like one of those Texas-born natives."

"Damn straight…and so are you when we park inside there. We're going to pretend to be Miguel and Otilia Perez: a couple of retired citizens who've been full-timing it down in the Rio Grande Valley at Weslaco, Texas."

"You think that we should *mingle* with Kai and those people?"

"Hell yes, Otilia. If we get friendly with our targets it will be easier to figure out the safest way to eliminate them."

Otilia sighed as she resigned herself to their situation. *Condenar! I'm not pleased with this. I prefer to not know the people we kill. This plan is too risky, especially when an ex-*

enforcer is one of the targets. "Listen to me, Miguel, we've always identified our targets, watched them, and then eliminated them when they were sleeping."

"Otilia, this is not one of our standard kills. We were hired to take out ten or eleven people here on the United States side of the border. It's not the same thing as walking into an adobe hovel across the border crowded with drunk cartel soldiers and using Uzi machine pistols to whack 'em, or sneaking into a house and cutting a sleeping couple's throats. We have to figure out how to do this thing and get our butts back to Mexico before anyone figures out what just happened." Miguel stopped in front of the RV resort's office and turned off the engine. "That's the reason the Betancourts insisted that you and I do this hit. We're the only enforcers who are smart enough to figure out how to nail these people. Just imagine, for one moment, how much shit is going to hit the fan when folks discover a bunch of murdered American citizens in an recreational vehicle resort." He opened the door of the motor home. "I'm going into the office to register. Wait here."

"You just now made a huge mistake, Miguel if you want us to pretend to be retired motor home campers."

Miguel turned back to Otilia and asked: "Yeah, what?"

"The women always go in to register and the husbands *never* turn off their diesel engines."

IIIIIIIIIIIIIIII 52 IIIIIIIIIIIIIIIII

Betancourts

Eduardo Betancourt leaned against the wall next to one of the bank of the prison's pay phones as he shouted into the mouthpiece in Spanish: "Damn it to hell, son, I told you that I want that Kai Ochita dead…and all three of those old thieving women who stole our money, as well…plus those four stupid curriers we paid to deliver our cash! It's been six months since that bunch of dishonest old putas and those assholes took our money and set me up to get arrested and go to this American federal prison. You can't, in your wildest imagination, visualize the crazy shit heads that I have to live with in here. Mother of God, son, if you don't get me extradited back to Mexico I won't be able to sit down on a chair without a cushion for the rest of my life!"

"I'm working on all of this, father, but it isn't easy to have a bunch of American citizens zapped in their own country."

"*I* know that! And *they* know that. That's why I had

you contact Miguel and that insane woman, Otilia. They're the most dependable enforcers the cartel's ever hired."

"They're expensive, father."

"I don't give a damn how much they want to do the job. Pay them an extra bonus to expedite the kill if you have to!"

"I was just informed this morning that Miguel and Otilia are making their move soon. They're all at a place called Stein's Ghost Town in New Mexico."

"Just make sure that they get it done!"

"Father, I'm sorry to have to tell you this, but our lawyers advise us to not continue persuing your extradiction back to Mexico."

"What? Why?"

"It seems that members of our rival border cartel are incarcerated in all of our prisons. It's rumored that they have ordered a 'hit' on you if you're sent back to any Mexican prison."

A long, silent pause.

"Send me one of those cushions shaped like a doughnut."

ⅠⅠⅠⅠⅠⅠⅠⅠⅠⅠⅠⅠⅠⅠⅠ 53 ⅠⅠⅠⅠⅠⅠⅠⅠⅠⅠⅠⅠⅠⅠⅠ

Stein's Ghost Town North Forty RV Retreat

Sunday afternoon. Every table in the clubhouse multi-purpose hall was occupied. Several retirees stood on the stage at the front of the room playing a variety of string and percussion instruments. One elderly woman was seated on a folding chair banging two tablespoons on her knee to the quick cadence of the piece they were playing: 'Five foot two, Eyes of Blue.' Another woman was standing at the microphone leading the sing-along. She held an empty Styrofoam dish in her left hand and directed the enthusiastic room of songsters with a plastic teaspoon in her right hand: "Five foot two, eyes of blue, but oh, what those five foot could do…has anybody seen my girl?"

A couple were dancing to the melody on the huge dance floor between the stage and the first row of tables. Several in the audience - obviously a generation older than the others - had misty eyes as they reminisced.

Miguel and Otilia sat quietly at the rear of the hall

listening and watching the scenerio. Kai walked to their table and smiled down at them. "Did you two enjoy your root beer floats?" he shouted over the din engulfing them.

Otilia smiled back and nodded. Miguel turned and looked up into Kai's face. "This is the first…what do you call it…root beer float I've ever tasted. It's good!"

"Oh, I thought you two are full-timing it."

"Yes, we are."

"You must not have been full-timing very long to not have experienced a root beer float," Kai answered.

"Miguel meant that it's been a while since he's had one," Otilia interjected.

"Oh," Kai said.

Kai stood by their table tapping his foot to the melody. "Well," he said after a few moments, "the guests sure enjoy singing the old-time songs."

"I noticed that you seem to be working here at Stein's Ghost Town North Forty RV Park," Otilia said.

Kai answered: "Yeah. It's nice out here in the desert. I like to ride my bike to all of the old mines and abandoned towns. It's peaceful."

"Yes," Otilia said, "and isolated, too."

"That it is," Kai answered. "Well, I guess that I'd better continue making the rounds. See you two about."

Miguel nodded.

After Kai walked away Otilia leaned close to Miguel's ear and said: "You're going to blow our cover, fool."

Miguel turned and glared back. "What did I say wrong?"

"These full-timers *all* know about root beer floats, estupido!"

"Yeah…what else?"

"You weren't singing 'Five Foot Two'."

"Get off my back, bitch, I know how to handle this situation."

"You'd better, Miguel, 'cause that Kai Ochita has a reputation for being a smart and clever enforcer. He's not some dumb-ass syndicate soldier."

"Yeah? Well neither am I."

"And listen closely, Miguel: don't you ever call me 'bitch' again."

#

Kai was sitting on the wooden rail fence enclosing the resort's firepit behind the clubhouse listening to the sing-song inside. Aldo strolled up. "Well, Kai, everything's running copasetic, just like we planned it."

"You bet it is, Aldo."

"Then why are you sitting out here so deep in thought?"

"I'm not sure, Aldo. I just got an odd feeling several minutes ago."

"What about?"

Kai stood and placed his arm on Aldo's shoulder. "Two of our guests. I'd like you and Rose to do some snooping for me. You remember that couple who drove in yesterday in the Gulf Stream motor home?"

"Sure. Louann had me lead them to space one-fifteen. What about them?"

"Well, I overheard the man tell Louann - when he was registering at the desk - that they are full-timers and that they've been staying at a RV resort next to Weslaco down in the Valley. But I happened to notice that a small sticker on the back of their rig had been scraped off. I think that it had indicated that it was a *rental* motor home. And just now I was chatting with them and he happened to mention that he'd never tasted a root beer float. Plus they looked too young to be retired."

Aldo looked out over the desert toward Stein's Peak for a few seconds. "So?"

"I've been knocking around RV parks for three years, and I've never run across a full-timer who was renting his rig."

Aldo turned Kai. "Maybe their regular motor home is in the shop getting repaired, or something."

"Maybe so, but *not* knowing about root beer floats?"

"Anything else?" Aldo said.

"She struck me as being smarter than him, but he was the one who got out of the motor home and walked to the office to register when they arrived yesterday."

"Is that all that's worrying you?"

Kai expelled a breath of air and smiled at Aldo. "This may seem silly, I suppose, but I've never - *ever* - seen a genuine full-timer in a large motor home turn off its diesel engine until, at least forty-five minutes, after they've parked it."

Aldo turned his head in thought for a few seconds. "You know, Kai, neither have I. Now *that's* something to be concerned about. You said that you wanted Rose and me to do some snooping?"

"If you don't mind."

"Hell, Rose will bust her butt when it comes to snooping. She *loves* snooping."

"Here's what I'd like you and Rose to do: figure out a

way to get into a conversation with them. Try to find out which park they were staying in near Weslaco. I know a guy in the Valley who delivers propane gas to the RV parks down in the mid-valley area. He peddles a little grass on the side. I'll get in touch with him and have him ask around if anyone in the RV resorts on his route knew - or noticed - a couple of full-timers in a Gulf Stream named Miguel and Otilia Perez."

#

Rose watched from her kitchen window as Aldo steered the park's golf cart into the parking space next to their new Holiday Rambler fifth-wheel. Kai had insisted that the corporation purchase a new rig for each of The Partners - who didn't already own a comfortable full-timers' rig. Nellie chose a Coachmen, the four fellows picked out identical Jayco trailers, and Louann and Marguerite selected matching Dutchman trailers.

"What's up?" Rose called out to Aldo.

"Kai wants you and me to do a little snooping around."

Rose smiled broadly. "Hot damn, I was beginning to miss all the baloney back at our trailer park in Kerrville. "Who're we going to snoop out?"

"You know that Hispanic couple who're parked in space one-fifteen in that big Gulf Stream diesel-pusher?"

"Heck, I can't remember every rig that pulls in here."

"Well, anyway, Kai was chatting with them earlier this afternoon at the sing-song and he said they didn't seem kosher to him."

"How so?"

"Something about their motor home being a rental… and the guy not knowing about root beer floats."

"Why would those things make Kai want us to check them out?"

"They told him that they were full-timers. Kai thought that they looked too young, also."

Rose raised her eyebrows. "Yeah, well Kai was right about one thing: full-timers *not* knowing about root beer floats. How're we going to handle this?"

Aldo sat back into the golf cart's seat and pondered a moment. "Tell you what: let's drive the cart over to their space and pretend that we're checking out their sewer hose connection. While I'm doing that you can contrive a way to get into a conversation with one of them." Aldo grinned. "You're good at that I've noticed through the years."

"How 'bout *you* doing the talking and *me* doing the checking? You're always gabbing with all the women."

Aldo nodded. "True," but I don't get near the amount of information you weasel out of the men."

"Oh, well what about the…"

"Just get in the golf cart, Rose, and we'll sort it out on the way over to space one-fifteen."

#

"Miguel, two of the park's workers are pulling next to our rig in a golf cart. What do you suppose they want?"

"I have no idea. Go outside and find out. We don't want them inside our rig."

Otilia stepped from the motor home and greeted

Rose and Aldo. "Hello. Is there something I can do for you?"

Rose struggled from the golf cart. "We're just making the rounds checking out all the black-water connections to see if everything's working as it should. When you build a brand new facility sometimes every little connection doesn't get its proper screwing or gluing. You know how it is."

Aldo left the cart and ambled around to the other side of the motor home. Rose stepped closer to Otilia as she said: "You have a real fine motor home here."

"Yes. We're enjoying living in it."

"Oh, so you're full-timing?"

"We are."

"Where'd you two stay the last few weeks?"

Otilia scowled as she answered: "Why do you ask?"

Rose laughed. Then said: "Oh, I guess that it's the nature of Rvers to want to know where other campers are coming from or going to. That's the way we RV gypsies learn about places to consider driving to. Now take Aldo and me; we like to run down to the Rio Grande Valley for a spell each winter. And summers we generally haul up to Ruidoso, New Mexico, or Buena Vista in Colorado."

"We drove here from the Valley," Otilia said.

"OK. That's quite an area. When we drive all that distance to the tip of Texas we like to stay at South Padre Island. They have a great county RV park down on the tip of the island. You ever stay there?"

"No, we haven't. Perhaps our next trip down we'll stop there." Otilia made a move to step into the motor home.

"Where *did* you stay down there?" Rose interjected.

Otilia lowered her shoulders and gave Rose an impatient stare. "I really don't believe that is any of your concern. Now please complete your inspection of the water 'thing' and go on about your business. It's our nap time."

"Black-water," Rose said hurriedly.

"Black-water?" Otilia queried.

"That's the connection we're checking.

"Whatever," Otilia muttered as she stepped into the motor home and closed its door.

Aldo walked back to the golf cart and slid onto the driver's seat. Rose climbed in and turned to him. "Kai's suspicions are right-on. I've never heard of a full-timer who didn't know what the hell you were talking about when you're discussing the shit-hose connection."

"Did you find out the name of the park they stayed last?"

"Nope," Rose answered, "she wouldn't say."

#

Aldo drove the golf cart around to the park's office and sounded the horn a couple of beeps. Kai stepped to the door and nodded.

"Your suspicions regarding that Hispanic couple in the Gulf Stream holds water with *our* take on them," Rose said.

Kai nodded. "I just called down to the propane truck driver I know in Weslaco and asked him if he ever ran across such a couple. He said that he couldn't remember any folks fitting their description, but that he would telephone all the RV resorts around Weslaco and ask the office gals. He knows all of them because he has to deal with them on a daily basis. He said that he'd call me back this evening as soon as he contacted them." Kai walked to the golf cart and leaned on the roof. "Thanks for checking out that couple."

"You think that the cartel sent them to find us?" Aldo asked.

"Could be. I heard a rumor a while back that the cartel bosses had a man and woman team of especially cruel enforcers that they kept on a retainer for murdering their priority enemies." Kai took a deep breath. "And we, The Partners, are certain to be number one on *that* list."

"Damn!" Aldo exclaimed, "What're we going to do?"

"We're going to have to move quickly," Kai said, "because big-time enforcers such as those two don't waste their time doing a hit." He placed his hand on Rose's shoulder as he continued. "Rose, you and Aldo roundup the other Partners and tell them that we have to have an emergency meeting tonight. Tell everyone to meet in my rig, but to not be obvious about it. Just casually, one or two at a time, saunter over and tap on my door. By then I will have heard from the propane truck driver. Then we'll know, for sure, whether or not this couple is a danger for us."

|||||||||||||||| 54 ||||||||||||||||

The Partners

The Partners sat silently inside Kai's fifth-wheel listening to him explain his suspicions regarding the couple in space one-fifteen. Nellie became restless mid-way through Kai's monologue. She stood abruptly and announced: "Let's go over there right *now* and confront them!"

"Hey, hey, now," Kai said to Nellie, "We have to be extra cautious with those two," he shook his head, "we have to get this right the first time, because we may not get a second chance."

"Well, for crap's sake, then, how're we going to defend ourselves?" Beto said.

"We're going to figure out a way to render those two harmless."

"That ain't going to be easy, man," Humberto muttered.

"Yeah," Jesse said, "you said that those two are highly paid killers; and good at it."

Kai held up his hands for attention. "Just try to

calm down, you guys. Remember how we eliminated Betancourt and his thug? We can all put our heads together and plan something similar to *that* to neutralize the threat from those two."

Prudence nodded her head vigorously as she said: "Yes! That's the humane approach to our quandary. We'll simply figure out a way to plan an *accident* for them. *That* will do away with our immediate danger."

"But Prudence," Louann said, "wouldn't causing them to have an accident be the same thing as murdering them?" She shrugged her shoulders and added with a thoughtful expression: "It wouldn't be the same as stabbing them or rocking them to unconsciousness, however. Would it?"

"So what?" Marguerite giggled, "they'd be *neutralized*, wouldn't they? Isn't that going to be our goal?"

Rose stood. "Pipe down for a moment you folks." She glared at the women. "I'm ashamed of you ladies for suggesting such things. Now let's follow Kai's line of reasoning and start thinking of some way to cause those two assassins to be sent to prison. That way they'd be out of our hair, so to speak."

Turk held up his hand.

"*What*?" Rose said.

"We worked together to successfully get Betancourt and his guy arrested but they still managed from inside the prison to arrange for *these* two enforcers to come for us. Wouldn't the same thing keep happening if we managed to frame these two? You know, everyone we screw will just order someone *else* to come after us. We'd *never* get off the hook."

All turned to Kai for an answer.

Kai sat down and studied the group for a few minutes,

then said: "I don't think so. It has been my observation that the 'mind-set' of the syndicate organization's honchos are basically self-centerd. There are *always* those next in line who are itching for an oportunity to step up a notch in the cartel's hiarchy. They quickly lose interest in ordering retribution for incarcerated ex-bosses."

Aldo raised his hand for attention. "Listen up," he said with conviction, "those cartel bosses aren't like other gangs. Take Rose's and my old-time biker buddies - the Hill Country Hellers - now those old boys are loyal to one-another. Heck, if Rose or me were to give them a holler they'd come a-riding to our rescue right this minute. They, in their own way, have class, even though they're gang members. Those dope cartel folks are plainly just thugs."

Marguerite studied Turk, Beto, Jesse, and Humberto. "*You* fellows worked for the cartel," she said in a hesitant manner.

"They were just 'gofers'," Kai quipped. "all they did was deliver street cash across the border."

Marguerite then turned her attention to Kai. She raised her eyebrows.

"I know," Kai said, "I was on their payroll, but I never hurt or injured anyone for the cartel. I just scared the bravado out of lowlifes who tried to cheat the cartel."

Kai studied The Partners. The three Kerrville ladies, for all intents and purposes, had similar backgrounds: higher middle income advantages, above average educations, moral foundations - at least from their own personal perspectives - plus a modicum of dignity. Yet, they greedily pilfered five-hundred thousand dollars. They justified their theft by the rationale that they were stealing from dope-dealers. But, nevertheless, they *stole* the cash. *Go figure*, Kai thought to himself. And the four fellows: cartel couriers. True, they weren't directly involved in the distribution of marijuana, cocaine, crack, or the other myriad kinds of illegal contraband, but they were - indeed - a *party* to those crimes.

He glanced at Nellie. A lady who lived by her credo of hard work, independence, and self-reliance. Yet she *gladly* accepted his invitation to join The Partners having full knowledge of the theft. And Aldo and Rose: a couple who trudged through their years together with optimism and humor, in spite of the swirling chaos engulfing the society about them, *voluntarily* joined the lady thieves by piggy-backing on the rationale that they were being of kindly assistance to three helpless old ladies. And lastly, himself. Kai Ochita: a student of philosophy and human nature using his learned physical skills to intimidate and strike fear into the minds of lesser men. He was *leading* The Partners.

Kai observed all of The Partners - basically *good* people bound together by stolen money and self-preservation - seated here planning machinations for the purpose of doing harm to other human beings. His degrees and studies of philosophy had taught him that: to be 'true to oneself' a person must have an altruistic nature. Otherwise that person is self-centered in his personal perspective. *How is it, then, that 'good' people can so easily justify their own unjust behavior?* Kai pondered as he perused his partners. Then an epiphany struck his thoughts: *Human beings aren't altruistic. Otherwise, winning or being 'first' would not be foremost in their psyche and they wouldn't scheme to take posessions away from one-*

another. Therefore, all humans are prone to transgress if their
actions will, in some way, be beneficial for their own self.
This must be why the board game called Monopoly is, and
has been, so popular.

Rose broke the silence. "Well, let's get to work planning a way to get those two enforcers off of our backs."

Kai said: "I've been giving this problem serious thought since my propane delivery acquaintance down in the valley called this evening. He said that not one of his contacts in the offices of the RV parks around the mid-valley area have knowledge of Miguel and Otilia Perez or the Gulf Stream they're driving. I'm convinced that those two are our enemies. So, the first thing that we have to do is contrive to get them out of and away from that Gulf Stream away from their weapons. The odds are that their weapons, whatever they might be, are stashed inside that motor home, not their tow car. We have to deprive them of their tools of their trade: their weapons."

"I can tell you, for certain, *that Otilia* woman isn't inclined to be willingly cooperative with any excuse that we can thnk up to get them to voluntarily step out of that rig," Rose said. "She got pissed-off at me for asking too many questions this afternoon."

"I betcha that I can get their butts out of there right fast," Humberto said.

"Yeah, how's that?" Turk asked.

"Any of you folks have vinegar and bleach stashed in your rig?"

"We do," Rose said.

"Good. Beto and I can sneak over there and flush 'em out real fast."

"How?" Aldo asked.

"Well, a few years back, a skunk got into my abuelo's little old tear-drop travel he was living in out in our back yard. We did a lot of figuring as to how to get that skunk out of Poppie's trailer. Finally someone came up with the idea of pouring a few cups of bleach and vinegar down the vent pipe to his grey water holding tank. The godawful smell coming out of the sinks caused that 'ol skunk to get out of Poppie's trailer muy pronto."

Prudence said: "Those two chemicals produce toxic chlorine vapor. It might kill them."

"I guarantee you that, if they're not asleep, they'll haul their butts out of that big ol' motor home long before the fumes get a shot at killing 'em," Humberto snickered, "that smell is *malo*, man."

"Now just how in the world are you two guys going to get yourselves up on the roof of that motor home without it feeling and sounding like an earthquake's rocking it?" Aldo said.

"Easy. The rear bathroom sink's vent pipe sticks out of the roof close to the side of those big motor homes. We'll set up one of the park's twelve-foot folding ladders next the rear of the rig so I can climb up and reach over to the vent pipe and pour the vinegar and bleach down it," Humberto said as he proffered a huge grin.

"What if they hear or notice you fellows?" Louann asked.

"All those two will hear, or see, will be everyone of *you* guys in the space between the rigs watching the fire pit, drinking beer, and playing loud conjunto music from my boombox."

"*My* motor home?" Prudence asked.

"Yep. We'll move your rig to space one-fourteen and throw one hell of a tertulia outside around the fire pit."

"A *tertulia*?" Aldo asked.

"A fiesta, man. It's a 'thing' we Mexicans do."

"Omigod," Marguerite snickered, "how on earth did you learn to do things such awful things such as this?"

Humberto chuckled as he answered: "Oh, I used to pal around with a fellow named Rex when I was a kid down in the valley. Me and him used to do a lotta shit like that."

"Come on, now, Humberto," Kai interjected, "we've talked about cleaning up our language around the ladies. They're still living in the 'twilight zone' of innocence."

Humberto looked down. "I'm sorry, ladies, I should have said: 'fun.'"

"OK, then," Aldo said as he rubbed his hands together, "let's get to work and get this deed done."

"Whoa. Not so fast, Aldo. We have to decide our next step," Rose quipped.

"Yeah," Turk said, "what do we do when they come running out of their motor home?"

"Grab them, tie and gag them, and secure them in Prudence's motor home," Kai said. "After we find whatever weapons those two have hidden in the motor home I propose that we haul their butts down Highway Ninety to Douglas, Arizona. That's about eighty miles south of here."

"Then what?"

"Turn them over to a vicious old smuggler I know down there who owes me a big-time favor. His name is Jorje. He hangs out a lot of the time in Matamoros, Mexico south of the border from Brownsville, but he lives with his son and grandsons in Agua Prieta just across the border from Douglas, Arizona. He's a 'sometime' informant for the Border Patrol."

"Kai, how can we trust such a questionable rascal?" Prudence asked.

"We can't. At least not completely, but ol' Jorje almost got himself and his boys into a really *bad* predicament with my cartel a couple of years ago. Another cartel enforcer had heard rumors about Jorje being an informant for the BP."

"What did you do to help him?" Humberto said.

"I'd rather not say."

Several moments of quiet contemplation hovered over The Partners.

"Why'd you help this old Jorje guy?" Beto asked, "You were a *cartel dude* yourself, man."

"Because Jorje was also keeping *me* informed about the illegal activities of a few Border Patrol Agents."

"But you said the old man *informs* on smugglers, too," Beto said.

"Only on *rival* smuggling gangs," Kai said.

"Why would you care what the two BP guys were up to?" Rose asked.

"Because I was recruited by the Homeland Security Agency to work as a special undercover agent when I completed my PhD at Stanford. My assignment was to infiltrate one of the drug cartels and learn everything I could about illegal activities back and forth across our border with Mexico."

Stunned silence permeated the interior of Kai's fifth-wheel. Finally Turk spoke: "Will you tell them or BP people about me and Beto and these other two guys?" He motioned toward Jesse and Humberto.

"No," Kai said.

"Why not?" Turk asked.

"I'll soon be thirty-three years old and all that I've done for the past few years is deal with low-lifes." Kai shook his head: "I'm sick of it."

Aldo offered a low whistle. "Wow, I thought that Rose and me had heard it all, but this takes the cake."

Prudence furrowed her brow as she asked: "OK. Now a lot of things are beginning to make sense to me, except for one thing: how does a man your age amass a half-a-million dollars in an offshore bank account while working for the U.S government?"

"No one in the agency was concerned about any monetary gain that I accrued from the cartel when I was acting as an undercover informant. I had to become as one of them. It was sort of a 'don't ask, don't tell' arrangement with my contact. Otherwise, I wouldn't have done some of the crap that I had to do in order to survive amongst the cartel members. The Agency wouldn't pay me near enough to do the things that I was doing for them."

"Are you still an undercover agent?" Louann asked.

"No. I resigned immediately after I caught up with you folks." Kai smiled at The Partners. "As you know, I'm a student of philosophy. I found all of you folks and your situations too interesting to walk away from. You feisty old ladies intrigued me with your audacity of first: stealing half-a-million dollars from a vicious dope syndicate, and second: inviting Aldo and Rose to share your booty and join you in your escapade. And, by damn, they *did* join you. Then," Kai looked toward the five elderly people, "the five of you: citizens of Tom Brokaw's 'Greatest Generation' - for crying out loud - convinced these four young illegal cartel money couriers to join your 'gang'. Your collective innocence, naivety, good will, and ultimate friendship fascinated me."

"We are *not* a *gang*!" Prudence exclaimed.

"If we're not a gang," Louann said, "then, what are we?"

"Partners!" Marguerite squealed as she clapped her hands.

"So why would this Jorje hombre help *us*?" Turk said.

"As I mentioned before, I saved ol' Jorje and his boys' lives a couple of years ago. He vowed to me that he'd return the favor one day. He even crossed himself and promised Jesus."

"I'm going to tell Jorje and his son that Miguel Perez and his woman companion, Otilia, plan to 'rat' them out to a rival dope cartel."

"What will Jorje and his boys do to them?"

"I have no idea, but whatever it is I don't want to know about it," Kai said.

|||||||||||||||||| 55 ||||||||||||||||||

The Partners, Miguel, Otilia

After two hours of animated discussion amonst The Partners, Kai stood next to the dashboard of Prudence's motor home and raised his hands for attention. "OK. I believe that we're all in agreement regarding the disposition of Miguel and Otilia Perez. Agreed?"

Nods.

"Then let's 'get it on'!" Aldo whooped.

Prudence, Louann, and Marguerite hopped up and began the process of preparing their motor home for vacating its space. Prudence busied herself with the dashboard controls: starting the diesel engine, raising the automatic stabilizers, checking the multiple gauges. Marguerite scurried about the enterior of the coach securing loose items such as kitchenware, books, vases, inside doors. Louann and Nellie stepped outside and started unhooking the electrical cord, the television cable, and beginning the tedious process of securing the sewer connections and water hose.

Aldo and Rose rushed to their rig to fetch two large sacks of charcoal, a can of lighter fluid, and bottles of vinegar and bleach. Humberto trotted to the park's maintainance building to retrieve a twelve-foot folding ladder. Jesse raced to Humberto's fifth-wheel to collect Humberto's boom box. Kai, Turk, and Beto each hustled to their on rigs to collect rope, duck tape, pillowcases, and bedsheets.

#

Two hours later, precisely at ten p.m., Kai stood behind Prudence's motor home as he peeked toward Miguel's and Otilia's rental Gulf Stream in the next space. The Partners had quietly - at least as quiet as possible for a diesel - moved Prudence's motor home onto the empty spot next to the Gulf Stream. Kai studied a flickering bluish light emanating from the living room area of the Gulf Stream. *They're watching television*, Kai deduced. He turned back and motioned to the rest of The Partners hunkering behind him. "Go," he said. On his command The Partners scurried to their assignments.

Aldo and Rose crept to the firepit between the coaches and emptied their two eighteen pound sacks of charcoal into its circle, then splashed an entire sixty-four fluid ounce container of lighter fluid onto the charcoals and lit them. Jesse turned on Humberto's boom box to its highest volume with a fiesty recording of "Me Perdonas Vida Mia" by the lively Conjunto Primavera Mariachi Band. Three Coyotes, a mile from the RV resort, turned and ran, helter skelter, away into the wilderness. Marguerite and Louann scuffled to the edge of the firepit and commenced dancing wildly about issuing long, drawn-out 'Mexican' yells. Humberto struggled to the rear of the Gulf Stream, a folding twelve-foot ladder riding on his back. Beto followed with a quart of vinegar in one hand and a quart of bleach in the other hand. Humberto hurriedly set the ladder. Beto thrust the two quart containers into the crook of Humberto's right arm as he scampered up the ladder. Prudence started the engine of her motor home and opened the door. Nellie, holding a laundry basket filled with rope, duck tape, sheets, and pillowcases, raced around to the right side of the Gulf Stream behind Turk and Kai. The three crouched beside its front door.

Inside the Gulf Stream, Miquel and Otilia jumped from a twilight slumber in front of their television set. "What the hell?" Miquel exclaimed. Otilia turned and started running to the rear of the coach where their weapons were hidden. Just as she reached the bathroom door, suffocating acrid vapors stung her eyes and throat. "Get outside!" she gasped as she turned and stumbled toward Miquel who was peering with confusion out of a side window toward the blazing firepit where Marguerite and Louann were dancing about yelling and whooping.

"Damned loco gringos!" Miquel shouted as he flung open the Gulf Stream's door and lept out into Kai's powerful Jujitsu hold. Otilia followed a milisecond later into Turk's grip. Nellie quickly placed duck tape over each of Miquel's and Otilia's mouths and commenced to wrapping and tying rope around their arms and bodies. Kai and Turk hurriedly slipped pillowcases over their captives' heads and began wrapping them in bed sheets. The three Partners then dragged Miquel and Otilia around the Gulf Stream to Prudence's coach and loaded them inside. Kai turned to Prudence and grinned. "Go," he said. Prudence closed her motor home door and pulled from the parking space heading toward the rear exit of Stein's Ghost Town North Forty RV Resort. Desination: Douglas, Arizona, via Highway Ninety.

The remaining Partners quickly damped the roaring charcoals, turned off the conjunto recording, quit their dancing and yelling, took down the ladder, entered the Gulf Stream with wet towels over their faces and opened up all the windows and vents and turned the air conditioners to their highest setting, then rushed outside to assist the other Partners in quelling nearby outraged RV guests who had been comfortably snoozing in front of their television sets tuned a re-run of The Lawrence Welk Show.

As Prudence adjusted the motor home's cruise control to a conservative speed of sixty-five miles per hour, Kai opened his cell phone and dialed. "Hey Jorje, you ol' rascal, it's Kai Ochita. I'm on my way to deliver the Perez couple I phoned you about. I'm headed toward Douglas on Highway Ninety in a Gulf Stream motor home. We'll meet your boys at the city limit sign on the north side of town in about two hours." A short pause as Kai listened. "You're welcome, compadre," Kai said into his cell phone.

||||||||||||||||| 56 |||||||||||||||||

Kerrville, Texas
Texas Hill Country Guadalupe Retirement Center

"What's all the excitement about?" Nancy asked the two ladies waiting for the elevator in the hallway on the second floor of the Texas Hill Country Guadalupe Retirement center.

"Mildred just received a card from the three girls!" Betty Bea exclaimed.

"Prudence, Louann, and Marguerite?"

"Yes."

"Do you realize that those three have been gone almost a year?" Mildred said.

"Well I'll be," Nancy answered with a shake of her head, "it surely doesn't seem that they've been gone *that* long."

"It was just a year ago that they up and skidaddled off the face of the earth in that motor home Prudence's silly old fool bridge partner, Mr. Jones, willed to her."

"Where are they? Are they still together?"

"Prudence writes that the three of them are still together and that they're living in campers out in the desert in New Mexico at a place called Stein's Ghost Town RV Retreat."

"Have they lost their senses?" Nancy asked.

"It says here on their card that they own an interest in that trailer park where they are staying," Betty Bea said.

"Let me see that card," Nancy said as she took it from Betty Bea's hand. She perused the message; then handed the card back. "They're coming here for a visit, she writes."

Betty Bea pushed the elevator button on the control panel with the tip of her walking cane.

"Jeannie, down in the office, told me that she knew all along where they've been."

"Well, for heaven's sakes, how would *she* know?"

"It seems that they've been in contact with the office the entire time they've been away."

"Well, of all the nerve of those three. They could have - at the least - let the rest of us know of their whereabouts all this time. I worried about them."

"I didn't," Mildred said, "they're big girls."

"Well *I* fretted about them. That *Marguerite* is somewhat of a character, you know, and is easily influenced by those other two."

"What else did Prudence write?" Mildred said.

Betty Bea studied the card. "She writes that the three of them are arriving by airliner in San Antonio next week and that they are renting a car to drive here to Kerrville."

"Did she say that they are coming back?'

"Not really. She just wrote that all three of them have some unfinished business here and that they intend to stay one week."

"Did Jeannie know what they've been doing all this time?"

"No. She just told me that they contacted her once a month to take care of whatever obligations they left behind."

"We knew that they had their furniture and things stored and that they relinquished their apartments. What other obligations could they have had?"

"Oh, just simple things such as mail-forwarding, if needed, and consulting with their CPAs and such. I imagine that they paid Jeannie to handle some other things for them."

"Now that I've given it some thought, it has been rather quiet around here since they ran off like the Three Stooges."

The elevator door opened and Betty Bea, Nancy, and Mildred stepped inside. Nancy pressed the 'down' button. "I hope that Lucille doesn't join us at our table for lunch," she quipped, "she tends to 'hog' the muffins."

#

Prudence parked the rental car on the street in front of the retirement center and turned to Louann and Marguerite. "Now let's review our reasons for coming back to Kerrville for a week." She closed her eyes for a moment and took a deep breath, "We're here to visit our friends and acquaintances. OK? Also, we're here to deal with our banking accounts and things like that. Right?"

"We know. We know, Prudence. Must you be *so* repetitious?" Louann said.

"Yes I must, because Kai was insistant about us having a full understanding of the seriousness of our mission while we're here in Kerrville."

"OK, we got it," Marguerite quipped with in a pout: "it's imperative that we *not* do or say anything that will make that man suspicious who has been asking Jeannie about us."

Prudence shook her head as she continued: "Well I hope so, because when I told Kai about the note Jeannie sent us ten days ago about some well-dressed Hispanic-sounding fellow walking into her office and inquiring about the three of us, Kai immediately became seriously concerned about our well-being and safety as well as the welfare of The Partners. "Kai believes that the stranger who inquired of Jeannie, about the three of us, *could* be a cartel hit man, or someone Eduardo Betancourt - or his son, Eduardo, Junior - sent over to Kerrville to locate us."

Prudence turned to face Louann and Marguerite as she forcefully reviewed their situation. "One more run-through: Jeannie called to inform us that a Hispanic-sounding man in an expensive looking suit dropped into her office a few days ago and inquired - specifically - about the three of us. That he wanted to know of our whereabouts. That he promised her a substantial monetary reward - if and when - she did hear from us she would telephone the number he left with her and leave a message for him. OK?"

Marguerite and Louann nodded.

"When I told Kai about Jeannie's note to us, he

immediately became concerned that the person who wanted to know of our whereabouts - and would pay her money to reveal that information to him - was someone sent by the cartel from which we stole the five-hundred thousand dollars. OK?"

Marguerite and Louann nodded.

"Kai then instructed me to contact Jeannie and a couple of our past acquaintances here at the retirement center and tell them that the three of us are on our way for a short visit. OK? Kai will ride his motorcycle back to Kerrville to be with us when the strange man arrives."

"Why doesn't Kai fly with *us?*"

"Because he wants to have the advantage and mobility of his Harley, he said."

Nods.

"And we're to instruct Jeannie to call the number that the man left her and say that the three of us will be here for three days for a visit. OK?"

Marguerite's eyes drifted toward the front entrance of the Texas Hill Country Guadalupe Retirement Center as Prudence spoke. She watched an elderly woman, led by a Miniature Poodle, slowly extend a 'pooper-scooper' toward a tiny, brown turd.

"Are you paying attention, Marguerite?" Prudence demanded.

"Yes'm boss lady," Marguerite replied with a bored demeanor.

"Well you had better be paying attention, because we could be in harm's way if Kai's intuition is correct."

Prudence opened the car door and stepped to the pavement. "Now let's go inside and visit Mildred, Betty

Bea, and Nancy. We have to finalize the chicanery we've been concocting."

Prudence's cell phone chirped. She fumbled about in her ladened purse and fished it out. "Hello?" she said hesitantly, then listened for thirty seconds. "I understand," she said, then closed the cell phone.

"What?" Louann asked.

"Kai's out on I-10 between Van Horn and Ft. Stockton. He said that he had to swerve off the highway to miss a whitetail deer."

"Is Kai OK?" Marguerite asked.

"Kai is fine, but his Harley is damaged. He said that he doesn't know how long it's going to take to fix it."

"What are we to do?" Marguerite queried with alarm.

"Kai said that if the cartel man shows up before he can get here that…"

"That what?" Louann said, her eyes wide with concern.

"…the three of *us* are going just going to have to '*wing it*' until he arrives."

||||||||||||||||| 57 |||||||||||||||||||

Eduardo Miguel Betancourt, Junior

Eduardo Miguel Betancourt, Jr. despised everything in the United States, except the dollars he received from the cartel's illegal commerce. Yet, at this moment, he found himself driving a rental car alone on I-10 through Boerne, Texas, of all places, toward his destination of Kerrville. He had booked a flight from Mexico City to San Antonio, moments after receiving the recorded telephone message from the woman named Jeannie in the Guadalupe Retirement center's office telling him that the three ladies are expected at the retirement center in Kerrville today. *Soon,* he was thinking, *I will avenge my father. Those thieving old women will pay dearly for stealing the cartel's money and participating with Kai Ochita and the others in the imprisonment of my father.*

Betancourt Junior had studied the area of south-central Texas that the Texans called the 'Hill Country'. San Antonio lay on the western edge of the Gulf of Mexico's coastal plains. Kerrville perched sixty miles northwest and approximately sixteen hundred feet above San Antonio on the edge of the Edwards Plateau. The scenery was mindful of parts of northern Mexico that he had visited, but minus the hovels of the peasants whom he and his father - as well as many other wealthy and educated Mexicans - considered to be their 'children'; annoying, but necessary. The privilegio needed servants to provide for their personal wants and comforts. *Let the gringos feed and house our excess,* he intellectualized.

||||||||||||||||| 58 |||||||||||||||||

Texas Hill Country
Guadalupe Retirement Center

Hugs and 'air kisses' as Prudence, Louann, and Marguerite entered Nancy's apartment in the retirement center. The six friends chatted excitedly for several minutes exchanging pleasantries, untruths, health issues, and bemoaned their collective loss of memory. Then: total silence. Finally, Betty Bea cleared her throat - peered over the rim of her glasses - and said: "*What* have you three girls been up to these last twelve months?"

Marguerite glanced toward Prudence and Louann, then blurted forth with: "We stole a half-a-million dollars from dope dealers and ran out west to raise hell and live *large* and now we've returned to nail the bad, bad, man who's coming here to harm us!"

Nancy shook her head and said, "You know, Marguerite, you've always had a problem with propriety," then directed her attention to Louann and Prudence. "Now what have you girls *really* been up to?"

Prudence shot a glare at Marguerite - sniffed twice - then smiled sweetly back at Nancy as she said in a perfectly calm tone: "I believe that Marguerite succinctly stated our status quo."

"Heaven help them," Mildred whispered to the ceiling.

Nancy slowly rose from her chair and walked painstakingly to her apartment's window and gazed thoughfully at a fluffy white cloud for a few minutes. Then turned back to the others and said: "You know, there's a wing of this facility in which you three belong. Perhaps we should all go to the office right now and see to registering you."

"No, Nancy. Marguerite and Prudence are both telling you the truth," Louann said. "We've come back to the retirement center to confront a Mexican cartel bad person!"

Nancy smiled sweetly. "The office staff hasn't left for the day yet, so if we hurry perhaps Jeannie can assist you with all of the paperwork and details you'll have to provide to become patients."

Mildred and Betty Bea nodded vigorously as they stood. "Yes," Mildred added, "we'll be happy to escort the three of you to the office right now."

Prudence stood and placed her fists on her hips. "Now listen to me," she exclaimed, "Marguerite, Louann, and I are serious. We're in dire straights. Harm's way. Deep doodoo. And we're telling you the truth. We can use your help, but if you insist on disbelieving us and suggesting that we belong in the west wing we'll just run up to Pauline's apartment and elicit *her* succor!"

"Why don't you simply call the local police?" Betty Bea said as she lifted her shoulders.

"Because they just could just possibly arrest us and our partners as well for the things *we* have done."

A prolonged period of silence. Not one of the six ladies looked at each other.

"Well," Nancy finally said, "dinner's going to be served soon. We're having tacos and enchiladas this evening, so, if we're going to make some sort of commitment here let's make it now. I like to get to the enchiladas first when they're good and hot."

"What can *we* do to help?" Betty Bea asked.

"Just let us stay in your apartment, Betty Bea, until the cartel man comes for us," Prudence said.

"Well, for heaven's sake. How long will you be in my apartment?"

"We calculate that he will appear here looking for us within two days or less."

"Well where will *I* stay until he arrives?"

"You can stay with Mildred."

Nancy made her way back to her chair. "Just what is it that you three plan to do in Betty Bea's apartment?"

Marguerite commenced to giggle as she stuttered forth: "We decided that it would be best if you do *not* have knowledge of our devious scheme."

"Oh? Well this sounds interesting," Betty Bea said, "I think that all six of us should participate in whatever you girls are planning."

Mildred looked upward. "Heaven help us *all*," she muttered.

||||||||||||||||| 59 ||||||||||||||||||

Eduardo Miguel Betancourt, Junior

Eduardo Junior parked his vehicle parallel to the curb a quarter of a block from the retirement home and studied the facility for several minutes before he exited. He didn't have a gun or any other weapon with him because he'd just, two hours prior, gotten off an international flight. He was pondering his next step. Should he, first, drive to a store and purchase a weapon before entering the retirement home to engage the three old women? Or should he peruse the facility first? He elected to do the latter. That way he could visit that Jeannie person in the office, find out if the old women had arrived, and ascertain their current whereabouts.

He glanced across the street from where he had parked his rental car and studied the abandoned movie threater. *Caramba,* he mused, "*that must be where our estupido couriers hid the five-hundred thousand dollars.* Anger returned to his emotions with a flash of adrenaline. *Screw it. That Jeannie woman said that Kai Ochita appears not to have come with them, so I'll just go find the old bitches and beat their brains out with my bare fists after they tell me where the money's stashed!* Then he grinned. *Father would like that.*

⑥0

Prudence, Louann, Marguerite
Mildred, Nancy, Betty Bea

The six ladies sat in Betty Bea's apartment listening spellbound to Marguerite's conceptualization of her contrivance to neutralize the bad man coming to place them in harm's way.

Marguerite continued with her soliloquy, seemingly oblivious to the other five ladies seated about the apartment. "And then," Marguerite prattled on, "when the bad man breaks into Betty Bea's looking for us," she grinned broadly, "he'll find *me* - stark naked - drying myself off with a bath towel as if I'd just come from the shower."

Instant chatter filled the apartment.

"Why *you*?" Betty Bea shouted, "it's *my* apartment!"

"Well I'll be," Nancy muttered as she closed her eyes and shook her head.

"Why *not* me?" Marguerite looked around the

apartment with an indignant expression, "Of the six of us *I'm* obviously the most qualified for such exposure."

"Maybe so," Betty Bea interjected, "but *I'm* the most worldly!"

Prudence slumped back into her chair and crossed her arms in a gesture of obvious disapproval."

Mildred, rolling her eyes, stared toward the ceiling.

Finally, a quiet moment.

"*Then* what?" Betty Bea asked with a hesitancy in her voice.

"Well," Marguerite continued, "during that precise moment when that bad man stops to take a *good* look at me - and he *will* take a moment to look - he's the male of the species, you understand - the five of you will jump from behind your hiding places and pummel him senseless with your walking canes. Then we'll all commence screaming and hollering. One of us will push the emergency call-button on the wall and when the attendents rush in we'll all swear - on our honors - that the bad man was attempting to ravish me." Marguerite looked about the apartment to each lady, then added with a sincere expression: "I honestly believe that a dirty mind is a terrible thing to waste, but *that* 'bad boy' has got to go."

"That ought to do it," Nancy sighed, "now let's hurry before the enchiladas get cold."

ⅠⅠⅠⅠⅠⅠⅠⅠⅠⅠⅠⅠⅠⅠⅠ 61 ⅠⅠⅠⅠⅠⅠⅠⅠⅠⅠⅠⅠⅠⅠⅠ

Kai

Kai leaned his Harley through the sweeping curve to remain on I-10 where it split off to link to I-20. The highway was virtually vacant as compared to his ride from Stein's through the congested corridor through El Paso. He accelerated to a higher cruising speed on this leg of the less trafficked interstate. He was concerned about Prudence, Louann, and Marguerite who were waiting for him at the retirement center in Kerrville. His anxieties were multi-fold: had he recklessly advised the ladies? Would the suspected 'bad man' take the 'bait' that he had suggested Prudence phone to Jeannie to pass on to the stranger? Would the unknown person arrive before him and harm the ladies?

The isolated mountain ranges of Mexico loomed low to his right on the horizon; shades of blues and grays capped by brilliant sunlit cumulus clouds. This stretch of I-10 - La Entrada del Pacifica - offered a soothing scenario for Kai to peruse as he virtually flew over the pavement. This trek, however, was fraught with tension. His normally acute attention was diverted. Five miles west of Kent a Whitetail deer bound across his path causing him to swerve to the shoulder of the roadway. Kai avoided a collision with the deer but the resulting one-hundred yard dash over rocks and road debris shredded both tires on his bike. He stood next to his disabled Harley and peered anxiously back and forth. A big-rig trucker approached from the east, slowed to a stop on the westbound shoulder of the highway, and hailed Kai. After a minute of inquiries and pleasantries the driver advised Kai to secret his Harley in the brush a few feet off the shoulder of the highway and ride west with him back to Van Horn. The truck driver told Kai that he didn't believe that he could purchase two Harley tires in the small village of Kent five miles east. Kai hid his bike several yards off the highway's shoulder and trotted across the pavement and climbed into the cab of the eighteen wheeler.

On arrival to Van Horn, Kai learned that there was only one tire available that would fit his wheel. The station manager called every tire dealer in town for a second tire, but to no avail. Kai asked the tire man to order one from El Paso, and that he'd pay whatever it cost to have it immediately dispatched to Van Horn.

Kai walked to a small café and ordered coffee. He opened his cell phone and dialed Prudence. "Hey lady, what's up?"

"Hi, Kai! We've just finished having delicious enchiladas here at the retirement center and now we're back in our friend's apartment planning how to capture that bad man who's been inquiring about us," Prudence said with excitement in her tone.

"Listen, Prudence, you and the girls had better get out of the retirement home and find a secure place to hide. I'm sitting in a café in Van Horn waiting for a new tire for my Harley. I blew out two tires out in the boonies on I-10 a couple of hours ago and I'm having to wait here until one is delivered from El Paso. I have no idea as to how long I'll have to wait for it to get here. It may take several hours, or more."

"Oh, Kai dear, don't worry. The girls and I have a *plan*."

"No, no, Prudence…no plan…just high-tail it away from there and hide somewhere safe until I arrive. You can't mess around with those cartel assholes!"

"Now, Kai, please tend to your use of proper language. We've had many discussions with you and the boys about proper speak."

"I'm sorry, Prudence. Now please do as I say."

"I told you, dear, that Louann, Marguerite, and I, and three of our friends here at the center, have devised a scheme to *neutralize* - as Humberto always says - that bad fellow."

Kai stood abruptly - accidently knocking over his coffe cup and eliciting a glare from the waitress - "Please, Prudence, stay away from that man."

"Sorry, dear, if you can't be here in time; well, it's *our* call."

"No! I beg you Prudence, just gather the girls together and vanish until I get there to take care of you."

"Our plan is foolproof, Kai, and we intend to go

through with it if you do not arrive before the bad person gets here."

Kai took a deep breath and closed his eyes. "Just what *is* this *foolproof* plan you ladies cooked up?"

"Well, it has to do with Marguerite getting naked to divert the bad man's attention so that the rest of us ladies can beat him unconscious with our walking canes."

Kai hollered: "Naked?" and sat back onto his chair with such force that it tipped over against an elderly customer seated behind him. She scooted her chair to the side and whacked his head with her spoon. "Loco!" she exclaimed. Then added: "Estupido!"

Kai scrambled from the floor as he wiped menudo from his hair and pantomimed an apology to the elderly woman. "Have you lost your minds!" he shouted into his cell phone.

The waitress flapped her apron toward Kai as she barked for him to vacate the premises.

"No! Do *not* do anything other than getting out of there and hiding somewhere else!" Kai said as he backed from the café's entrance. At that precise moment Prudence whispered excitedly over her cell phone: "Oh, goodness, I have to hang up now, Jeannie's on Betty Bea's line. Betty Bea says that the bad man is on his way up to her apartment in the elevator as we speak."

"Get the girls out of there right *now*!" Kai shouted.

"Can't. Too late. He's tapping on Betty Bea's door."

"Don't hang up, Prudence! Let me listen to what's happening," Kai pleaded.

"OK, OK, Kai…I'll lay the cell phone on the table so you can hear everything."

Kai pressed his cell phone hard against his ear as he

listened to Nancy yell: "Hurry Marguerite…get your clothes off!"

A pause.

Scuffling sounds.

A click of a door lock.

A loud exclamation with a Spanish accent: "Chihuahua!"

Another pause.

Then sounds of whacking and moaning.

Silence.

"Hello?" Kai said into his cell, "Hello?"

"Yes, Kai, I'm here."

"Prudence? Is everything OK?" Kai gasped.

"Oh my, yes. The attendants are coming in the door now. Wait a second. Start screaming *now*, girls."

Screams. Scuffling sounds.

"Hello, Kai? This is Marguerite. Everything's under control here, so don't you worry yourself sick, now."

Nancy's voice from the background: "For heaven's sake, *Marguerite*, you can put your clothes back on now."

|||||||||||||||| 62 ||||||||||||||||

Texas Hill Country
Guadaulupe Retirement Center

Kai stood outside of the entrance into the center's second floor dining hall of the retirement center as he peered nervously inside. It wasn't difficult for him to spot 'the ladies' - six bobbing gray-haired heads swiveling to and fro, mouths in fervored motion. He noted the empty chair at their table. It was waiting for him. Kai took a moment to breathe deeply and slowly in an effort to 'center' himself. That was a common practice that he had perfected prior to his judo matches during his university days. He made a private wish that Nellie was standing here beside him for support. Then, with a confident expression, he stepped into the dining hall with an air of confidence in his bearing. Marguerite was the first to notice Kai's approach to their table. She waved excitedly. "Over here, dear!" she called.

Kai smiled as he made his way through the tables of

smiling old-timers to his seat with the ladies. Every eye in the dinning room struggled to focus on Kai.

"Hello," he said to all.

Prudence stood and said with a flourish: "Ladies, may I present to you our dear friend and partner, Mr. Kai Ochita!"

Kai grinned broadly around the table as he said: "Let me see, now," he nodded at Betty Bea. You must be Betty Bea." Then: "and you two are Mildred and Nancy." He stepped around the table and gave a peck on the cheek of Prudence, Louann, and Marguerite.

"My, my," Nancy said, "how did you know who was *who*?"

"My partners described each of you for me."

"Oh dear," Nancy murmured to Mildred, "he has a ponytail."

"So what?" Betty Bea replied, "So does my grandson."

"I do so hope that he doesn't use vulgarisms or profanity."

Betty Bea glanced sidewise at Nancy and whispered: "Who gives a flying fart?"

Nancy raised her eyebrows and replied softly: "Plus he rides a motorcycle."

"So does BJ," Betty Bea said.

"Who's that?"

"It's a long story," Betty Bea replied.

"Sit, sit, sit, Kai, and tell our hostesses all about our Stein's Ghost Town RV Retreat," Prudence said.

Kai smiled as he said to the six ladies: "Our RV retreat is the result of hard work, dedication, and true friendship on the part of these three lovely ladies, a sweet old married couple, and four reformed fellows who bind us all together."

"Don't leave out you and Nellie," Louann interjected.

Kai nodded, "I would *never* leave out Nellie."

Marguerite sat forward and affected a pouty expression, "I wanted Kai for *me,*" she whispered to Louann.

"Fat chance," Louann snorted.

ııııııııııı EPILOGUE ıııııııııııı

Stein's Ghost Town RV Retreat
One Year Later

Kai stood and tapped his spoon on his wineglass for attention. The Partners gradually ceased their animated chatter and smiled back at him. The multi-purpose room of Stein's Ghost Town RV Retreat had been reserved exclusively by the Partners for this private celebration dinner. Each Partner had opted not to wear their regular attire of jeans, shorts, culottes or tennis shoes or western style boots for the occasion. This evening marked the first anniversary of the opening of the RV resort. Each had worn their 'going-to-Tucson' apparel.

"I can truthfully say to each and everyone of you, my best friends and partners, that this past year has been one of hard work, determination, and belief. It has taken long hours of daily application of each of our individual skills, much thought and planning, and a fierce dedication to our mutual goal of owning, managing, and earning an honest profit from our endeavors.

"Don't forget our escape from the bad guys!" Rose called out, followed by raucous cat-calls from the four fellows and clapping from the three ladies.

Kai proffered a 'thumbs-up' gesture.

"But our continuing success with our RV retreat isn't the *whole* picture," Kai said softly. "That success, in itself, has been quite a remarkable accomplishment, especially considering the make-up of our partnership. He looked about the table. "Four fellows who were couriers for an illegal narcotics synndicate. Three dignified ladies from a ritzy retirement center. A married couple who happily have been together for nearly sixty years." Kai turned to Nellie. "And a lovely lady from the Netherlands who incidentally - and I don't use the word 'incidentally' lightly for this announcement, just received notification that her hard-earned thesis from her university in the Netherlands has been accepted. Nellie now proudly holds the title of PhD."

The Partners stood in unison and clapped for Nellie.

Kai continued: "I have another exciting bit of news: Nellie, just this day, received notification that she has been awarded a generous grant from Alliant Internationl University in Mexico City to study the possible migration of ancient Inca Indians from the Sierra Madre del Sur region of western Mexico to the Animas Mountains of western New Mexico." He turned to Nellie and motioned for her to stand for her second ovation.

"But that's not all," Kai continued after the Partners quieted. "Our gracious ladies, as you all know, have had overwhelming success this past year with their outstanding entertainment programs for our visitors. Their directing of the guests in mini-musicals and other activities has resulted in write-ups from two RV travel magazines."

Applaud.

"And these guys: "They've each developed skills in all facets of the RV industry."

The four fellows nodded their ackowledgements.

Kai then turned to face Rose and Aldo. "I can't say enough about these two characters. They've been our 'anchor'. Rose asked me to announce, this evening, that they're retiring."

Boos and chiding.

Kai held up his hands, "But *not* leaving for good. They'll return here and substitute for the rest of us when we're on vacation or ill."

Cheers.

Aldo rose and said: "We know some good ol' boys back in the Texas Hill Country who've been our buddies for many years. The Hill Country Hellers. They're old worn out bikers. There's only four of them still kicking about. They'd like to come back with Rose and me and take a look at this fancy RV resort we put together. So, from time to time, Rose and I are going to be rejoining you fine friends and Partners."

Applause.

Rose and Aldo stood and bowed. Then Rose said: "Did Kai mention that the novel he's been writing about illegal dope cartel wars along the border has been accepted for publication by a major publisher?"

The Partners whistled and clapped.

"Hey!" Humberto shouted, "We all done good!"

Then Nellie stood and waited until everyone had

settled down. "I, too, have an announcement," she said with a sparkle in her eyes, then held her left hand to display an engagement ring. "I asked Kai to marry me and he said 'yes'."

Whoops and hollers.

THE END